Leann stepped cl **seeming not to c...** **both her hands.**

They were soft and warm, and he had the feeling that if he let go, he would spend the rest of the night trying to reclaim them. He could tell she didn't want him to do anything but what they were doing. Standing on the dance floor, gazing at each other, touching, with a half smile on her face.

He got it. She was as torn as he was.

But she still didn't move away from him. Maybe because they were in a sea of adolescents, maybe because the music was a little nostalgic, maybe because she was off duty as a cop or maybe because she wasn't sure who he really was: friend, foe, stranger, admirer.

Sometimes he wasn't sure, either.

And Gary's feet refused to leave the dance floor.

Dear Reader,

Welcome to book three of the Safe in Sarasota Falls series, set near the Jemez Mountains in New Mexico.

Leann Bailey, our heroine, is a bit different than the ones from my earlier books. She's a cop, so her job is keeping other people safe, especially her two sons. She's too busy for romance and she has trust issues. Things become even trickier when Gary Guzman shows up in town and she can't seem to avoid him. Soon she doesn't want to. But falling in love means her heart isn't safe.

Leann is my second cop heroine. She's tough but fun. It's a balance most women have to manage. "Hey, Mom, you're tough but fun." "Hey, professor, you're tough but fun." "Hey, editor, you're tough but fun." I could go on.

Above all, this is a romance, and when Leann falls for ex-soldier Gary, she's met her match in the "tough but fun" arena. Hmm, maybe those three words could be in their wedding vows! "Dearly beloved, we are gathered together to take these two tough but fun..."

I enjoy hearing from my readers. Please visit me at pamelatracy.com to find out about my other Harlequin Heartwarming books.

Pamela

HEARTWARMING

The Soldier's Valentine

———

Pamela Tracy

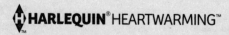

Recycling programs
for this product may
not exist in your area.

ISBN-13: 978-1-335-51064-8

The Soldier's Valentine

Copyright © 2019 by Pamela Tracy Osback

Printed in U.S.A.

Pamela Tracy is a *USA TODAY* bestselling author who lives with her husband (the inspiration for most of her heroes) and son (the interference for most of her writing time). Since 1999, she has published more than twenty-five books and sold more than a million copies. She's a RITA® Award finalist and a winner of the American Christian Fiction Writers' Book of the Year Award.

To the Haag family: Stephanie, Steve and Nolan.
I get to write adventures for Harlequin,
but I get to live adventures—camping,
body surfing, Universal Studios, Legoland
and more—with the best traveling buddies
in the world. Most excellent of all,
the adventures are filled with laughter.

CHAPTER ONE

THE ONLY THING Officer Leann Bailey hated more than domestic disturbance calls were domestic disturbance calls that involved her family.

She pulled into the familiar parking lot of Meteor Park, located a mere block away from where she'd grown up.

Evening on a school night meant plenty of empty spaces. She pulled into one and turned off the engine.

Leann had chosen to return to the small town of Sarasota Falls and raise her boys. She had not chosen to return to the neighborhood of her childhood, a house that wasn't a home and siblings as damaged as she was.

Thanks to her spoiled, slightly neurotic younger sister, she didn't always have a choice.

"I can deal with this," Leann muttered to herself, yet she didn't move from behind the wheel. Every time, every single time, she was called to this side of town, to deal with Gail's issues, it was a step back in time: a time she didn't want to remember yet alone police.

Her badge grew heavier on her chest as the toxic bubble of childhood memories appeared. Her parents, Ted and Allison Crabtree, served on various boards, gave to charity, threw great parties and were respected by everyone in town—except their own children.

"Silver-spooned kids, didn't none of them live up to their parents' expectations," Leann had overheard her doctor's receptionist say somewhat sadly.

It was true, the silver spoon part.

Clark, her older brother, had moved to Los Angeles, gotten a degree from a small college and now was a private accountant. He'd not returned ever, even at Christmas. His silver spoon was tarnished.

Leann, instead of becoming a doctor, lawyer or at least marrying well and staying married, had become a cop. Her silver spoon had been pawned to help pay the bills when her oldest boy was a baby.

Still, she'd done better than her sister Gail who was on husband number three and lived in their parents' guesthouse. Gail lived under the misguided belief that she deserved more than one silver spoon.

"Move," Leann told herself, trying to shake away the invisible restraints keeping her from exiting her vehicle. Unless she missed her guess, she was due a front-row seat as Gail's husband number three was promoted—or would that be demoted?—to ex-husband number three.

As the crisp New Mexico air permeated, battling the smell of oil, sweat and metal, she took yet another precious moment to organize her thoughts, assess the situation.

The moon was full in the sky, casting gray shadows on the skateboarders who sailed across the concrete area designated for their use. Only the older kids remained, those who were out of school or who didn't care about school. Leann rolled down her window and listened to their muted laughter. A small late-night birthday party was winding down as parents packed up gifts and food. A limp piñata hung from a tree about to lose its tentative connection to a low-hanging branch, and a young child's tired whine provided background music.

A young couple sat very close together on a bench. They paid no attention to the family, skateboarders or argument happening in the distance. Leann envied them. They were so into each other that their love drowned out reality.

Leann wasn't so lucky; she could hear her sister's voice, could even make out the words.

"You absolute jerk! You quit your job without reason and now want me to lend you money so you can make a car payment?"

Leann knew exactly where her sister was: to the left of the birthday party, straight behind the lovebird couple and on the playground. It had been a favorite getaway for her and Gail during their youth.

Leann's ex-husband, Ryan, had proposed to her there—she'd been sitting on the swing; he'd been kneeling before her in the sand—on a moonlit night just like this one, a week before high school graduation.

She'd been newly turned eighteen, pregnant and willing to dream. He'd been six months into eighteen, pressured by his parents to do the right thing and about to get to boot camp.

Gail's voice grew even louder. "Loser!"

This shrill exclamation interrupted the young couple, who stood, gave Leann a what are you waiting for? stare and walked slowly away.

"I can't believe I married you!"

The birthday party parents started moving faster, perhaps inspired by the rising tone of Gail's voice, and gathered their kids, ice chest and limp piñata before hurrying down the sidewalk toward the small man-made lake. Ever a cop, Leann scanned the parking lot to see if a minivan was waiting for them. No, so they must live nearby. Besides her squad car, there was a dark blue Ford truck, New Mexico plates, with a good-sized dent in the left side. Hmm, not a vehicle she recognized. Could be one of the skateboarders had finally gotten a job and some transportation. She hoped so, because otherwise it might be a recent acquire of her brother-in-law's and the vehicle payment he needed to make.

Leann checked the computer for anything new and then radioed in her time of arrival: nine fifteen. She'd get a few smirks when she got back to the station. Gail and Ray's feuding was legendary in Sarasota Falls.

No sense delaying. She opened the door and almost got one leg out when she saw a dark mass heading in her direction, moving fast across the grass, not making a sound. Her mind reached for possibilities even as she returned her leg to the vehicle and reached out to close the door.

She didn't have a chance.

The dog nudged the door the rest of the way open, his head butting its way in, and then stopped—butt outside but head inside. "Woof!"

"What the—?"

"Wilma, come!" A man's voice, louder than her sister's even, came sharp and clear, commanding.

Wilma? This dog's name was Wilma? Based on its size, it should be Brute or Thor, Cujo or Genghis Khan. Not Wilma. Wilma was the nice Flintstone.

"Off," she ordered.

The dog didn't budge, just grinned at her, openmouthed, tongue out, drool dripping, weighing at least sixty pounds she guessed. It was big, brown and reminded Leann of a dog she'd had years ago. Without thinking, she said, *"Varaus,"* meaning "Off" in German. At the same time, she pushed and the dog retreated maybe two steps where it remained, head tilted to the side as if expecting more.

"Wilma, come!" The voice, louder this time, was deep and rich, without temper. If her dog, Peaches, acted so wild and wooly, she'd be adding a little sass and showing her who was boss.

"Gey," she said, and surprisingly, the dog

fully backed away from the vehicle, so she could extract herself just in time for the owner to finally jog into view. He was almost six foot, dark, possibly Hispanic, and had straight black hair. "The harness broke," he explained.

"What you should be saying," Leann suggested, the foul mood caused by her sister making her use a tone she normally wouldn't have used, "is, thank you, Officer. I needed the help."

He looked at her, eyes penetrating. A wave of emotion—long suppressed—reached the part of her that still believed in Prince Charming. Wow. Her hormones hadn't taken notice like this since she'd turned fifteen and realized kissing wouldn't be so weird.

He attached the leash to the harness circling the dog's upper body before saying, "Thank you, Officer."

She was about to cajole him into adding "I needed the help," but she heard Ray finally hit his breaking point with Gail by shouting, "You weak-kneed princess. I know—"

Leann quickly jogged up a small embankment, hurried down the grassy knoll and, not even out of breath, announced, "You know nothing." Hmm, she'd left the door to the squad car open. If the dog hopped in, good. When she got back, she'd assist Mr. I-Don't-Need-Help with manouevering the dog out again. That would be way more fun than stepping into the middle of this dispute.

She skidded to a stop next to her brother-in-law. "Ray, calm down. Gail, don't you think there's a better place for you to have this fight, er…discussion?"

"I didn't want Mama to hear," Gail said softly. Tears rolled down her face.

Leann wasn't moved. Gail should have been a movie star. She cried at will, no effort or emotion necessary. Also, she was a master at being the center of attention.

"I didn't quit my job, Le—, er, Officer Bailey," Ray grumped. "I got laid off. There's a difference. I'll start looking for a new job come Monday."

Leann made sure her face didn't so much as twitch. She was a cop more than she was family just then. Good thing, too, because she suspected he hadn't been laid off; he'd most likely been fired for lack of effort if experience counted for anything.

Gail had a right to be annoyed. Ray worked for a leasing agency doing landscaping and repairs on their real estate property and rentals.

Leaves didn't stop needing to be raked, and trash didn't carry itself to the bin.

A snort sounded to Leann's left. She looked, realizing the sound had come from Wilma the dog. She moved her gaze up the grassy knoll to Wilma's owner, who sported a look of disdain. Great, even total strangers could look at her family and guess "dysfunctional" almost immediately.

Wilma strained at her leash and tried to pull the man toward Leann, who took a few steps closer to the swing set.

"Bleip," she ordered the dog, telling it to stay. Turning to the man, she said, "Control your dog, sir. And if you have no business with these folks, could you please move along." Then she turned back to face her sister, and said, "Gail, you head home, not the guesthouse, but the main house. I'll call Clarissa and tell her you're on the way. Ray, go to your brother's house for the night."

"No, I'm going to my own house," Ray said.

Gail immediately protested, "It's not your house. Tell him, Leann."

"Or I can bring you both into the station and book the pair of you for disturbing the peace." Leann shrugged.

Ray mouthed a word that Leann pretended not to hear. "Fine. I'm going."

Gail marched away. In a matter of minutes, she was nearing the sidewalk by the softball field. She had only a block to go to arrive at their parents' home.

"I got laid off," Ray said to the man holding onto the dog. "It happens."

The man didn't so much as shrug.

Leann took out her cell phone and hit a button. Clarissa answered at the first ring, her voice—as always—upbeat and reassuring. Leann knew at least one person in the Crabtree home had her back.

"Gail's coming to see you. Let her in the back door, give her some cookies and coffee, listen to her cry and please try to calm her down."

The housekeeper laughed, like she always did with their overly dramatic episodes, and promised warm cookies for Leann, too, if she wanted them. She did; her thighs didn't.

After ending the call, Leann studied the man and dog. Wilma promptly dropped to the ground, rolled onto her back and waved paws in the air. She either wanted her stomach rubbed or she was having a fit.

Leann admonished, "It's not wise to follow a police offer to an incident."

He nodded, his face somber, but one corner of his mouth twitched a bit. "I'm sorry. I just wanted to make sure…" His words trailed off. "I've just never seen an *incident* handled quite like that. You able to boss the entire town? Is that why even Wilma listens to you?"

Leann didn't answer. She was tired and it was none of his business. She assessed the situation. "Do you not have someplace you should be?"

Something changed in his eyes, a wariness that hadn't been there before. Nevertheless, he chuckled. "I'm staying over at Bianca's Bed-and-Breakfast. You can call her if you want."

"I might do that."

He fell in step beside her as she made her way back to the police cruiser.

The nearness of him, how the night shadows swayed, made her walk faster. She wasn't scared of him; after all, she held the baton, she had a Glock and his dog listened to her more than it did to him.

No, with him beside her, she felt a little more worried about her reaction to him. It had been a long time since she'd been around a man who made her notice his nearness, made her aware of the heady scent of masculinity and how fun a walk in the park could be. So, she walked faster. When she got to her cruiser, he stayed on the sidewalk and watched as she opened the door.

He stopped her right before she got in the car with, "Was that German?"

"Yes."

"How did you know to give Wilma orders in German? I've had her a week and it never occurred to me."

She didn't want to share her past, about living in Germany, the military life and leaving her ex-husband, so she merely quipped, "Guess I'm smarter than you."

He chuckled again, and it reminded her of the way he'd spoken to the dog, not losing his temper, not getting excited, just calm and low-key.

She slid behind the steering wheel, started the the engine and backed out of the parking lot. Heading in the direction of the station, she first quickly glanced in the rearview mirror.

He was gone.

Maybe she wasn't smarter than him. After all, he'd gotten her name thanks to Gail and Ray, but she—a cop!—had neglected to find out his.

CHAPTER TWO

GERALDO "GARY" GUZMAN opened one eye and glanced at the clock. Just past four. *That dog sure knows how to bark.* His mind registered the fact even as his body automatically exited the bed. A whole month out of the service and he still had the soldier mind-set.

Once his feet hit the carpet, he grabbed a pair of old jeans from the floor, pulled them on and then took Wilma out to the back of his aunt Bianca's bed-and-breakfast to do her business. She took her sweet time, exploring the bushes for the enemy, and then looking at him expectantly.

"Do your business," he ordered. It was the one command she seemed to understand in English but only if he squatted, which made him feel like a three-year-old.

Hours later, it wasn't her I-need-to-go-to-the-bathroom bark that woke him. It was a loud crunchy gnawing. He opened one eye, rolled over so he could see what she was doing and realized his tennis shoe was now mangled.

She also knew how to chew clothes, furniture and pretty much anything else in her path. And, she always decided to gnaw loudly on a bone or persistently bring a chew toy to his lap just as he'd settled down to watch television.

Gary realized if he was to save the other shoe, he had to do something to distract her. He got into his jeans again and led the dog to the back door, taking her outside. Once he'd let her run around for a while and sniff every inch of the backyard, he let her inside and turned to go upstairs. He wanted one more hour of sleep. That had been his goal since exiting the army. He wanted to sleep when he wanted to sleep, eat when he wanted to eat and do nothing when he wanted to do nothing.

Wilma was worse than his commanding officer.

He'd made it only halfway through the kitchen when he stepped on something: a mangled personalized Bianca's Bed-and-Breakfast oversize coaster. His aunt was being a good sport, but she'd suffered from Wilma's high jinks and had two guests complain about the dog's barking.

"I'll add dog friendly to the inn's description," she'd brushed it off when he'd apologized.

At least now, thanks to the cop from last night, Gary had an idea. He sat down at the computer in the family room, plugged in the inn's password and started researching.

He'd just hit Print and the paper was still warm in his hand, when his aunt Bianca came up behind him.

"I just had two interesting phone calls, both concerning you."

He turned around. "Really? Why? About the dog?"

"One of them was about the dog. Our neighbors who live in the green single-story a few houses down. Guess the husband's having trouble hearing the television."

As if knowing she were the topic of conversation, Wilma barked. Gary glanced down at his list, found the word for quiet and loudly said, *"Ruhig."*

Bianca Flores raised an eyebrow, Wilma barked louder.

"I'm sorry," Gary said but Aunt Bianca held up her hand.

"Don't worry about it. The husband is the kind who'd complain about a crack in the sidewalk even if he'd been the one to put it there."

"I'm working with her. She'll learn. She's smart." He checked the paper in his hand and tried again. *"Ruhig!"* This time, the dog listened. She turned and headed for the door to the backyard, lay on her back and began chewing her own paw while a giant bone lay unloved right next to her.

At least she wasn't barking.

"The second call," Bianca continued, "was from one of our local police officers wanting to know if I had a thirty-something male with a dog staying here at the bed-and-breakfast."

To his aunt Bianca's credit, she didn't show any more concern about the call from the police than she had about the noise complaint. She'd always been the aunt to step in when the Guzman brood needed a soft place to land. That didn't mean, though, that she was blind to their faults.

Gary grinned. "Let me guess. It was an Officer Leann Bailey."

Bianca nodded. "You were out late last night. Something happen?"

"Quite a bit." He handed her the list of commands he'd just printed off. "Thanks to Officer Bailey I found out the dog understands and obeys—well, sometimes obeys—German. Who would have thought it?"

Bianca gave Wilma an appreciative look. "Leann lived in Germany for quite a while, I remember. So, how do you say, 'Quit chewing the table leg'?"

Gary laughed. "Those words aren't on the list."

Bianca took the paper out of his hand, studied it and handed it back. "What happened last night that had you figuring out Wilma understands German?"

"How well do you know Officer Leann Bailey?"

"Her father used to be my financial adviser, so I know the family quite well."

"Last night, Wilma and I had a little run-in with her at the park."

"What—?"

This time it was Gary who held up a hand. "Nothing to worry about. Wilma took a liking to her, tried jumping into her squad car, but had to settle for giving her a hug."

"Wilma probably smelled Peaches," Bianca offered, heading for the kitchen, probably knowing Gary would follow. Gary followed.

"I didn't notice the smell of peaches." Gary thought back. He hadn't noticed any smell except for the ripe grass and strong pine scent coming from the trees.

Bianca laughed as she started making lunch. "I'm talking about Leann's dog. Peaches. She's a big mutt, tough looking, like a bear, but gentle as a kitten."

"And to think she made fun of Wilma's name." Gary sat at the table. It felt odd, not having anything to do, but he'd been out of the military only a month, and his mind hadn't wrapped itself around the term *civilian*.

Bianca raised an eyebrow. "Oh, you had a whole conversation with Leann?"

"Just enough to figure out she can control Wilma better than I can."

"How did the training go?"

"Not so good. I can't believe Max neglected to tell me Wilma only understands German! I spent a whole hour ordering Wilma to sit and offering treats. She sat, but not when I asked her to, and she still expected the treats. She jumped on me a least a dozen times and almost dragged me down a small hill when she spotted a cat."

"Now that you know about the German, it will help. What was Leann doing at the park?"

"Husband-and-wife dispute."

"Ah," Bianca said, "by the swings."

"How did you know?"

"That would be Gail and Ray Goode. They

argue at least twice a month and usually do so in the park. Gail doesn't want her parents to hear. They're the disapproving kind, not the helping kind."

"Officer Bailey handled it differently than I would have, but she handled it well. She separated them, sent the husband to his brother's and sent Gail to the main house and someone named Clarissa."

"That would be the Crabtrees' housekeeper."

"Crabtree?"

"Gail's parents, her maiden name."

"They have a live-in housekeeper?"

Aunt Bianca nodded. "And a full-time groundskeeper."

"So, they get special consideration from the cops?" Gary didn't think his brother Oscar, who was also a part of the Sarasota Falls police department, would go for such behavior, but maybe Leann was different? Yet that hadn't been the sense of her he had last night. He'd been impressed with the police woman and how she'd handled the scene with her sister.

Bianca deftly set bread on the cutting board—lunch meat to the left of it; cheese and tomato—and started making their lunch. "What I should have said just now was that

Crabtree happens to be both Gail's and Leann's maiden name."

"Sisters?" Gary sucked in his breath and relaxed a little. "That explains a lot."

"I wonder why Leann called here instead of asking Oscar about you."

"She was so busy with her sister, I think she forgot to ask my name so doesn't know Oscar's my brother. Not very cop-like." Gary had been military police among other things.

"She's a good cop, dedicated and—"

The bell over the front door rang. Bianca set down her knife, glanced out the window checking the dog's whereabouts, quickly washed her hands and headed up front. Yesterday, she'd done the same thing and Wilma had snatched the bread.

Gary recognized the voice that said, "Hey, Bianca, good to see you."

Leann Bailey in the flesh. Gary grinned. So, the lady had decided to follow up her phone call with a visit. He sometimes had an effect on women. Usually, though, it was when he was in uniform.

He followed his aunt to the foyer and studied the cop in question. He'd liked her better standing with the moon to her back. She was equal in height to his aunt, but where Bianca was soft and dark, Leann was toned and fair. He noted how well she wore her blue uniform.

"You looking for me?" he asked.

Bianca, a half frown on her face, told him. "I guess I didn't take their complaint seriously enough. Officer Bailey's here, something about a noise ordinance."

Leann nodded. "Right now, I'm just issuing a warning, but—"

"I'm Gary Guzman. You met me last night."

"Guzman," Leann muttered before turning to Bianca. "I can't believe I missed it. Oscar's brother?"

"And my nephew. Younger than Oscar by two years," Bianca supplied.

"Better-looking, too," Gary put in.

He watched as a myriad of expressions crossed Leann's face. There was surprise— probably a result of last night's meeting or maybe his relationship to Oscar and Bianca. Annoyance—no doubt she didn't like sur- prises. And detachment—she probably didn't want to warm up to him while on duty.

"About Wilma," Leann said. "You're going to need to do something about her barking."

"I'm working with her. Now that I know she understands German, I'll be able to ratchet up the training." He pulled the piece of paper from his back pocket and showed her.

Leann didn't look impressed.

"It will just take a few days," he promised.

"She's a good dog," Gary inserted, "but I've only had her for a week."

"Ah," Leann said.

This time Gary could read her face. The smile reached her pretty green eyes, which suddenly registered a positive impression even as she said, "A rescue?"

"No," Aunt Bianca said.

"More or less," Gary put in.

Leann looked from one to the other.

"My friend Max has been in Germany the last three years, came stateside for a few months and was just deployed six days ago to a place he couldn't take Wilma. It's temporary." Gary didn't mention the arm-twisting from Max, or the adamant "No" consistently given by Gary, followed by Max finally showing up at the tiny apartment Gary was crashing at.

"Good of you to take in Wilma," Leann said.

"No, good of me to take in Wilma." Aunt Bianca shot Gary a look.

"I'll let the neighbors know this is only temporary and that you're working on the problem," Leann said, suddenly back to being a cop. Gary liked the impressed lady better. He wanted that look back.

"We'll think of something," Aunt Bianca said.

Footsteps sounded on the porch. The bell over the door tinkled as a short man, definitely military, leading a midsize border collie, pushed his way in. Aunt Bianca immediately smiled and asked, "Do you need a room?"

"No, I'm looking for Gary Guzman."

"That's me," Gary said, looking from the man to the dog. He didn't recognize either and had the feeling he didn't want to.

"I'm William Benedict, and I'm desperate," the man began. "I got called up a week ago. I'm leaving in the morning and my sister just found out that she's pregnant with triplets. She already has two kids not even in school. She can't handle Goober now. I heard you took in Max Juergens's dog."

Aunt Bianca's, Leann's and Gary's eyes all went to Goober, a beautiful black-and-white dog who didn't look at all like a Goober.

"I'm staying with my aunt temporarily..." Gary said, noting the way Officer Leann Bailey watched him.

"Look," William said, "my mother died six months ago. Goober was hers. I promised I'd take care of the mutt. I went online, and there's places—families even—where I can board the dog, but, well—" his voice softened "—she was my mom's, and Goober's sensitive if not a little high-strung. She needs someone who will pay attention to her. I hear you have time."

Time. Gary's enemy right now because he just didn't know what to do with it, how to spend it. One thing he could do was give good ole Max a call and a virtual kick in the butt.

"I'm not at a place where I can take care of…" Gary faltered as he noticed Aunt Bianca, who was shaking her head no. Unfortunately, standing next to Aunt Bianca was Leann, who was already bending down, stroking Goober's ears and whispering, "Good girl. Such a good girl." The dog—all bright-eyed with a ring of white around her nose, chest and both back feet—gave a polite woof and wagged her tail.

If Leann touched Gary that gently on the face, and if he'd had a tail, he'd be wagging it, too.

Leann switched her gaze from Goober to Gary, her eyes indicating disappointment. Great, she expected him to refuse to help.

He didn't need, want, another dog, even temporarily, and especially not one "sensitive and a bit high-strung" and taken on just to impress a woman he barely knew. The way that William referred to Goober indicated he wasn't attached to his mom's dog. In the military, *temporary* could be years.

Gary made the mistake of looking at Goober, who was looking back at him as if she already knew and loved him. "Your mom named her Goober?" Gary asked.

Not a chance he could take the dog. Aunt Bianca was running out of coasters; Gary was already almost out of shoes.

"Actually, my mom let one of my sister's kids named it."

"She's a great dog," Leann said. She went to her knees in front of the dog, both hands streaming down the sides of Goober's head.

William's smile for Leann became a frown as he faced him. Gary quickly spoke up.

"I'm going to get a job. It's just…" For some reason, Gary felt it important for Officer Leann Bailey to know he intended to be gainfully employed. For some reason, he didn't see Leann as someone who would be impressed with a man taking a break to find himself.

Heck, he wasn't always impressed with himself lately, either.

"It's just that there are a few things Aunt Bianca wants to me do first," he finished.

"Yes, and helping out at an inn really doesn't give him much time to work with dogs." Bianca focused on Leann and suggested, "Maybe you could take her?"

Leann stepped back from Goober and shook her head. "I've already got a dog, a turtle and hamster. All of which my sons promise to take care of, but I wind up doing most of it. Plus, when my boys go to stay with their grandparents while I'm on the job, they take Peaches. I doubt very much that they'd welcome a second dog." With her hand still stroking the top of Goober's head, she gave William a stern look. "Why on earth didn't you call first and save yourself a trip?"

"I didn't call," William explained, looking solely at Gary, "because I was afraid you'd turn me down. I drove three hours to get here."

As if cued, Goober gave a little bark and gazed adoringly up at Leann.

Gary rarely did anything rash. Being rash could put his team in danger, civilian lives in danger, but he wasn't in Afghanistan or Syria now.

"What's one more?" he said, reaching for the leash and bending down to pat Goober. "Come on over to the table—" Gary looked at the bag the man carried "—and let's see what all you've brought with you."

"Gary," Aunt Bianca began. "I—"

"I promise I'll make this good," Gary said.

Benedict, clearly knowing when strategy was needed, jumped in with, "I've got her toys and favorite blanket in the car and enough food for a month."

Gary led the way to the table. Behind him, Aunt Bianca coughed. She didn't have a cold.

Without looking, Gary knew Officer Bailey was smiling. Still, he looked, and sure enough he'd managed to win her approval. Usually, his uniform or wit did the trick. This time, he'd needed Goober's help.

No, more likely, Gary needed other types of help because he'd just taken on a dog he knew nothing about, from a person he knew nothing about, and all because he was trying to impress a woman he knew nothing about and who lived in a town Gary didn't intend to make home.

He made the mistake of looking at her. She looked back and he was lost.

Man, she had beautiful eyes.

The cop, not Goober.

It'd be Gary's luck, Goober probably obeyed commands issued in Chinese.

CHAPTER THREE

LEANN LEFT BIANCA'S Bed-and-Breakfast try-ing to wrap her mind around this newcomer. Gary Guzman was all hard edges and mys-tery. But, buried under all that baggage, he had heart. Otherwise, he'd not have taken Goober, or Wilma, for that matter.

She quickly filled out an incident report and then radioed the station to see what was up. It was the only thing she could think of to take her mind off the dark-haired, dark-eyed soldier who'd wandered into her town.

"Nothing's happening," said Lucas Stillwa-ter. On the Sarasota Falls police roster, he had seniority. He'd been an officer for more than twenty years. He'd started talking retirement three years ago, had started the paperwork even, but then didn't file. A month ago, the paperwork resurfaced, was updated and now waited in Lucas's outbox: not turned in. Lucas was having a hard time retiring.

When he did, though, Leann was going to

be a squeaky wheel. She'd done her time and was ready for a promotion.

Leann started her patrol vehicle and headed down the familiar road, driving by the town's busiest convenience store, where she once prevented a robbery, then on past the high school, where the coach was always leaving lights on, either the stadium's or his vehicle's, and then she started thinking about lunch.

Oscar drove by in his cruiser, giving a honk and waving. She waved back. Why couldn't he have been hired after Lucas retired?

She loved her job. Loved that as Sarasota Fall's first and only female officer she had obligations that she met and that she made Sarasota Falls a better place, a safer place. Something changed inside her when she dressed for work. It was like she shed all her insecurities and became someone strong, someone to be respected.

Not because of who her parents were but because of who she was.

She needed that promotion, deserved it, so she could stand on her own two feet. Not that she didn't appreciate her ex-husband's parents, who provided free child care and unconditional love for her kids. Leann was the force that kept them from spoiling her boys the way they had their own son. Sometimes she succeeded.

She'd always be grateful for the school clothes they purchased, the sport fees they paid and the holiday meals. She just didn't have the money—even with her job and with child support.

Ryan Bailey was an absentee father because of his military duties, but in his place were his very attentive parents.

They were a huge help. Although, the reality was that they were getting older and she had to think of the future. The extra income from the promotion would be enough to make a difference financially and help offset the cost of child care, if it came to that.

Until then she'd have to make do on her own.

Meanwhile, there was something—or rather someone—in her way. Gary Guzman, dog lover extraordinaire, had a brother named Oscar, who didn't have her insecurities and who had a resume that made her work experience look like she was a trainee.

Goober. What a name for a dog?

Darn, here she was contemplating her promotion and thoughts of Gary Guzman interfered. Good thing he was aimless. Not a chance she'd ever be interested in him. She had a mortgage and two sons. She didn't trust men as a rule, thanks to her own father and her ex-husband. She saw nothing to trust in Gary. And she was annoyed that he dared invade her thoughts—again. She stopped a driver and gave him a citation for having expired tags. Then, she wrote another quick incident report, circled Main Street once and headed for the Station Diner. She'd grab a bowl of soup and cup of coffee before continuing on. Who knows how many more expired tags she'd be battling today.

She pushed the door open and walked into the familiar diner. She'd started coming here in junior high with her best friend, Patsy, and Patsy's family. Her parents wouldn't deign to frequent a "dive" like this. Leann loved the place. If one of her children spilled a glass of water, a waitress handed over a towel and no white linens were ruined. Here, a person could joke with the folks at the next table because the tables were so close. The laughter was muted at the places her parents liked, and children were seen but not heard.

She shrugged out of her jacket, aware of the Glock 17 tucked in its holster, and looked down the aisle toward her favorite booth in the back.

William Benedict nodded at her and went

back to his pancakes. If she'd just turned Peaches over to new owners, she'd be drowning her sorrows with chocolate. She supposed pancakes could do the trick, and Benedict did look a bit distressed.

"Coffee," she called to Joe as he peeked his head around the door frame. He responded with, "You know where it is."

She helped herself and headed for her favorite booth and the man who occupied it. "Mind if I join you?"

"Go ahead," Benedict answered.

She settled in, added two packets of sugar to her coffee and studied the soldier across from her. He wasn't lean like Gary. Benedict was more the compact but stocky type. He'd be fast and furious, she figured. Not like Gary, who'd be fast and fluid. Benedict had a regulation buzz cut and she wondered if Gary's hair had stood up that straight. Now it was short, but not military short.

She shook her head, trying to dismiss the image of Gary. She wanted to talk to Benedict.

He apparently wanted to talk to her. "Will Goober be all right with Guzman? I mean, why were you there?"

Leann immediately flashed on Gary and Wilma from last night. Gary might not be the most polished handler, but he'd been out with his dog, trying his best. In her book, that took heart. She blew a mist of steam from the top of her coffee, took a sip, still too hot, and said, "Someone complained about barking. It's nothing. Goober will be fine, but I really think it's strange you took a chance driving all this way to drop off a dog with a complete stranger. What if Gary said no?"

"My orders were not to take no for an answer," Benedict said, wiping a smudge of syrup from his shirt.

"Orders?"

"Guzman's commanding officer is worried about him. He told me to take the dog, leave it in Gary's truck if I had to, and retreat."

Leann almost spit out the coffee she'd just inhaled. "Retreat? What?"

"Gary's having a bit of trouble adjusting to civilian life. We all do. When Max told the commander how much time Gary was spending with Wilma, Commander thought another dog would be just the thing."

"That's pretty presumptuous," Leann noted.

"You're telling me. And, just how the commander knew I had a dog I didn't want is pretty amazing, too."

"How could you not want Goober?"

Benedict merely shrugged. "I'm never home."

"Was Goober really your mother's?"

"Nah, she was my sister's, who really is pregnant with triplets. Her youngest boy, turns out, has asthma, so I took the dog to help them out. Which," he added, "I have done."

"Do you even know Gary?" Leann asked.

"No, we've had different deployments. I hear he's a decent guy."

Leann couldn't respond to that. She knew a few decent men, worked with them. She didn't want to continue that thread because one of those decent guys might get her promotion.

Benedict rolled his eyes. "I was going to put Goober up on Craigslist. Last time Goober had puppies, that's what my sister did. But, I could never disobey an order from the commander."

Leann thought back to Bianca's Bed-and-Breakfast this morning and wondered what demons were chasing Gary that had his former commanding officer sending him dogs to take care of.

GARY REREAD CHAPTER FOUR AGAIN. It had a checklist for training an adult dog. Unfortunately, the author of *How to Train Your Dog in Three Days* hadn't taken into account a dog that only understood German. So far today,

Gary had requested that Wilma come a dozen times. Wilma ignored him a dozen times.

Instead, she ran back and forth across his aunt Bianca's backyard, skidding up dirt and leaving a gift in the garden that Gary quickly cleaned up.

"Any progress?" Bianca called as she stepped onto the back porch.

"No."

"It will happen."

"I'm not so sure."

"I remember when your dad was about twelve, and he came home with some old mutt he'd found abandoned by the railroad tracks."

Gary stopped. His aunt rarely mentioned his father. Sometimes he even forgot that his father was Aunt Bianca's little brother. She seemed so much like everyone else, the good side, his mom's side.

"The dog, oh, I don't remember his name," she continued, "but he'd obviously been on his own for a long time. He had no social graces."

"Like Wilma?" Gary said, trying to bring the conversation back to now, these dogs, himself, not his dad.

"No, Wilma's a good dog. She just misses her owner. Berto's dog was missing half its fur and half an ear. It would run around in circles, jumping for hours." Aunt Bianca laughed. "Drove our mother crazy. But, your father never gave up. By the time he got finished with that dog, you'd never have known he was a wild stray. Roberto was always trying to take care of animals and people."

Gary almost pointed out how his father hadn't taken much care of his own family. But, something in Aunt Bianca's expression changed his mind, so instead he changed the subject and said, "Goober doesn't act like Wilma."

Aunt Bianca glanced over at Goober, who followed at Wilma's heels, herding the other dog. "She's older."

He turned his attention back to Wilma, who'd given up trying to impress them with her running and turning skills and was now rolling on her back.

Gary patted his left leg and once again called for Wilma in German. The dog remained on its haunches. Goober, however, trotted obediently over and looked up at Gary.

"You so remind me of Berto," Aunt Bianca said.

Gary felt a knot forming between his shoulder blades. He shook his head. "No, I'm not like him."

"You are. More than any of the others—"

"Aunt Bianca, I'm not like him."

"Anna's about to graduate college. Hector's finishing his doctorate. You and Oscar are here. It's time to think about the past, about your father. I've never believed he just walked away. He came here all those years ago, and it was like he was on a mission. There was something going on. I just wish I knew what happened."

The knot tightened and so did his stomach. "I don't want to talk about it."

Aunt Bianca stopped rustling the fur on top of Goober's head. "That's the problem. We didn't talk about it enough. Your mother and I were so careful not to upset you kids. We should have questioned things more when your father disappeared."

Gary froze.

"Do you remember that your father was last seen here in Sarasota Falls?" Aunt Bianca queried.

Gary did know that.

"I just think," Aunt Bianca continued, "there's more to find."

Gary really wanted to run, disappear, which he was good at. But he was stuck and, unfortunately, starting to think of a few what-ifs.

"No," he finally said. "My mom tried to find him, waited and…"

The expression on Bianca's face said differently. "Aunt Bianca, I know that my dad's leaving was bad, but that doesn't mean we didn't care or notice him gone. And, I'm sure the police—"

Aunt Bianca interrupted with "could have done more."

Where was this coming from? Why now? Taking a deep breath, he walked toward his aunt and put an arm around her shoulder. "Aunt Bianca, your family helped settle Sarasota Falls. No way would an effort not be made to find him. As for me and my siblings, we missed him every single day. But, we got by. Sometimes that's the best you can do." Gary bent down, picked up one of Wilma's toys and threw it as far as he could. Wilma took off running.

"No." Bianca's voice was now matter-of-fact. "It's not the best. It's the easiest."

Gary hated this, hated that she was taking him to a dark place he'd not revisited in a long, long time.

"Your mother too easily believed that he'd left her. I questioned his leaving, and at first she listened. But as more time went by, she stopped believing in him. But why? Something kept him from coming back."

"Maybe because he had a girlfriend," Gary ground out. It's what he'd always thought, feared, but never mentioned to his mother. Instead, he'd internalized it. Maybe that's why he'd never wanted to marry and made darn sure to never get close to someone who wanted to marry him.

Aunt Bianca shook her head. "No, not a girlfriend."

"Maybe it was because he was tired of having all us kids. Oscar remembers the last fight our parents had."

"He'd never walk out on you children."

"He did," Gary insisted. "My mother was beyond hurt and she didn't declare him dead for years."

Aunt Bianca raised her hand. "The family needs closure. Think about it. That's all I'm asking."

Wilma whined a bit and this time when Gary took the toy and threw it, it sailed over the back fence, no chance for Wilma to retrieve.

"Look," Aunt Bianca said, relaxing a little, "Goober's owner said it best. You have time. So, I'm now asking for a favor. Figure out what really happened."

"Almost twenty years later?"

"Yes, if anyone can do it, you can. You can ask Leann to help. She's trying to make a name for herself. Solving a cold case might be the very thing."

Working a cold case alongside a pretty detective was not a good idea. Of that, Gary was sure.

CHAPTER FOUR

WEDNESDAY WAS LEANN'S day off.

In truth, as she turned into the elementary school's parking lot, she mused how this day probably wouldn't be too relaxing. Number one on her schedule was to switch her cop persona for her mom persona.

If she were lucky, she'd do a decent job.

The problem with being a cop, Leann thought while standing at the back of her son's sixth-grade classroom, was she'd grown used to issuing orders and having them immediately obeyed.

That didn't work in a sixth-grade classroom, especially when she was dressed in tennis shoes, old jeans and a bright red button-down.

"Mom," Tim whispered, "don't embarrass me."

She shot him a look that had just last week sent a computer hacker to his knees in fear. Tim, however, was made of sterner stuff and huffed away. Honestly, working a ten-hour shift yesterday bringing down bad guys—Gary, dog owner extraordinaire; the outdated tag guy; and two speeders—was easier than helping in her older son's class. And, to add insult to injury, she was helping with a Valentine's Day art project. First problem—Leann wasn't artistic. Second problem—she'd not been anyone's Valentine in—she quickly counted in her head—five years.

No, six.

"Mom," came a groan.

For the next hour, Leann worked her station. Every fifteen minutes she got a new group of eleven- and twelve-year-olds. She provided paint, clean paintbrushes and wipes to clean their hands with. Pinecones went from brittle brown to bright pink or red. Some pinecones were saturated; others were spotty. Most of the girls didn't get any paint on their hands but cleaned them anyway. Most of the boys got paint on their hands, shirts and pants. Tim—she was no longer allowed to call him Bug, her pet name for him—managed to get paint on his ear. She quickly whipped out her cell phone and took a photo, which earned yet another roll of the eyes and an exasperated, "Moooom!"

Finally, the kids trudged off to PE and she and Patsy, the mother who'd thought up this punishment, helped the teacher clean up. In two days—once the paint dried—the students would glue on fake eyes and kissy lips and add pipe cleaners for arms and legs. Then they'd add a heart to the Valentine people. Leann figured it would have been easier to hand them a piece of paper and some colored pencils.

Patsy Newcastle, mom and Pinterest fan extraordinaire, never lacked for ideas. She'd found the Valentine's people art project on Pinterest and had fallen in love. No surprise. Last year, Leann had helped the sixth-graders—then fifth-graders—make flowerpot people for Christmas, pinto bean turkeys for Thanksgiving and giant, hanging black licorice spiders for Halloween.

Leann felt sorry for Aaron in fourth grade. Anything art related was really limited, so Leanne usually took home extra unused material from Tim's class so she and Aaron could make the projects. He liked making the giant licorice spider the best and probably would still have it hanging from his ceiling if he hadn't eaten it.

She wasn't so sure she still liked Patsy, who was saying, "I've already got an idea for Easter."

"Are we even allowed to celebrate Easter in school?" Leann cautioned.

Patsy narrowed her eyes. "I'll take responsibility."

And, Leann would back her up. Patsy had been her best friend since their own sixth-grade year. The only private school in town had closed down, and, gasp, the Crabtree children had been forced into attending public school.

Leann loved it. The first day, she'd sat across from Patsy, who secretly passed her a stick of gum, and their friendship had been cemented. They'd become even closer when they gave birth to their first babies on the same day. Ryan hadn't made it back to town and to the hospital until it was time to drive Leann and little Ryan—her ex insisted on naming the baby after himself—home. Patsy's husband, however, had bounced between rooms, handing out chocolate cigars to visitors—Patsy had dozens; Leann had two: Patsy's husband and Gail—and making sure both women had plenty of chocolate. Later, Patsy confided that half the time when he handed out a cigar, he'd said, "We have a boy! And so does Leann."

The day Leann's divorce finalized she stopped calling Ryan by his first name and switched to his middle name of Timothy, now Tim. So far, he hadn't questioned it.

Exiting the classroom, they made their way past the playground—earning Leann a "Hi, Mom!" from Aaron, who was swinging and not embarrassed of her at all—and through the school office to their cars. Patsy wasn't going back to work. She'd married a doctor and now acted as his receptionist, meaning she could make her own hours.

"I've got your boys after school," Patsy reminded her. "Don't worry. I'm thinking pizza and *Star Wars*."

"I'm thinking pizza and homework," Leann countered.

"I'm thinking a free babysitter is worth the price." Patsy's laugh choked off almost before it started. "I'm sorry. I shouldn't tease about this."

Leann shook her head. "Don't be. I knew Ryan would exit out eventually."

"Nothing will change," Patsy predicted. Her tone, however, didn't support her words. "When do you see the lawyer about the new custody arrangements?"

"Tomorrow."

"I can come with you."

"No, I'll be fine."

"You don't have to always do everything by yourself. You have friends." Patsy got in her car, rolled down her window and added, "I certainly don't hesitate to make you do things with me, even if you'd rather do anything else. Don't forget you're both attending and helping with the Mother/Son Valentine's Day dance Saturday after this one."

"No kidding," Leann said. "Both my boys have offered their opinions about my presence. Aaron thinks it's cool, but Tim assures me no one will be attending. No one. He insists the school will be empty."

"Being a sixth-grader's mom is not for wimps," Patsy cautioned. "Neither is being a cop. I hear there's a good-looking newcomer in town and that twice you've threatened to arrest him."

"What?"

"I gave you every opportunity to bring it up," Patsy said. "You could have mentioned Gary Guzman when we were setting up the art project or just now as we're fixing to leave, but no, not a word. I have to bring it up. What kind of best friend are you?"

"The kind that doesn't bring up unimportant things. The kind who doesn't go around arresting good-looking newcomers."

"Ah, so you admit he's good-looking." Patsy

emphasized the word. "Leann, I've seen him walking his dog. The man is gorgeous."

"Dogs," Leann corrected. "Now he has dogs. As in more than one. And, he's unemployed and ex-military. I've already been a military wife. Rewarding, but she wanted a personal challenge for herself. Nope, nope, not the man for me. I could never trust him. I can't believe you want me to go all doe-eyed over someone I'd never be able to trust."

"Actually, yes, I do. You need a life, especially now that Ryan's moving back." Patsy's voice practically oozed as she tried to add humor to what Leann considered the worst news ever. "Gary is Oscar's brother, which means he's nothing like your ex, and I'm sure he's a good guy. Go have some fun. At the very least, Gary could remind Ryan what a mistake he made letting you go."

Leann shook her head. Patsy watched way too many romance movies and truly believed in heroes. Leann knew better. What she didn't share with Patsy was that the gorgeous—and yes he was—Gary Guzman, however, wasn't just unemployed. He was also living on his aunt's charity and, by his own account, was not at a place he could take care of others.

"Ahem!" Patsy was louder this time. "You're off in la-la land, definitely not like you."

"Sorry," Leann said. "I've got a lot on my mind."

"Any of it have to do with Geraldo Guzman?"

"Geraldo?"

"That is his first name. You knew that, right?"

"No." Since the first meeting, she'd been one step behind. First, not getting his name at all and now not having the whole name.

"It's a manly name."

Leann almost gagged. One thing was for sure, Patsy wasn't subtle. She was trying to get a rise out of Leann, but it wasn't going to happen. "I… Oh, never mind. I need to get back to work." Then, she rolled up her window and drove away, making sure not to look in the rearview mirror, where she'd see Patsy either bent over laughing or, worse, with a contemplative look on her face as she tried to figure out ways to get Leann and Gary together.

Not happening.

Worst timing ever.

Patsy had always dragged Leann into activities she'd never have ventured into on her own. And, Patsy had what looked like a perfect life. Her two children, a boy and girl, had been blessed with the willing-to-do-homework gene. Leann's two boys hadn't. Tim on a good day remembered he had homework but didn't do it. Aaron, a fourth-grader, couldn't even spell *homework*, so he claimed.

She didn't pressure her boys. She expected them to do their best, worked with them when they struggled, and pushed only when she had to. They knew they were loved.

Something that, when she was their age, she'd not experienced. And, quite honestly, she'd not experienced it as an adult either. She doubted she ever would.

A NOISE REVERBERATED, LOUDLY. Gary's eyes snapped open; sleep interrupted. He rolled and in one fluid motion crouched facing the door. His eyes took a moment to adjust to the light so he could note windows with their blinds down but allowing in sunshine—too bright to signal morning—that accentuated a light burgundy door with a glass ornate knob. A white robe advertising Bianca's Bed-and-Breakfast hung on a hook.

It took a few deep breaths before his heartbeat slowed and the adrenaline rush ebbed. He could accept that he was in Sarasota Falls, in a bedroom.

Downstairs came voices, his aunt greeting new guests and the chaos new guests carried with them; simultaneously, Wilma began to bark.

It was a safe kind of chaos, which, unfortunately, had induced Gary to head upstairs a few hours ago to check his cell phone and make a few calls. He remembered lying down, thinking to be lazy as he checked his phone but falling asleep for no reason...

The way his heart was beating, he knew he'd not fall back to sleep, not that he wanted to, and he needed to get Wilma quieted before the neighbors called the police again.

Hmm, would Leann be the responder?

No, his luck wouldn't work that way. This time he'd get his brother. Come to think of it, he didn't want to tell either of them that he'd been napping away the late afternoon with nothing to do and no one to notice.

Quickly, Gary changed out of his jeans and into shorts, T-shirt and his jogging shoes.

His workout routine had the additional perk of making his aunt Bianca laugh. Something about his having a Bianca's Bed-and-Breakfast bath towel spread on the backyard grass, jumping over it and doing squats, tickled her funny bone. Then, Wilma gave him grief when he'd added her to the jogging regimen. Their time leash jogging had been a combination of his forcefully dragging her along or giving up and letting the dog sniff and meander whenever she wanted.

It meant Gary got half a workout.

Gary did, however, understand and appreciate the solid offensive stance Wilma assumed during cat reconnaissance.

Today, though, newcomer Goober proved to be a willing participant and eagerly took to the harness.

When Gary started his run, Goober trotted alongside in perfect sync. Surprise, surprise, Wilma followed Goober's example. Maybe tomorrow he'd ditch Wilma, just take Goober, and see if he could do a four-minute mile, weighed down by a sixty-pound backpack and with a collie as his formation.

Something about the evening felt right, so instead of heading to the park and jogging the trail, Gary headed through some residential areas where cars were turning into driveways and individuals or families were exiting: parents who just finished work or parents who'd finished work, picked up kids and finally arrived home.

He and his siblings had walked back and

forth to school, no need for keys as four houses in a row, on their street, had belonged to relatives. There'd always been an aunt with a cookie or an uncle wanting Gary to help rake the leaves. Plus, there was a key under a rock in the backyard. Probably still there.

The neighborhood changed, the houses got smaller and the yards looked more lived in. Gary's jog turned into a slow trot as his conversation with Aunt Bianca reared its head and memories materialized. The home he'd grown up in had been the last on the block, the old farm of some long-ago immigrant, and it had been added to by so many generations that it looked like three houses all leaning against each other.

He stopped, no longer smelling the juniper or feeling the faint pain in his thigh where a piece of shrapnel had carved a quarter-sized hole.

Theirs had been the house with the best yard. He'd grown up playing kickball, dodgeball and hide-and-seek, until his father had disappeared and hide-and-seek became a term his mother used disparagingly.

"Hey!"

The word wasn't directed at him, but it was loud enough to get Gary's attention. Goober's ears perked up. Wilma was too busy investigating a patch of grass to notice.

Two boys tumbled from a house about four lots away from where he stood. The older one clutched a football. Squaring off in the front yard, they began tossing. Within a minute, Gary could see that the taller one clearly had skill but no patience with the younger one, who seemed better at chasing the ball than catching it. The younger boy also had zero control when throwing.

"Hey!" The word became the chant of the older one as he got more and more frustrated.

Gary smiled. This could have been a scene from his childhood. He and Oscar with their younger brother, Hector, who'd always been more brainy than brawny.

"Hey!" Not a chance was the older boy going to get a workout. He seemed to know it, and his cheeks went slightly red even as his lips pressed together in ire. "I might as well be playing with a girl," he finally spat.

Gary almost laughed. His sister, Anna, ran faster than big brother Oscar, threw farther than baby brother Hector and caught better than Gary—not that he'd ever admit the defect.

"I'm telling Mom," the little guy croaked.

"No need," said a familiar voice.

What? Did the woman have a beacon that drew him to her? Gary watched as Leann stepped out from the front door. Her hair was longer than he'd thought, and a bit redder, like mahogany. He moved off the sidewalk and onto grass where he watched from a safe distance, somewhat hidden by a tree. Goober obediently sat at his feet. Wilma pulled at the leash, heading toward Leann and her sons. Not a chance. Gary liked where he was, what he was watching.

The older boy made a strange hissing sound. Gary recognized it. It was the sound of a youngster who knew he was about to be bested and didn't like it one bit.

"You don't count, Mom," the kid said. "You're a cop. That means you can throw a football."

"I could throw a football long before I became a cop," Leann responded. "And, I've never, not once, thrown a football at a criminal."

Gary had a sudden image of Leann throwing a football at some punk running away from a convenience store robbery.

"I have, however," Leann said, "thrown footballs at my boys. Both of them!" With that, she snagged the football from the younger boy's hands and spiraled it to the older boy, who jumped, managed to get his hands almost on the sides but lost his grip.

"Ha!" Leann said.

"Ha," the younger boy echoed.

For the next few minutes, the front yard was filled with the younger boy tripping over his feet; the older boy scrambling, trying to catch easily and throw fiercely; and his mother not giving an inch until finally when the ball landed in a neighbor's yard. All three of them charged for it and fell in a heap, laughing, until the younger boy's hand shot in the air, ball carefully balanced.

Goober let out a low whine expressing her desire to inch closer, get to know them, play. Gary understood. He wanted to join in the fray, too.

What was it his aunt had said? Oh, yeah, that Leann had a story worth telling.

Gary turned and walked away. He knew all about stories, especially the kind his aunt read. She still believed in happily-ever-after. He wanted to, thought maybe his brother Oscar had managed to find it, but Gary too vividly remembered his mother's love story, which ended with his father walking off the page. Never returning.

Aunt Bianca believed Gary could actually

find out what happened to his father. Maybe that's what he should focus on because he sure didn't need to be focusing on single mother Leann Bailey, who was all I-can-out-football-you-and-look-great-doing-it.

She was all about stability; he was all about just making it from one day to the next.

CHAPTER FIVE

"HE FILED HIS PAPERWORK."

Leann didn't let her steps falter or her face register surprise when Oscar Guzman made the announcement the moment she entered the station late Thursday afternoon.

"When?" she asked.

"Yesterday at the close of his shift."

Leann knew Lieutenant Lucas Stillwater had been on duty until almost midnight because of an automobile accident with serious injuries.

"Chief Riley say anything yet about it?"

"No."

She and Oscar looked at each other, something vaguely different in the air. Just yesterday, they'd been contemporaries looking toward the future when they both would want the same promotion. Now, they were competitors, each wanting—no, needing—the same job.

"Thanks for letting me know," she said.

Oscar nodded.

Leann headed for the restroom, where she checked her hair and uniform. She was the first female cop in Sarasota Falls' history. She had to shine because she not only wanted to prove herself, but she also hoped to pave the way for the next female officer.

Her years on the force had been an uphill battle that she'd won! Was still winning.

Next, she sat at her desk, logging onto her computer while also listening to the messages on her phone. They were brief and unimportant. She spent a few moments reading the two priority calls—nothing pending. Oscar, who managed to get to work ten minutes before shift began, filled her in on a malicious destruction of property incident.

Preliminary work done, she stood and headed for the cruiser. She checked the backseat and trunk before finally sliding behind the wheel ready to start her shift.

The malicious destruction of property had to do with a woman Leann knew through her youngest son. Just one more happily-ever-after that wasn't going to happen. The divorce had finalized yesterday, and the husband wasn't taking it well.

Once again, Leann sent up a quick thank-you prayer that for the majority of her children's growing-up years, her husband had been across the ocean.

That was all about to change, and in two hours she'd be sitting across from her lawyer and finding out the changes her ex-husband wanted since he was moving back to Sarasota Falls.

The car in front of her ran the red light at Main. She hit the siren and then issued a warning to the driver. Leann then drove to the high school and cruised the parking lot. Following that, she did a wellness check on Sarasota Falls' oldest resident, who lived alone and who sometimes forgot to go grocery shopping. After ascertaining the lady was keeping company with a bowl of cereal and watching a rerun of *Judge Judy* on TV, Leann called in a seven and headed for City Hall for her appointment at the law office of Fred Balliard.

Swallowing, she made herself rethink "her" boys and changed it to "their" boys. Ryan, at first, had paid a bit more child support because she'd returned to Sarasota Falls without a college diploma or much work experience. When she'd made it through the academy and was hired by the police department, his support had lessened. He'd also tried to get his payments down by claiming his parents were acting on his behalf and shared custody.

Now he was exiting out, wanting to negotiate the future and share custody. Leann was worried about losing child support. She really needed the lieutenant position.

She was also worried that Ryan would dash into his sons' lives, make a splash and then disappear. She didn't trust him to stay.

He hadn't stayed with her.

Sure made giving a ticket over expired tags seem trivial.

An hour later, she was greeted and offered a bottled water by the receptionist. Leann took a long drink before choosing a too-hard chair in a too-fancy waiting room, cooling her heels and worrying.

The door opened and Tom Riley, the chief of police, walked in. He was in street clothes, coming in on his own time because a cop's time was never really their own.

"I didn't know you had an appointment today," Leann said.

"Last-minute thing. You okay?" He stopped in front of her.

"I'm fine."

"You don't look fine," he observed.

"I'm still pretty amazed that Ryan's not only leaving the military but returning here." *Amazed* was a good word: *dismayed* a better one. She'd wanted him to be career: always gone, seldom around.

Chief Riley smiled, greeted the receptionist, refused a bottled water, took the seat next to Leann and wisely changed the subject. "I hear you met Oscar's brother Gary."

"At the park Monday night. Then, yesterday again because his dog was barking."

"Today it's both dogs," Chief Tom Riley corrected. "I fielded a call today from their neighbors."

"They complain about everything."

"What's your impression of Gary?"

"He's very different from Oscar."

"How?"

Leann thought a moment and then shrugged. She had no real answer, just an uncomfortable feeling that she'd met a man she couldn't figure out. "I don't know. Call it intuition."

Chief Riley merely smiled. He'd gotten so much easier to get along with since he'd married last month. Oscar said that having someone to go home to was making Chief Riley soft.

Tom had overheard and accused Oscar of

the same thing. Oscar, married just over a year, didn't deny it.

Sitting in her lawyer's office, about to face life changes thanks to the return of her ex-husband, Leann knew there wasn't a man alive she'd trust enough to marry.

The silence ticked by. Even the receptionist's fingers, flying across the keyboard, seemed muted. Finally, Chief Riley asked, "You had a chance to check out the whereabouts of Jace Blackgoat?"

"I thought I'd try to head out to Russell's later. See if Jace has been around," Leann said.

Russell Blackgoat was the grandfather Leann wished she had. "How much trouble is Jace in?"

"Did you read the report?"

"I know he's been in a bar fight over in Taber, but that's two hundred miles away."

Chief Riley nodded, and Leann wondered why the chief was so concerned. Not only was Sarasota Falls safe compared with many of the cities surrounding it, but the police force was top-notch and thankfully, well-funded. They'd even hired a new officer just last month. Zack Bridges might not look old enough to wear the badge but he'd gone through the police academy and was sincere.

A loud ping sounded. The receptionist hurried back into the room, picked up the phone and said, "Yes, Mr. Balliard." She listened for a moment, and then said, "Leann, you can go on in."

Leann gave a tight smile and entered Balliard's office.

Except for white and dark brown—paint, carpeting and woodworking—the only bright color in the room came from a picture of the American flag that hung behind the desk.

"Please sit down, Leann." Balliard, a tall African American man wearing a dark suit, striped tie and white shirt, shook her hand and directed her to the seat in front of him.

She sat and looked at the lawyer who would be representing her now that her ex was trying to reestablish a connection with his sons. He shuffled a few papers and then smiled at her, waiting.

"What I really want," Leann said, "is for custody, visitation, child support and such to continue as it is now."

"I have to be candid, Leann, that's unlikely," Balliard said.

"What does Ryan's lawyer have to say?"

"Ryan's moving back home, already has

gainful employment and intends to be an involved parent."

"I don't trust him," Leann said. "He forgets birthdays." She didn't add that when Tim was a baby, Ryan wouldn't even change a diaper. Her main memory of his early parenting was asking her to keep Tim quiet, so the baby wouldn't interrupt Ryan's TV watching or video gaming.

"Honorable discharge, commendations and a paper trail of consistent child support. Add in his parents assisting with the boys' care, and Ryan's got a good case."

Leann sighed. Joint custody would definitely mean less or no child support: her biggest fear. She'd been raised never having to worry about money. Then she'd married Ryan and worried a little bit, but the military offered base housing, a decent salary, and so on, and the fact that their bank account wasn't something to brag about didn't bother her. When she'd divorced Ryan, though, she'd discovered what having no money really meant.

She'd called her parents for help once. She'd never do that again.

She didn't care, not for herself, but she did for her boys.

Words Leann didn't allow her children to

say almost bubbled out. She'd had a plan. Ryan said he'd be giving Uncle Sam twenty years. Had he stayed true to that plan, Tim would be nineteen and Aaron seventeen. No worries, not really. Now, Ryan was exiting before he'd put in twenty years, affecting his pension and retirement.

"Okay," she said, keeping her voice strong, "what are my options?"

Balliard folded his hands and leaned forward. "Leann, more than a lawyer, I'm your friend. I've known Ryan as long as I've known you. Try to work this out without lawyers. What you'll pay us might equal Aaron's first semester in college. Talk with Ryan, maybe the two of you can be reasonable. Consider the man he is today rather than the boy you married and divorced. Remember, what you decide affects the boys."

"They only know him from brief visits."

"You have to be realistic. Ryan's parents have told your boys all about his glory days. I've been to that house. It has to what amounts to an only-child hall of fame."

Leann closed her eyes, pictured the hallway, which indeed boasted Ryan's history from birth to deployment. The only photo they'd taken down was the one of Ryan and Leann's wedding. It hadn't been a fancy ceremony since they'd gotten married by the justice of the peace. She'd been three months pregnant. The ink on his enlistment papers was still wet.

Sometimes she wondered how they'd have done if she and Ryan had waited. If she'd gone off to college while he put in his first four years. They'd have matured, had time to be kids before they had kids.

Balliard broke into her thoughts. "You need to prepare for his return home and the loss of some support."

Tears welled, spilled over, and Leann fought to keep her voice steady. "I can do that."

Balliard reached across the desk and put his hand on hers. "Look, from here on out, every move you make, every concession you give, should be for the well-being of Tim and Aaron. If you keep that in mind, your ex-husband will have to do the same, because if he doesn't, the courts won't look favorably on him." He held up a hand, anticipating her retort. "If the courts don't look favorably on him, neither will your sons, and no matter what, he's their father."

The one thing Ryan had done extremely well: fathered two awesome kids. For the next few minutes, Balliard went over the custody agreement from a decade earlier, letting her know what she could expect to stay the same and what she'd have to be willing to negotiate.

She struggled as Balliard's words meant giving up control, meant trusting her ex-husband. Finally, her lawyer ended the session, asking her to schedule another appointment after Ryan returned.

She exited Balliard's office and headed for the lobby. She'd known Ryan all her life, had been his science partner at Sarasota Falls Elementary when he'd been struggling to get passing grades. He'd given her a used eraser as a thank-you. In high school, junior year, he'd sat in front of her every class. She'd been a Crabtree, and he'd been a Bailey. It had been the beginning of their relationship and what seemed like her quickest ticket out of town.

She'd always known that in some ways she'd orchestrated their romance, had wanted it more than he did. She'd wanted away from her parents' house and to not be dependent on them for anything. College would have been on their dime and their terms. She wanted to stand on her own. She'd also been in love and thought it would be better to have Ryan at her side. Then, she'd gotten pregnant and college had been a distant dream, rather than immediate one.

She owed him and could be the bigger man, er, woman.

In the waiting room, Chief Riley was on his cell phone, giving someone directions. Good, she didn't want to answer his questions.

Leann pushed open the door to the hallway, hurried to the drinking fountain and took a long drink, hoping to open her airway, push away the raw feeling that had accompanied her from the lawyer's office.

Detachment. They'd pounded her over the head with the word at the academy. She could do it.

"You okay?"

She recognized the voice. The phrase "kicked when you're down" crossed her mind. Gary wasn't the last person in the world she wanted to see at the moment. That would be her ex-husband.

"Fine."

"You look a little frazzled," he said, matter-of-factly. His eyes glittered, dark and moody, in the same way they had that night he watched her sister and brother-in-law fight/whine on the playground. "Come to think of it, the first time I met you, you looked frazzled."

She frowned.

"You need to sit down or something?" he queried.

"No, I'm fine."

He looked over her head, studying occupants' names as well as their office numbers.

"Why are you here?" she asked.

"I'm looking for Frederick Balliard."

"He's the third door on the left."

"Drei?" he queried.

She stepped back and almost smiled.

"That's right," he said. "I've started learning German online. Thanks to you and Wilma."

Against her better judgment, Leann had to admit that Gary's appearance wasn't the only thing she admired. She also admired his quiet confidence.

Something about him felt familiar. If Leann were the trusting type, given time, she might be able to become close with him. But, no.

She trusted his brother Oscar, somewhat. After all, they had foiled robberies, pulled children from an overturned school bus and even busted a meth lab last month. The Sarasota Falls Police Department was small. Until Zack's hiring, she and Oscar were the newest officers. She'd signed on over five years ago when Ryan was just entering first grade. Oscar was on his second year now. There had to be a tiny shred of trust involved in their relationship.

She and Gary, however, had no relationship.

"Did you just come out of Balliard's office?" he asked.

"Fred's office. I've known him all my life."

"And even though you've just left the office of a man you've known since childhood, you're tightly wired and exasperated. So, you were in there because of some case you're working on."

He hadn't asked a question. No, he'd made a statement, and she could answer honestly. "No, not a case I'm working on. Something else."

"Something else, eh? Something personal."

She opened her mouth, intent on dismissing him, with attitude, but Gary reached out and carefully tucked a strand of hair over her left ear. "I believe you have white paint on your ear."

Then, he walked around her and headed down the hall and through the door she'd just exited.

She frowned, annoyed that he'd left her speechless, and wondering why no one else had mentioned the paint on her ear. Well, if she knew anything it was that doing an art project in her son's class was bound to leave behind residual damage. How she'd missed paint on her ear, though, was beyond her.

Almost against her will, she fingered the top of her ear, the ear that still held the heat of his touch.

CHAPTER SIX

GARY HAD ALWAYS loved spending time with his aunt Bianca. She'd been the one who'd pushed him—not quite a teen—out the door, handed him—an angry kid—his skateboard and said, "Don't return until you're too exhausted to talk back."

His own mother had kept a tight rein on her brood and had only tightened her grip after their father was gone. She'd followed Gary to the skateboard park as if afraid he, too, would disappear. He pushed her away with both hands. He knew he was the son responsible for the most gray hairs. Every once in a while he thought about calling to say he was sorry, but the words never came, so he did the next best thing. He sent her money and when he came home, he fixed things around the house. It was Aunt Bianca's place in Sarasota Falls, however, where he'd always felt he could breath. Something about small towns and open spaces.

Since she didn't have any guests currently

staying at the B and B, she'd invited his brother Oscar's family for dinner.

"I saw Officer Bailey today," Gary informed Oscar after taking the biggest chicken leg before his brother could.

"Officer Bailey?" Oscar's wife, Shelley, queried, taking a napkin and brushing something off the high chair tray. Little O, Oscar and Shelley's one-year-old, didn't notice.

"He met Leann the other night and now can't stop talking about her." Oscar scooped most of the mashed potatoes onto his plate and then passed the almost empty bowl to Gary.

"What?" Gary frowned at the empty bowl that landed in his hands.

Shelley stared at Gary. "Have we ever heard you mention a woman before? You never tell us about anyone you're interested in."

Aunt Bianca stood and took the empty mashed potato bowl. She winked at Shelley.

Oscar laughed, but to cover it he pretended to choke on his green beans.

"Whoa. I'm not interested in Officer Bailey, or anyone else for that matter," Gary said.

"Why not?" Shelley queried. "She's great."

"Because," Bianca said, handing Gary a now full bowl of mashed potatoes, "she's settled. Happy here in this ole small town. Knows what she wants. Gary, here, is afraid that if he let himself like a woman, *really* like a woman, he might be tempted to settle down."

Oscar choked again. This time Gary wasn't sure his brother was pretending.

"I'll admit," Bianca countered, "I was surprised when Leann came back to Sarasota Falls to stay. In fact, I almost fell off my porch I was so surprised."

Gary started to say something but noted the rapt attention his brother and sister-in-law were paying to Bianca.

"Why did it surprise you?" Shelley asked. "My dad said Leann and Ryan were born and raised here, although, much too young to get married."

"They were. And, Leann married Ryan Bailey to get away from her parents. He was a good kid but had no direction. When Leann left him, I'd have expected her to go anywhere but here. She's got grit, that girl. Doesn't matter where she settles, she'll do fine."

"Her parents are rich. Surely she'd come here for their support," Shelley sputtered.

"Sometimes glitter hides imperfections," Bianca said. "Think about it. Have you seen Leann's parents with her boys? Do they watch

Tim and Aaron while Leann works? No, Ryan's parents watch over the boys."

"Aunt Bianca's right," Oscar said. "Leann talks about Ryan's parents, and she talks about her sister and her parents' housekeeper, Clarissa. I've never heard her say anything about her own parents except that they disapprove of her being a cop. I know they don't help her."

Shelley frowned. "I always thought she had the perfect life."

"No life is perfect," Aunt Bianca said.

"If it makes you feel better," Oscar offered, "I feel you've given me a perfect life."

Shelley smacked him, and then looked at Gary. "Where did you see Leann today?"

"Did she come out here because of the dogs, again?" Oscar teased.

"No, I ran into her just as she left Fred Balliard's office."

Oscar nodded. "I'd forgotten. She was meeting the lawyer because of her ex."

"That explains her mood," Gary said, finally getting around to putting a heaping scoop of mashed potatoes on his plate and passing the bowl to Shelley.

"What do you mean?"

"She was on edge. What's happening with her ex?"

"Ryan's getting out of the service and coming home." Bianca handed Little O a green bean he'd just thrown at her.

"I thought he was in for life," Shelley commented.

"I saw his mother at the grocery store," Bianca put in. "She said he should be home in the next week or two."

"And," Oscar reported, "he's already hired a lawyer to get his child support reduced."

"Ohhhhhh," Shelley whispered. "This makes it hard."

"What?" Gary knew he was missing something important, but the way the Guzman clan was bouncing around, no way could he keep up.

Oscar wiped some sort of orange glob from his son's chin and said, "Lucas Stillwater submitted his retirement papers this morning."

"So?" Gary knew Oscar wanted a promotion. This was good news.

"So," Oscar said, "there are two officers vying for his position."

Gary whistled, the truth finally dawning. "You and Leann, and now Leann's really going to need the money."

"And so are we," Oscar said, giving his wife a look that almost made Gary want to step out of the room. His brother had found his soul mate, and their commitment to each other was tangible.

Little O chortled, and Bianca caught another green bean midair and stilled: her eyes gleaming, her lips curling into a wide smile. "Another baby?" she guessed.

Shelley nodded.

"Bro!" Gary said.

"When?" Bianca asked.

"I'm three months along."

For the next ten minutes, Little O banged on his high chair tray catching the excitement, sending green beans flying, while everyone else focused on Oscar and his family's future. Gary was relieved they weren't addressing his lack of future.

After all, he wasn't addressing it himself.

Finally, Oscar changed the subject from new baby to something else. "That's one of the reasons I wanted to come to dinner tonight. It's last minute, but Shelley and I are going to take a brief vacation. A buddy of mine had booked a cruise for him and his wife. They can't go now, so I purchased the tickets from him."

"Where to?"

"Alaska. We'll fly to Long Beach, and then we'll be gone six days. I talked to Mom, and she's dying to look after Little O while we have a second honeymoon because come next June we're going to be busy."

"We should be saving our money," Shelley advised.

"We can make it work."

"Make it work" had been Oscar's mantra most of his life. Not Gary's. While Oscar tried to save the world, Gary focused more on the damage left behind. The problem was he'd never thought enough pieces were left behind to make anything "work" again.

"It's a good idea," Aunt Bianca said. "Maybe if your parents had done something like this, they'd—"

Oscar gave her a look. Clearly this wasn't what he'd expected her to say.

"She's been talking about our father for days," Gary put in.

"What's going on, Aunt Bianca?" Oscar managed just the right look, one that Gary never managed: concern mixed with intent. All Gary could manage was disbelief.

"I've asked Gary to look into Berto's disappearance."

Oscar set down his fork and stared at Aunt Bianca. Finally, he said, "Wow, I didn't see that coming."

"It's time," Aunt Bianca said.

Oscar nodded. "I agree."

"What?" Gary broke in. "You've never said a word about our father's disappearance, not since right after it happened."

"Because it made both Hector and Anna cry," Oscar defended himself.

Gary leaned forward. "So, you're telling me that if our father is in, say, Florida someplace with a new wife and kids, you'd like to find him and say, 'Hey, Dad'?"

"I'm not saying that at all," Oscar said. "When he first disappeared, Mom was all 'Something happened,' then that changed. I've always wondered what. Do you know, Aunt Bianca?"

"I don't. I do know that Berto came here for a reason. He was agitated. I tried to get him to confide in me, but he wouldn't."

Gary tried to remember his father. He remembered laughter, and roughhousing, and fart jokes. Most of all he remembered the day his mother told him and his siblings that their father wouldn't be coming home. Oscar had been all of twelve; Gary ten; Hector eight; Anna just six.

While Oscar took charge, Gary took to the streets; Hector escaped into books; Anna clung. She might well have saved them all. Every time Gary turned around, she'd been there: following him to the skateboard park, grabbing one of his Xbox controllers, sitting next to him spooning Fruity Pebbles into her mouth.

Shelley gave Oscar another look—Gary interpreted it as "We'll be talking later"—and got up.

Shelley pulled Little O from his high chair, brushed off a few crumbs but left a still-wet orange glob stain. Right now, everyone called the kid Little O because they were trying to differentiate. Shelley tried the "Junior" bit a few times but both Oscar and Gary gave her the evil eye. She'd also tried Ozzie. No better.

So, little Oscar—better yet, Little O—it was.

The kid would hate it once he hit fourth grade. No one wanted to be called little. Gary pushed back from the table and started to excuse himself. He needed to get out of here before Aunt Bianca brought up the search for his father again. He'd already half committed. It would take only a nudge for him to completely take on the task.

"Wait, Aunt Bianca's bringing the dessert now," Oscar said, "and we have a favor to ask."

"Name it, but not babysitting." Maybe, though, Gary considered, babysitting wouldn't be so bad. He'd just make sure he had help. Someone like Officer Leann Bailey. It might be the perfect ploy to get her next to him. He needed to make up for their exchange outside the lawyer's office. He'd known the minute he'd seen her in that hallway that she was upset. He had no clue why he'd decided to push her buttons.

Maybe because they were there and could be pushed.

"It is a form of babysitting, just not Little O. I need someone to watch Peeve while we're in Sedona," Oscar said.

Gary shot a look at his aunt, who was shaking her head and stating, "We've got two dogs too many."

Goober and Wilma were outside, mostly because Wilma was a beggar and wouldn't leave the table. She'd poke her nose in a lap, lay it on the table and scold in an indignant "Aren't you going to feed me?" series of loud barks. Goober, although incredibly well behaved, probably wasn't above snatching anything Little O happened to drop. Wilma, of course, would get there first.

"Too many dogs, I know," Oscar said, "and

I wouldn't ask except we can't take him on a cruise. He's not a service animal."

"I run a business," Aunt Bianca reminded him. "Personally, my answer is yes to Peeve and no to the other two dogs. Gary, what are you going to do? It's time to make up your mind."

"I…" What was he going to do? He didn't want to apply for jobs; he wasn't staying. And, two dogs made traveling a bit difficult even when you knew what you were doing and where you were going.

"I should have said no to both Wilma and Goober," he admitted. "Now I'm stuck."

"It's a good thing someone in the family knows how to make decisions as well as get what she wants." Aunt Bianca stood, walked out of the room and soon they heard the old rolltop desk in her office open. After a moment, she came back with the big envelope Gary had picked up from her lawyer's office on her behalf.

Shelley cleaned up the rest of the table and wiped it down, and Aunt Bianca laid three photos as well as a deed in front of her nephews.

Gary stared at a picture of slender green trees rising high in the sky, grass that needed cutting and a decrepit cabin in the midst of it all. There was a hole in the red tin roof, two of the beams holding the porch's roof up sagged, and the rock chimney was missing more than a few rocks.

"A beautiful mess," he muttered.

"Like your dog ownership," Oscar added.

At that, Shelley snickered, Aunt Bianca laughed out loud and little Oscar crooned along with them all.

"I need to make some changes to my will," Aunt Bianca said. "Not right away, and before I do, I want to see what I have."

"You own this?" Gary asked in awe.

"It belonged to my great-grandparents. I'm ashamed at how I've let it go."

"It looks pretty good," Oscar observed, "for being that old and let go. Shelley and I have been out there a time or two?"

"Where is it exactly?" Gary asked.

"Just inside city limits, about three miles down County Road 6 and off to the west. It's a mile from the base of the Jemez Mountain."

"Blackgoat land?" Shelley said.

"They still own over a hundred acres. Our family bought at the same time, not as much, forty acres just behind them. For a while, both families raised sheep."

Both Gary and Oscar raised their eyebrows.

"What?" Aunt Bianca queried. "You mean you didn't know how long the Guzman family has been in this area."

"Guess not," Gary admitted.

"The Guzmans were here when this area was little more than a settlement. There's a rumor that one of our relatives even tried to name the town Dead Bull's Corner."

"Sounds like something a Guzman would do," Gary deadpanned.

Shelley studied the photos. "It still has an outhouse. That's what I remember."

Bianca nodded. "Yes, but indoor plumbing was added in the sixties. Until your father disappeared, it was kept up. It's just been the last seventeen years that it's fallen apart."

"Exactly how long our father has been missing," Oscar noted.

"The cabin was left to Roberto and me. When your mother had him declared legally dead, it came to me."

"Why aren't you using it, or selling it, or something?" Gary asked.

"The last time I saw Roberto," Aunt Bianca said, her voice quavering, "he was standing on that porch noticing how much work needed to be done to the beams. He was going to fix it up. Oh, he'd talked about it before, but this time he sounded like he really meant it. I don't know. In the back of my mind, I think I've left it be because I kept expecting he'll show up one day and be glad I saved it for him."

"And you no longer feel that way?" Shelley asked gently.

"He had no intention of coming back," Gary said.

Bianca gave Gary a look, one that would have stilled a weaker man, but Gary wasn't weak. Gary had never believed his father would return. He'd made his little sister, Anna, cry more than once by telling her the hard truth, and to this day, whenever Gary thought of his father, he became angry and often felt frustrated.

"No," Bianca admitted. "Not after all this time."

Using one finger, Oscar pushed the photos closer to Gary. "We went there as children. Do you remember?"

Gary shook his head.

"Your mother didn't like it much," Aunt Bianca said. "She got bit by a spider the first time she visited and that ended her forays into the woods forever. It's time to fix it up. If nothing else, I can rent it out. Make some money."

Looking at Gary, Aunt Bianca said, "You should move out there, Gary. Take the dogs, take time to think about your future, and while you're doing that, fix up the place and see if there's any hint of what Berto was really doing out there."

"I'm out of your price range," Gary half joked.

"When you were young, you'd work for kisses."

"That was Oscar, not me." Gary pushed away from the table. He felt a little like he'd just been given orders and would have to head someplace he didn't really want to go. He'd be all alone out there, and since leaving the military, he'd been wary of solitude.

Right now, though, he seemed to be a dog magnet, had no place to call his own, and it was starting to drive him crazy. Aunt Bianca, with her infinite wisdom, probably knew that.

"It would take me a couple of weeks to make it livable," he finally said, aware that everyone was watching him. "A couple of months to make it livable for anyone else."

"You can borrow our camper," Oscar offered. "Live in it."

"You never let me borrow your things."

"Yes, but I want you to watch Peeve."

"Borrow the camper," Aunt Bianca suggested and gave him "the look." He had two, no three, dogs to take care of and she had a business to run and complaining neighbors.

Yup, Oscar—as always—was taking charge of his future, while Gary was being forced to dwell on his lack of one.

Gary was a loose end that needed to be tied. He didn't like it one bit.

CHAPTER SEVEN

THE BOYS' GRANDMOTHER, Tamara Bailey, opened her front door and ushered Peaches, Leann and the boys inside. The boys weren't happy. Going to Grandma's for a sleepover, while Mom worked the graveyard shift, no longer held much appeal. They preferred it when Grandma came to their house and slept in the guest room.

According to Tim, Grandma coming to their house made total sense. After all, their stuff-think Xbox- was there, and inevitably, they'd forget to bring something when packing for an overnight.

Peaches, however, was overjoyed. Grandma's house had different smells and a bigger backyard.

"Every thing all right with you?" Tamara asked.

Leann set school backpacks by the front door, checked that school IDs were inside and then stuffed a dollar in each, so that tomorrow, the boys could buy ice cream after they ate their lunch. Straightening, she said, "Yes. Everything's all right. I'm thankful that Zack's been hired. You've probably heard Oscar is taking a much-needed vacation."

Tamara nodded.

"So, yes," Leann continued, "There are portions of my life that are going well."

An expression Leann couldn't read passed over Tamara's face as she stood aside, letting two stampeding boys and one exuberant dog slide by her toward the living room.

It had to be hard, dealing with an ex daughter-in-law and returning son and not knowing which questions to ask or what to expect in terms of answers.

"Ten minutes," Leann called to her sons, "and then be sure to take the dog out."

"Milk and cookies are on the kitchen table," Tamara added.

The cookies would be homemade. No doubt Tamara would be handing Leann a container of cookies to take to the station, a station that was still so woefully understaffed that Leann had to ask, "With Oscar taking time off, can you watch the boys more often this coming week?"

"No problem at all. I'm just sad you have to work so much."

Leann was, too. It was a constant war within her heart, needing to work and so wanting to be with her boys.

"When does your shift end?" Tamara asked.

"In twelve hours, give or take, but Zack has a doctor's appointment in the morning and is coming in right after. I'll stay on patrol until he shows up and catch up on my sleep while the boys are in school."

"Good, you need to take care of yourself."

This was the moment when Tamara held up a hand for Leann to wait while Tamara quickly fetched the cookies. Not this time. Tamara, instead, had a few more probing questions. "I hear Lucas Stillwater turned in his retirement papers."

"He turned in the papers this morning. It will be a huge change. He's been there forever." He'd also been Leann's field training officer and had believed in her when many others hadn't.

"You still wanting to move up the ranks?"

"I'm considering it."

"Good thing Sarasota Falls is such a safe place to be," Tamara said brightly.

Leann knew Tamara meant those words sincerely. Only one officer had died in the line of duty, and that had been Chief Riley's partner and best friend.

Ten minutes later, Leann had the cookies and was on her way to work. She wasn't a real fan of working the zombie shift, but sometimes it worked in her favor. It meant very little sleep but it also meant she was there when her boys finished school. She could supervise home-work and stay for soccer practice.

The cookies disappeared as soon as she set them down on the counter of the break room. Leann didn't eat any; she needed to avoid any extra curves right now. Fishing an apple out of her lunch box, she checked the patrol car, secured her weapons and began patrol.

She stopped by Main Street Church. Even though the dusk of evening had already changed from muted gray to dusty charcoal, the Women's Auxiliary Club was just now streaming out the doors. Her mother belonged, so did the mayor's wife, and anyone who was anyone in the small town of Sarasota Falls. Leann didn't slow down, but before she could make her getaway, her mother waved to her. Leann called in her location, parked and ex-ited the vehicle.

When she finally stood in front of her mother, Allison Theodora Crabtree, she was made to wait while the last of the church ladies had shut the doors to the vehicles. A few shot Leann sympathetic looks. Either her mother didn't notice or she didn't care.

"You wanted to talk to me?" Leann urged.

"I did. I understand Ryan will be here next week."

"Possibly."

"You know," her mother said coolly, "he's the father of your children. It wouldn't hurt you to see if you can't work out your differences for the sake of the boys."

"Mother, believe me, Ryan doesn't want—"

"Maybe if you shed that uniform and kept decent hours—"

Leann bit her tongue. What she wanted to toss out was "And give up helping others? And Ryan respects what I do." Yikes, she'd actually given her ex a half compliment.

Her mother tossed one last grenade. "I heard you've been hanging around one of the Guzman brothers."

Ah, Leann knew where this was going. "I responded on a disturbing the peace call. Nothing else."

"What you don't need," her mother said, "is to get mixed up with someone with no prospects and little to speak of in terms of a secure future."

Leann interpreted that as Gary Guzman had no position in the Sarasota Falls hierarchy. Bianca did, but it wasn't very high up the ladder, at least according to Leann's mother.

"He's visiting his aunt, Mother."

"I saw him coming out of the grocery store. He looks just like his father. It would be the worst kind of mistake for our families to mix."

"Mother, Gary and I are…"

Her mother paid no attention to Leann, never had, and headed for her car, talking loudly as she went. "I do wish you would get control of your life. Your father would give you a job at his investment firm."

Stuck in a small room, either answering the phone or checking numbers, emailing clients about changes in their portfolio or following the stock market…no thanks. Leann would rather drive an Uber. Besides, next to parenthood, being a cop was her life.

Opening the car door, her mother turned to add, "You need to start making better choices. And, Ryan is a better choice."

Immediately what came to mind was the image of Gary, whose Sarasota Falls lineage went all the way back to the town founders.

Something that her parents couldn't claim. There'd been Crabtrees in Sarasota Falls for only the last, hmm, Leann didn't know. Maybe sixty or seventy years, meaning if there really was a ladder, Bianca would be at the top and the Crabtrees would maybe be on rung three.

So, her mother's aversion to Gary had to be something else.

What?

FRIDAY MORNING HAD been a round of packing, cleaning out his room at the B and B and heading to both the grocery store and the hardware store. As for food, man, he was going to miss Aunt Bianca's cooking every night. As for the hardware store, he bought just enough to get started on the kennels. The dogs, as if sensing something unusual, had barked more—at least Wilma had. Goober just stayed close to Gary.

Oscar showed up bright and early Saturday morning. Still, it was well after ten when they both left Aunt Bianca's driveway and hit the road.

At noon, the Jemez Mountains came into full view. Gary studied the various deep, rich colors of the sloping volcanic ridges. From a distance he saw the valleys as well as the woods. He tried to recall this trip, but he couldn't. He clutched the steering wheel of his truck and all he could think was, "Wow, this is far from town."

The dogs didn't seem to mind. They stared at the passing scenery, tails wagging, and accepted the ride.

Just ahead, Oscar turned off New Mexico State Highway 4 and onto a gravel road, which eventually turned to dirt, and Gary was privy to watching the back of the camper bump along.

Finally, they arrived. His aunt Bianca's property was marked by a weathered sign that read Guzman.

"Shelley and I have been out here a couple of times," Oscar said after stepping down from his truck. "We mostly walked the forest. The cabin's in pretty bad shape. More than once we found evidence that someone had squatted."

"They must have been pretty desperate," Gary remarked, hoping as Wilma took off for the trees that she'd return. Goober stayed at his side.

Together, he and Oscar chose where to set up a campsite. Gary had lived in most primitive spots, places where the trees hid danger and where sleep didn't come. This wide-open space didn't feel right. While it shouted "Safe wide-open space!" he knew looks were deceiving. Nothing that looked this good could be this good. Somewhere there was a shell waiting to be stepped on.

Gary knew more about generators and leveling than Oscar, but Oscar understood pop-outs and gray water. When they were done with setup, there was not only a decent bed, but also a working bathroom, shower, kitchen with microwave and television. Hopefully Gary could get reception. In the military, he'd often slept on the ground in the rain using his pack for a pillow, so this was luxury. The dogs loved it.

"I'll bring Peeve out here right before we leave," Oscar said. "That will give you time to get a proper place set up for Wilma and Goober."

Goober heard her name and returned to Gary's side. Wilma, however, had disappeared into the trees. Gary knew where he stood in the pack; he'd be chasing Wilma down, not the other way around.

"Sounds good," he said. "First thing I'm going to do is build kennels for the dogs. I don't want either of them running lose while I work on the roof."

"I'm beginning to think you actually like being a dog keeper. Aunt Bianca says you're learning German just so you can speak to Wilma."

"To get Wilma to behave and be a good dog," Gary corrected.

"Call it what you want." Oscar checked the generator and then advised, "Make sure to take time to go introduce yourself to Russell Blackgoat."

Gary remembered Shelley saying Blackgoat land was next door. "I look forward to meeting him."

"You'll like him. He's got a shooting range in his backyard. Zack, Leann and I come up every once in a while and target practice."

"Zack?"

"New hire at the station, just a kid."

"I'd like to get some practice in, too, once I get going on this project."

Both men turned to stare again at Aunt Bianca's cabin. "It has potential," Oscar said. "When we get back from the cruise, I'll come out and lend a hand."

"I'd like that."

For the last ten years, Gary had seen family only during holidays and if he were stateside. Spending time with family was a perk. Maybe Sarasota Falls would do for a while. No, not to settle, but to rest a bit. He gazed at the cabin, trying to remember ever visiting it, trying to imagine Berto Guzman standing on the porch. His dad had been a flannel-shirt, baggy-pants kind of guy, always smiling.

"Your father had big dreams but experienced little payoff," his mother once told him.

Gary's great-grandparents had built this cabin. A photo of them was in Aunt Bianca's living room. They were stoic and steady, like this cabin had to be to survive this long. They'd raised eleven kids and had been married fifty-eight years. "You'll do great," Oscar said.

"I know." On one hand, Gary liked the idea of restoring the cabin to its natural beauty. On the other hand, he'd be out here in the middle of nowhere without neighbors. He didn't do well in crowds, but instinctively knew he needed to be in the thick of life-living, breathing, experiencing the day-to-day challenges. And, noise kept the nightmares away. Maybe because he'd rarely slept alone once he'd enlisted. He'd always been in a barracks, on a bunk somewhere or hunkered down in some hole with the unwashed bodies of his comrades next to him, trying to sleep while the next battle either engaged or disintegrated.

He looked at Wilma and Goober.

Hmm, maybe they'd be enough.

"Hey," Gary said, "before you leave, did Aunt Bianca bring up our father to you before I arrived?"

"Not really, not like she did yesterday. You have any idea what brought it on?"

"No, except she got all melancholy about the way I'm with dogs and the way Berto was."

"I lived with her and Peeve was with me. She didn't make a connection."

"Maybe it's something else," Gary mused. Then, asked, "Do you think there's really anything worth investigating? I mean, could there be something to find here about his disappearance?"

Oscar shook his head, but he didn't look completely convinced. "I'm sure that when Dad was reported missing Aunt Bianca told the authorities to come out here to the cabin. I'll check the station's old files and see if there's anything. Should have done it long ago."

"Why?"

"I've always wondered what happened. Haven't you?"

Gary shook his head. He'd stopped wondering during his twelfth summer, the summer he'd gone camping just about every other week. Usually, he was with his uncle Ricardo and cousins. Sometimes, though, he'd shared a tent with his best friend, his best friend's father and three or four other kids. It kept him focused and out of trouble.

Didn't matter if he had a father or not, that's what the twelve-year-old Gary figured.

As if Oscar knew what his kid brother was thinking, he tousled the top of his head and said, "Our dad loved us. Aunt Bianca's right. We can look into this."

It was some time later when Oscar drove away saying something about needing to get to work. Gary didn't have time to note how alone he was because he spent the next while driving around on the quad Oscar had lent him, to find Wilma, and he'd not have gotten the beast returned to the camper without Goober's herding her. When he got back, he walked the property and determined where he'd build the kennel.

The dogs had to come first, and once Peeve joined them, it'd be three dogs in the small camper. And that would be three dogs too many.

Thus, he ordered the dogs back into his truck and headed into town. He purchased a few groceries and then stopped at the lumber store before heading to his new home.

Silence, except for wind, surrounded him. Tree limbs bent and waved as the late afternoon made its presence known. Wilma and Goober barked and bounded from the truck. Wilma ran off to explore the trees and Goober followed.

"Bring her back," Gary shouted to Goober as he unloaded the ten treated posts from the back of his truck. He needed to dig ten holes, at least two feet apart, and then he'd mix the fast-setting concrete to secure the poles.

He turned toward the truck, then looked at the poles, before glancing back to where the holes needed to be. The only thing he'd forgotten to purchase was a shovel, and Gary really didn't want to go back to town.

A shed stood a short distance from the house. It was a long shot, and the odds of a workable shovel slim, but it was worth a look. Old air and dust puffed out at him when he pulled the rickety door open. The shed was loaded, full of old tools, most needing to be thrown away or shown a little tender loving care. He knew how to scrub, how to use linseed oil, but such a job had to be way down on his to-do list. *Stay on task,* he told himself because really, what a great place to explore.

He'd been right to take a chance.

He spotted a vintage metal collapsible shovel

in fairly good condition. He bent to pull it from under an old wooden table when he saw what was next to it.

A rifle. Old, with yellow on the handle.

Carefully, Gary moved the few things that were on top of it and freed it. Letting out a whistle, he tried to figure just what he'd stumbled across, but the only window in the shed had long ago ceased letting light in thanks to the dirt and spiderwebs.

Gary stood, aiming the rifle muzzle down. He doubted, even if it were loaded, that it could fire, but firearm safety had been ingrained during his stint in the military. Outside, he heard an engine taper off and the sound of a car door slamming.

He pushed open the shed door with his butt and stepped outside, assuming he'd greet Oscar, who must have forgotten something.

Instead, Officer Leann Bailey stopped just twenty feet from him, surprise quickly switching to annoyance on her face. She whipped her gun from its holster, took a solid stance and said, "Put the rifle on the ground, kick it out of reach and put your hands in the air."

That's when he remembered the weapon in

his hands. Not the best way to greet a cop you wanted to impress.

She sure did turn up at the most inopportune times.

CHAPTER EIGHT

"I WAS LOOKING for a shovel in the shed," Gary explained. "And found this rifle under a table. When I heard a vehicle drive up, I thought it was Oscar returning."

Leann didn't move, just waited. Her hand, the one holding the gun, didn't flinch.

Gary carefully set the rifle on the ground and nudged it away with his foot. His eyes never left hers but his lips were tipping up in a half grin even as he put his hands in the air. Finally, he stepped back, and she sighed in relief—not aloud, though, because she didn't want to appear weak in front of him. She looked down at the rifle and whistled before stepping closer.

"That's a Yellowboy."

"It was too dark inside to tell much of anything," Gary said.

"Any other weapons in the shed?" she queried.

"I haven't had a chance to look. I just set up this morning."

She glanced over at the camper, its door wide open. One chair, with a small table and ice cooler next to it, was on the outdoor carpet in front. There wasn't a lived-in look. There was, however, already a temporary, desolate look.

"Which is probably why I caught the trespassing call just an hour ago," she said more to herself than him.

Gary raised an eyebrow. "Someone called me in as a trespasser?"

"Your nearest neighbor, Russell Blackgoat. You probably need to head on up and introduce yourself. He's lived here all his life and keeps a good eye on things in this area."

She watched as Gary turned his head to the west, at the telltale smoke of a distant chimney. He'd known which way to look, so he'd already scoped out the area.

"Why didn't he call Aunt Bianca before calling the police?"

"Because he really thought you were a thief, or worse, and didn't want her to come out here to investigate."

Gary had the good sense to nod and get rid of the grin.

"So, what are you doing here?" Leann asked.

As if answering, Wilma barked and came

bounding out of the woods and straight to Leann.

"As you well know, I've got two dogs right now," Gary explained. "When Oscar leaves on his second honeymoon, I'm watching Peeve, which will make it three. Aunt Bianca runs a bed-and-breakfast, not a kennel-and-kibble. Three meant I needed to temporarily relocate. Plus, I've always wanted to flip a house, and, well, Bianca has one that needs flipping."

"Makes sense." Leann holstered her gun, bent to give Wilma a brief but vigorous rubbing. "Apparently I spent some time here as a child. I'm trying to remember."

Leann looked back at the cabin and imagined its potential. "This is a great place. I'm surprised that Bianca hasn't done something with it. I've been out here twice, thanks to Russell. Both times I had to get partying kids off the property."

"It is the middle of nowhere," Gary said. "Peaceful."

Gary had such a conflicted expression on his face as he studied the leaning porch beams that Leann couldn't keep from smiling. Somehow, when looking at him, peaceful wasn't an adjective that seemed to belong to him. She thought about their first meeting at the park:

not peaceful. Then, she thought about him dealing with Goober's owner: not peaceful. Maybe their meeting at the courthouse qualified as peaceful for him, but not her.

She took a breath, noting the heady scent of trees, grass and more. The wind sent a stray strand of hair fluttering against her cheek. Relaxing, she began, "So, Bianca thinks you have skill enough to hire you to transform this?"

"Hire me? Not really. More like I'm earning my keep."

"Chief dog master and renovator."

"Among other things." Gary reverently picked up the rifle from the ground and looked at it. "You called it a Yellowboy?"

"Now that I think about it, it's probably a replica."

"Can you tell the difference?" His right hand went near the trigger, not on it. She noted the confident way he stood, how strong he appeared. The weapon was pointed down with the butt close to his shoulder.

"The replicas," she informed him, "have a half-cock safety notch on the hammer."

She took the rifle, her fingers briefly touching his, noting again how physically aware she was of his proximity, and turned it round and round in her hand, touching the loading gate and the yellow receiver, studying the hammer.

"No, not a replica." She stepped closer to him, telling herself he was just Oscar's brother, holding the rifle so the top of the barrel was easily visible. "It has all the basic markings. Should be worth some money if it works and you don't botch the cleanup."

"You speak German and know antique guns. You just might be the perfect girl."

"Woman," she corrected before she had time to blush.

"Woman," he amended.

She handed him the gun. "Check the shed for more firearms. Last thing we need is some fool—" she looked him up and down "—finding the weapons and possibly shooting himself."

"I don't fool around..." he paused, looking at her and added with emphasis "...with guns."

She wanted to argue, but believed he was right. Sometimes it felt like everyone was better at shooting a gun than her. She already knew that Gary had been military police and more, meaning she needed to admit, "You probably, no definitely, can handle a gun better than me. I keep barely passing every time I have to qualify for marksmanship—with modern weaponry."

"No one's great at everything."

Nice. But his words didn't make her feel any better.

He looked down at the gun in his hand and repeated, "So, how do you know so much about guns?"

"I watch *Pawn Stars.*"

"And you remembered everything from one episode just in case you ever ran into an ex-soldier and needed to identify a rifle he'd just found?"

She shrugged. "When my ex-husband and I were in Germany, we lived next to a man who owned one of these. Hans had inherited it from his great-grandfather who'd been a soldier in the Russian-Turkish War."

The fatigue of working a twelve-hour shift had to be affecting her because Leann felt a smile curling as she thought about those long-ago days. Learning so much about history had been fascinating and made her wonder if she should have pursued it. Was it too late to do something for herself? At the time, she'd been desperate to find anything that she and Ryan could do together, some hobby they could share.

"Ryan," Leann said, realizing she'd just been standing there, dazed, while Gary looked at her concerned, "and I learned so much from him. He taught me how to clean and assemble quite a few types of guns."

Something she didn't share with Gary was that the gentleman had taught her how to cook and bake, as well. Her childhood hadn't involved a stove, making a bed or even doing her own laundry. She'd been overwhelmed that first year. Hans had been an answer to a prayer.

"Hans sounds like a person I'd like to know."

"He's a true gentleman." She almost added that true gentlemen were rare, but something in Gary's expression stopped her. Some other emotion had manifested in his eyes. She couldn't quite describe it, though it drew her to him.

Moments ticked by. She tried desperately to think of something to say, something that didn't sound lame or was boring procedural work stuff.

Gary, however, spoke first. "Best way to protect the town and its good people is searching the shed with me. There might be other weapons. You wouldn't want me to find anything I couldn't handle."

"I doubt there's much you can't handle." She

couldn't stop her cheeks from heating. Best to leave now before he said anything else to make her regret— or worse, rethink—her "never again" rule.

Instead, she said, "Give me a minute," and called Chief Riley to let him know she needed to clear a shed of potential firearms.

"How did that happen?" Chief Riley groused into the phone. "I sent you on a trespassing call and now you're inventorying firearms?"

"I'll explain it when I see you." Leann hit the off button, fetched a flashlight from the trunk of the police car and made it to the shed before Gary so much as moved. Good. She wanted him to know she was efficient. She reached for the shed's door handle and pulled; it stuck. She started to pull harder, but a body came too close and an arm went around her.

For a moment she couldn't breathe. As Gary opened the shed door easily, he opened something inside her, too. Something that made her lose her breath and consider turning to look up at the dark and handsome face, readying her lips for the kind of kiss that…

She tried to enter quickly, ducking under his arm, striving to vanquish traitorous yearnings. All she managed to do was bump her head on a beam. Goober followed them, nosed around and decided to wait outside. Smart dog.

"Where were you stationed in Germany and when?" he queried, following her into the shed. "I spent some time there."

She turned on the flashlight. "Schweinfurt. We lived there for two years. Aaron was born there."

"Your son?"

"My ten-year-old. Do the math and that will tell you when. I have a twelve-year-old, too. He was born stateside. They're a handful." She said the last sentence a little louder than she needed to. In her experience kids were a great way of discouraging potential suitors: preteenage boys were especially off-putting.

"Hmm."

Good, she'd given him pause. Moving the flashlight up and down the floor, walls and over all the junk piled there, she wondered at what might be buried. "Where exactly did you find the Yellowboy?"

Gary showed her the area under the table. She got on her knees, used the flashlight and pulled out screwdrivers, lanterns and even a length of rusty chain but no weapons. She did the same for a few other corners, trying not to notice the smell or the evidence left behind by animals that'd made the shed home.

"I don't see anything, but that doesn't mean you're weapon free. If you find anything else, hand it…" She looked around the shed, at all the piles of junk. "…or bring it over to Bianca's."

"I'll do anything you ask, Officer Bailey."

His sweet, slow drawl had her heading for the doorway, scooting past him and careful not to touch.

He followed her, Goober at his side, and waited patiently while she dusted off her hands and climbed behind the wheel of her vehicle. Relieved, she put the key in the ignition.

"Hey, Bailey," came a gravelly voice.

Russell Blackgoat, breathing heavily, seemed to come out of nowhere and pounded on her hood. "You've been over here forever and I don't see you loading him into the back. I came to make sure everything is all right. What's going on?"

Leann got out from behind the wheel, ready to scold Russell for walking this far. It was half a mile from his place. Good thing it was mostly downhill or the octogenarian might not be breathing at all. He could have fallen… Before she could open her mouth, Gary opened his.

"Hello, sir." Gary's hand was out poised for a shake; a look of respect was on his face.

"I'm Gary Guzman, Bianca's nephew and Oscar's little brother. I'm going to be fixing up the place a bit. This fun girl is Goober."

Russell grasped Gary's hand before bending to pet the dog. "Goober, huh? I imagine the rotti mix who's been jogging around my house is yours?"

"That would be Wilma. How far away is your house?"

"Half mile. Fool names for dogs."

"I agree, but I didn't name them. I'm watching them for friends who are doing tours overseas. My best friend is in Afghanistan."

"I was in Vietnam. Oscar's told me about you."

"The Seventy-Fifth Ranger Regiment."

"I was with the 213th Field Artillery Battalion, Eighth Army. Sorry I called the po-po on you."

"Po-po?" Gary raised an eyebrow.

He did that a lot, and she hated that she noticed. "My boys have educated Russell on cop slang," she supplied.

"I help with certain Boy Scout assignments," Russell further explained.

"He's the only man in town who knows how to tie a trucker's knot."

"And she found me," Russell said. "Now, once a year every ten-year-old Boy Scout in town comes out to my place so I can teach them."

"I can tie a trucker's knot," Gary said.

"Good to know," Leann said. "I'll divide Aaron's troop in half. Some to Russell, and some to you."

Gary shook his head. "But, I'm not staying."

"If you're fixing up this place, you'll be here awhile," Russell predicted, looking at the ramshackle building. "Six months, maybe seven, and that's pushing it."

"Won't take that long."

"Ha, you've never restored an old home, have you? Or—" Russell suddenly looked affronted "—are you going to tear it down and start with new? New's not better, you know. This place had good bones. Things people build today have ugly, weak bones. Have you seen the new library in town? Made out of nothing!"

"I'm not tearing it down. I'm restoring. And, it's not that big a place. No, I haven't seen the library."

Russell's breathing had finally settled down

to normal. "You got one big hole in the roof that you can see."

"Sheet metal is the way to go."

"If you buy new, though, rather than checking the metal yard, it won't match the rest of the roof."

"I can paint."

Russell guffawed and mumbled something about "old barn tin," which Gary—looking interested—immediately latched onto.

Leann left them chatting as if they'd been friends forever. "Men," she muttered, trying not to mind that Russell hadn't even come over to shut the car door for her and chat a bit like he was prone to do.

Trying not to wish that Gary had done it instead.

Her shift long over, she returned to the police station. The place always smelled a bit like the lemon floor polish used by the cleanup crew. Saturdays were busy, however, and so the station smelled more like sweat and cheap perfume.

Leann contributed to the sweat but not to the perfume. She didn't want to give away her position if she were trying to sneak up on someone.

Walking across the lobby, she nodded at

Lucas Stillwater, who sat behind the front desk listening to a woman complain about dog barking.

At least this time it couldn't be Goober or Wilma.

Oscar came out of the side door and went over to say something in Lucas's ear. They both looked up at Leann and then checked the clock hanging over the front entrance. It was half past eleven.

Chief Riley called something from the back and Oscar shouted, "Leann's here."

"Send her in."

Leann headed for the chief's office. He was staring at his computer screen and frowning. "Close the door," he said without looking up.

"I wanted to talk to you," Chief Riley said, "about Lucas's retirement."

Leann nodded, her throat going dry.

"There are two of you putting in for his job."

"Yes, sir," Leann acknowledged.

"You have the right attitude and the drive," Chief Riley said, "and an outstanding record."

"Thank you. I have a college degree and have been with the Sarasota Falls Police Department longer than Oscar." It felt wrong to talk up herself. But, she wanted the promotion— deserved it.

"I'm going to be honest," Chief Riley said. "Six months ago, your qualifying score at the gun range was seventy percent."

Leann knew that. Knew that had she scored a 69 percent, she'd have been put on probation and would need to retake the qualification.

She hadn't been able to spend enough time training. First, she had two kids and they had to have every minute she could find. Second, since being on the force, she had shot her gun only once, so the need didn't seem to be there. Thankfully.

Sarasota Falls wasn't a large town with a lot of folks where every call meant edge-of-the-seat danger. No, here she was more likely to direct traffic, or help Mrs. Brennan find her lost cat. Leann's sister generated the most calls. No way would Leann need a gun when it came to Gail and hubby number three. Although, Ray had once come into possession of a stolen car, quite by accident.

"Leann?"

"I promise I'll get a higher score next month," she said.

"Oscar's last score was ninety-six."

"And if I should get a ninety-five, I'd lose the promotion due to a point? Is that what you're telling me?"

Chief Riley shook his head. "I'm thinking a score of eighty-five would look good on your paperwork. And, the fact that the mayor has a say in who gets the position should make you want that score to be as high as possible."

"I—" She swallowed. The mayor was good friends with her father and knew how much Ted Crabtree hated having a cop for a daughter.

Chief Riley ended the conversation with, "Officer, I think we have an understanding."

She nodded and left his office. Her stomach felt the hammering of a million nervous butterflies. "You can do this," she told herself. She'd gone to the academy. She'd run the miles and done the push-ups. Passed every exam with honors. There'd been ten women in the class, then five, then three. She'd been the only one to make it to the end.

The only people who'd come to her graduation had been her two boys, brought by her best friend, Patsy, and her parents' housekeeper, Clarissa. Her parents neither acknowledged nor supported her career.

Sitting at her cubicle, she tried to finish her trespassing report concerning Bianca Guzman's place. She'd managed only five words when she noted Chief Riley exit his office and glance at the clock. Then, he waited patiently while Lucas assured the same complaining woman that people were allowed to park on certain streets at certain hours.

The lady huffed and left.

Leann listened a moment, finally overhearing Lucas say, "She was gone exactly two hours and two minutes."

"You sure?" Oscar said. "You were dealing with the parking lady."

"I still managed to look at the clock and write down Leann's arrival time."

Huh? Her arrival time?

"I said three hours," Oscar said. "I'm the closest."

"No," Chief Riley objected. "I said an hour and ten minutes. That's fifty-two minutes."

"But three hours is…" Oscar's words tapered off. "You're right."

"I totally blew it," Lucas said. "I predicted four hours and thirty minutes."

"A month ago, you'd have been right. Put my little brother alone with a single female, and he'd have kept her occupied for hours," Oscar said.

Leann's hackles went up.

"But, Leann's different," Oscar said. "I've told him to curb the romance."

What? Leann bit back the slew of words that started to surface.

"And," Oscar continued, "Gary's not himself. He's a bit more aimless than usual."

"Okay, 'fess up. Why are Gary and I being scrutinized?" Leann demanded, giving Oscar her most annoyed look.

Oscar grinned. "We did a pool with each of us estimating how long you'd spend out at the old cabin ascertaining that Gary wasn't a trespasser."

Leann turned to Lucas, aghast. "You thought I might stay out there for more than four hours?"

"Oscar says his brother mentioned your name once or twice, or twenty, so…"

Oscar nudged Lucas and gave a cease-and-desist glare.

Gary had mentioned her once or twice or twenty?

Great. Her coworkers thought that just because a guy was good-looking, she might take longer on a call. Still muttering, she went through the hallway door, making sure it slammed behind her. Taking a soda from the fridge in the break room, she tried to gather her thoughts.

She was annoyed, mostly with herself. She'd

never spent two hours on a trespassing call. Especially one that didn't really involve a trespasser…and seemed like such a good guy.

CHAPTER NINE

THE HARDWARE STORE made up in effort what it lacked in appearance. The owner not only provided expert advice but also knew his way around what type of fencing Gary needed and something called garden staples that Gary had never heard of. The dogs waited in the truck, beaming approval as Gary loaded a few supplies into the back.

"Remember, both of you are only temporary," he reminded them.

Wilma barked, but Goober gave him a look that said, "Wanna bet?"

Along with Sarasota Falls' hardware store manager, Gary utilized Russell's wealth of knowledge, too. Who knew that there was a market for used roof tin? Russell did, and even gave Gary two names to call. The elderly gentleman had walked down to Gary's place the last two mornings, mostly to share coffee, but also to predict the weather. Gary could always tell when Russell was on his way because Goober would give three sharp barks and then disappear up the dirt road. The next time Gary saw the dog, she'd be herding Russell, making sure he stayed in the middle of the road, right to Gary.

"Never thought I'd let a dog boss me around," Russell joked.

"Never thought I'd operate a home for wayward dogs," Gary returned.

"Probably keeps you from being lonely."

Gary had to agree, although it was hard to be lonely when Russell showed up in the morning and left in late afternoon. Between Goober trying to get Wilma to play and Russell's talking, it was never quiet either.

Russell always had something to say, most of it helpful or at least entertaining. This morning, Russell studied the flooring Gary had installed. "I like what you did with the untreated wood. Glad you finished the last of it this morning because it's going to rain later on today." Gary looked at the sky. It was gray and cloud-filled like it had been since Leann drove away on Saturday—two whole days ago.

"You sure?" Gary asked.

"I'm always right." Russell huffed and walked a few steps around the perimeter Gary had set out and leaned against a post.

Gary kept working, but had to admit that sometimes Russell fascinated him. "Rain won't hurt this flooring. Plus, if it rains it will give me a chance to find where my weak spots are. I don't want my dogs standing in cold or mud."

"They're dogs," Russell said.

Gary looked at Goober and Wilma. Didn't matter if they were dogs, they were *his* dogs, albeit temporarily, and he would do anything to protect them.

Russell chuckled and headed for one of the chairs. He immediately fell asleep, which allowed Gary to work in peace until the distant sound of thunder came.

"I don't know that I'd go to this much trouble for dogs that weren't mine." Russell pushed himself out of his chair and came to observe.

"Dogs are the least of my troubles," Gary said. It was true. The dogs were keeping him sane. Russell, too. The old man had been a steady voice of reason.

And, in truth, the cabin, at least in the daylight, intrigued him.

Nights, though, were a different story. They were long and the sounds weren't familiar. Granted, Gary had slept here only two nights, but so far he didn't much care for being left to his own thoughts. His last deployment had rid him of that desire.

Plus, Gary's father had been here, right before he disappeared.

As if sensing the turning of Gary's mood, Goober left Russell and came over to nudge her nose against Gary's hand, strongly suggesting it was time for a petting.

THE NEXT MORNING, Russell was offering some fairly good advice while Gary was back to work on the flooring for his dogs' kennel, layering over the untreated wood decking with nontoxic paint that was both rot and weather resistant.

He'd slept better. Maybe the pattering of the rain on the camper's roof soothed him. Gary didn't know. Standing up, to give his back a rest, he told Russell, "I've spent more money on this kennel than I'll ever see a return on."

"That's because you're doing it well," Russell replied, and looked at Goober, who waited outside the makeshift fencing so she'd not get the paint on her paws.

She whined, clearly wanting to be next to Gary instead of separated.

"I think that one favors you." Russell came to stand next to the nearest post. He had about a five-minute delay when it came to keeping up with Gary.

"I like her, too." His family had had dogs during his youth. Animals that came to the family either because they'd shown up one day and hadn't gone away or animals given because someone was moving, allergic or just plain didn't want the pet anymore. Taking in strays had started with his father, Gary realized. It was an old memory, one Gary had either pushed back or forgotten until this moment, but Gary could remember his father sitting on the living room couch, a dog spread out on the coffee table, while he applied salve to some wound.

Which dog had that been?

Even stronger came a more recent memory. Gary's sister, Anna, sitting at the couch, same coffee table, with a cat wrapped tightly in a towel, while she tried to force a pill down its throat.

Gary didn't have the time. Never had. He'd been busy with sports during high school and busy with the military after that. Wilma and Goober were the first pets he was solely responsible for. Not that they were his, not really. All Wilma wanted was Max, but Gary hadn't heard from his buddy since he'd dropped the coaster-eating dog off.

Now, on the other hand, Goober had decided Gary was hers and stuck to his side when she wasn't trying to herd Wilma into behaving. Gary had a bad feeling about William Benedict, Goober's owner. He'd not responded to Gary's texts and emails.

"That one likes you, too," Russell said, jutting his chin to the left. A police cruiser wound its way up the dirt road.

Gary rolled his eyes and asked, "You didn't call in another trespassing report, did you?"

"No, not me."

"Could be my brother," Gary predicted, though he knew it wasn't. Oscar was out of town.

"Nope," Russell said.

"You're right. Oscar drives slower. Maybe it's Lucas?"

"Nope," Russell said.

Leann parked her vehicle next to his truck and then took her sweet time talking on the phone before finally joining them. "I'm getting all the permits," he told her before she could say a word.

"I'm not here for you." She was all business,

as usual, ignoring him and focusing on Russell. "You're not answering your phone."

"Course not," Russell said reasonably, "I'm here."

"I'm not just talking about your landline. I'm also talking about the cell phone your granddaughter got you for Christmas."

Russell had the good sense to look guilty. "I keep forgetting to charge it."

"She's called you all morning and got worried enough to contact me."

"There's nothing for Lydia to worry about." Russell looked slightly indignant. "I walked here. Does me good to get some exercise. And, Lydia worries too much, just like you do."

"Give his granddaughter my cell phone number," Gary suggested. "Russell's been coming here every morning since he made that trespassing call. She can try here if he doesn't answer, and if she's worried, I'll go check on him."

Leann frowned. "That's too easy and makes a whole lot of sense."

Gary smiled.

Russell rolled his eyes. "You came all the way out here just to tell me my granddaughter's trying to get ahold of me?"

"I came out here to make sure you were all right."

Leann wore a look he'd seen before, on the face of a young woman in Manbij. It was just after ISIS had lost its hold on the town. That woman had been hurrying through the streets, her voice frantic as she called a name Gary couldn't pronounce then and couldn't remember now. Gary had been told she was searching for her mother.

He didn't know how that story ended.

"You're a lucky man, Russell," Gary said.

"What? I am?"

"You not only have a granddaughter who worries about you but a cop who's willing to drive all the way to the outskirts of city limits just to make sure you're okay. I'm a little jealous. After all, for a moment I thought Leann had come all this way to see me."

"I'd send Oscar to check on you," Leann scoffed. Something in her face changed, became thoughtful. "Oh, and Russell, would it be all right if the boys and I come up one evening this week, and I get some target practice in?"

"Sure. You want me to help?"

"Anything." With that, Leann punched a button on her phone and then handed it to Russell. "Talk to Lydia, tell her you're okay."

Russell nodded, took the phone and headed for the chair he'd been snoozing in earlier. He sat, said a few words, and then started nodding and uttering, "Uh-huh."

"Bossy," Gary whispered to Leann, half joking, half serious.

"Sensible," Leann responded.

"Tell me your cell number, Officer Bailey, and I'll call you. That way you can save my number."

She frowned but did it, adding, "I'll make sure Russell shares it with his granddaughter."

She took a few steps toward his construction site. "What are you making?"

"Kennels."

"You've got quite a bit done. I thought they weren't your dogs?"

"They're not, but Wilma keeps running off and—"

"You need to stop her. She could get hurt."

"I know that. Which is why I'm building the kennels," he said patiently. "Wilma's the problem child, er, I mean dog. She obeys Max and merely tolerates me."

Leann looked Gary up and down. He started to laugh, liking the assessment, but then she said, "You need to show Wilma that you're alpha."

"I am alpha. You should have seen me order her to hit the dirt and give me thirty, but she played dumb."

She blushed and wasn't sure how to answer. "As far as the dog training goes, you're not in the army now. Dogs are a bit different from soldiers."

Gary opened his mouth to answer but her cry of *"Kommen"* silenced him. The next second a bark sounded in the distance.

"I've said *Kommen* to her at least a dozen times," Gary grumped. "She pretends she doesn't understand."

"Probably the accent," Leann said at the exact moment Wilma burst from between two trees, running with pure abandonment, and skidded to a stop by Leann's feet. Then, Wilma looked up expectantly, waited for praise. Leann scratched the dog behind the ears and then smiled sweetly at Gary—clearly indicating look-what-I-can-do-and-you-can't—and innocently watched Russell sitting with the phone pressed against his ear. "Should I go remind him that his granddaughter can't see him nodding?" Leann wondered out loud and grinned.

Gary wasn't sure he wanted her to change the subject. He'd not held his own just now, not with the dogs and not with Oscar throwing around wrong assessments, and Gary wanted a redo. But, he had a feeling that he wasn't quite ready for a redo with Officer Bailey—at least not on the topic of dogs.

"It means he's listening," Gary said.

Leann nodded, watched Russell for another few moments and then murmured, "You're right. Good guys who listen deserve a break."

"I take it your ex-husband didn't listen well?" Gary queried.

"I wasn't thinking of my ex-husband," she surprised him by answering. He'd have bet money she kept her personal life close to the cuff, not sharing, especially with someone like him: a virtual stranger.

Maybe she felt safer because he was a stranger.

"Who were you thinking of?" he asked.

"I was thinking about my father. The last time I talked to him on the phone, he did all the talking and I just nodded."

"How long ago was that?"

"The day I showed up back in town and called to see if he'd let me and my sons—his grandsons—stay with them until I could find a job and a place to live."

"And he did all the talking?"

"I'm not sure why I'm telling you this." She headed for her patrol vehicle.

"He did all the talking?" Gary followed her, his words urging her to continue. Aunt Bianca had mentioned the disconnect between Leann and her parents. He'd wondered but hadn't expected to learn the truth.

She opened the door, and with one foot on the floorboard, the other still on the ground, said, "I didn't do much of the talking. The only words he let me say were 'Dad, I need help,' and then he proceeded to tell me that I'd embarrassed my family name and why he and my mother wouldn't give us a hand. If I hadn't hung up on him, he might still be telling me. Then he had the audacity, when I became a police officer, to complain about my choice of career."

She sat, straight and stiff behind the steering wheel, hesitating before closing the door, and added, "But today I wear a badge, I've got a college degree, a three-bedroom house, I pay my bills on time and my kids don't want for anything. Turns out I didn't need his help." She looked Gary in the face. "Or anyone's."

Gary wanted to tell her that everyone needed a hand, needed someone, but he tended to share her feelings. It wasn't lost on him, though, that he was here thanks to his aunt's helping hand.

"Oh," she said, almost as an afterthought, "I saw your brother looking through one of our cold cases. When I asked him, he said this place might be the last known residence of your father."

Oscar was already looking into his aunt's claim. Interesting.

"My father walked out on us when I was ten. Aunt Bianca says this was the last place he was seen." Gary looked toward the neglected cabin. He'd been in there yesterday, walking over dirt-crusted floorboards and furniture that had been at best secondhand-store rustic.

"My aunt got it in her head that Oscar and I should keep an eye out for any hint of what happened to Berto."

"Berto?"

"Roberto Guzman, my father."

"And your aunt thinks something happened here."

"It's what she's saying now."

"Well, I hope you find what you're looking for." With that, she slammed the vehicle door shut, turned the ignition and backed up.

Too late Gary remembered that Aunt Bianca had suggested getting Leann to help. Maybe it was for the better, though, because Leann had opened up just enough to let him know how off-limits she was and that she also had father issues.

Heck, he had father issues too.

He watched her cruiser until it went around the bend and only a wisp of flying dust from her tires evidenced her movement. Then, he checked Russell, who still nodded at whatever his granddaughter was saying.

Gary pulled out his cell phone and punched the number that connected him to his mother. When she answered, he found himself smiling. "Hey, Mom, can you email me a photo of Berto?"

It took him a minute to convince his mother to find a picture of Berto, close to the age Gary was now, and message it to him.

"You're wasting your time," his mother groused.

"No," he countered, "Aunt Bianca is. Guess where I am?"

Thirty minutes later, he hung up. His mother had promised she would be by to visit real soon, and that he should take care to avoid spiders.

Once a mother, always a mother, he figured. He'd forgotten to say, "I'm sorry for the misdeeds of my childhood." Guess he'd do that when she came for her visit.

Russell came to stand next to him. "Yup," Russell stated matter-of-factly, "Leann's going to be trouble."

"What do you mean?"

"I mean you've only been here a few days and she's been by twice. There's got to be a connection."

"She's been here two days because of you," Gary corrected. "First that silly trespassing call and now your granddaughter."

"Fate is a funny thing," Russell said. "It puts someone in your path right when you need her most."

"You're imagining things."

Russell only smiled. "I was married for more than three decades. Knew I'd found a keeper the moment I met my wife. I miss her every day."

"I'm not the marrying kind."

"I've heard that before."

Gary laughed. "Really, from who?"

"From Leann. And, you're the first one I've seen her cozy to in a long time."

"I wouldn't call it cozying exactly."

Russell chuckled. "You should take her out,

do a comparison, figure out which way it leans. If it's cozying or harassing."

"She's a good cop."

"She's a good woman. I'm thinking you're crazy about women."

Gary laughed again. "Plus, she's got two kids. Not something I'm willing to take on."

"A lot of people say that at first."

Gary thought about Oscar and Little O. Little O was Oscar's, no doubt. But, Oscar wasn't the biological father. Didn't matter.

Nope, the right woman, a cool kid or kids, and a man might become so settled that he lost himself. Gary knew just how to distance himself from her. "We're not right for each other. We'd clash. I just know."

"You sure you have her pegged, eh?"

"Yes."

"Sometimes it's the one who challenges you that's the most fun. My wife chased me out of the house once." Russell laughed, his eyes crinkling on the edges. "I'd taken a huge piece of chocolate cake that she'd baked for a social function. Couldn't help myself. Darned if she didn't have a rolling pin as she sped behind me, hot on my heels. I'd give anything for that day to happen again." He nodded toward the disappearing vehicle. "Best way to test the water is to jump in."

"I don't swim."

Russell scoffed.

"Okay, I do swim. I'm just very cautious about the deep end." Then, in an effort to get Russell off the subject of Leann, Gary asked, "What did your granddaughter want?"

"She says I'm not allowed to walk down to your place anymore. She's afraid I'll fall, not be able to get up and no one will know."

"She's got a point."

Russell didn't look happy. "I've walked these woods since before you were born."

"Your knees were a lot younger back then."

Russell looked at his knees. "Stupid things," he muttered.

"I'll lend you my quad. If I need it, I'll drive up and get it."

"You'd do that?"

"We're neighbors and comrades. Plus, I make my own schedule." What Gary didn't say and would never admit was that right now, he had trouble being alone and the old man's company far outweighed the time spent fetching the quad.

Russell nodded and said, "Neighbor, you'd better take me home. I need to do a few things."

Meaning, Gary thought, that it was Russell's nap time. It took Gary a few minutes to clean up. Then, he opened his truck's doors, herded the dogs into the extended cab, helped Russell into the passenger seat and ran him home. He walked the old man in. Just as he was about to head back out, his phone pinged, and he brought up his emails.

True to her word, his mother had found a photo of Berto. He stared at the image. He'd seen this photo before. His father leaned against an old red truck, one that belonged to Uncle Ernest. It wasn't all that different from the blue one Gary drove. Berto had on loose jeans, a black T-shirt and a jean jacket. His hair was dark, and a faint stubble covered his jaw.

"Hey, Russell, do you think I look like him?"

Holding out his phone, he showed the photo. Russell took it, studied the likeness for maybe half a second and said, "Yup. Been a long time since I thought about Berto, even longer since I thought about him being this young, but you are the spittin' image."

"You knew my father?"

"Quite well."

Gary didn't like what he was feeling. It was anger, like he always felt, but this time a bit muted as if something akin to hope had been mixed in.

"From the time he was a child. He was at the cabin a lot. Your grandparents were still alive, of course. He and my daughter were about the same age and great friends. Odd, really, because your dad was all fixing cars, playing pool with his friends and camping. My daughter was all nail polish, beauty pageants and hair salons. I thought for a while they'd become a couple, but then she took off."

"I'm sorry. Her leaving had to be hard."

"It was, but I got two grandchildren out of it. Sometime when you can stay longer, I'll show you their pictures. My wife and I pretty much raised them."

Then, Gary returned to his truck and was soon bumping down the dirt road, aiming for town.

He probably said the words *no way* a dozen times as he drove into town. He couldn't get the image of his father out of his mind.

After securing the dogs in Aunt Bianca's backyard, he helped a few guests out to their cars with their luggage, earning himself a little over five dollars in tips—which he put in a tip jar on the front desk. In the kitchen, he watched Aunt Bianca finish dicing potatoes for what appeared to be pot roast. The Crock-Pot stood waiting on the counter.

"Smells good already," he commented.

"You're always welcome to stay."

"I might do that." Gary helped himself to a glass of milk and then sat at the table watching as she deftly swept the carrots from the counter into the palm of her hand and then dumped them in the Crock-Pot. "I wasn't expecting you today," she said. "How's it going out at the cabin?"

"Good. I've got the kennels a third complete. I've been researching the best roofing. And, Russell comes by and helps every morning."

"Helps?" Aunt Bianca laughed.

"He helps himself to my coffee and then helps me out by giving me advice."

"He probably has good advice."

"I'm all ears when he talks about preowned tin roofing," Gary agreed before asking, "Do you know his granddaughter?"

"Lydia might be a few years older than you. She's nice. She'd have stayed here, lived on Blackgoat land, but her husband wanted the big city."

"Russell says he helped raise her. How did that happen?"

"It's quite a story," Aunt Bianca said. "Russell and his wife had just the one daughter. Well, now that I think about it, she wasn't Russell's. She was by his wife's first husband. Her name was Angela, and she was a beauty. She was your father's age, and he thought she hung the moon. Your grandparents were still alive, and Berto spent lots of time with them at the cabin."

"I wish I could have met them."

"They were something. I can't imagine living without plumbing or modern electricity, but they did. Russell's family, too, for that matter."

"What did Angela do for fun?"

"She drew. Here, come look." Aunt Bianca led him into the dining room. He'd noticed the large framed pencil drawing of dense trees amid cloud cover. Now, Aunt Bianca tapped her finger on a signature: Angela Blackgoat.

"She was good."

"Good enough to be in galleries," Aunt Bianca agreed, "but that wasn't her passion. Angela was in every theater production at the high school and even won some local pageants. Her picture is on the wall at the Station Diner. A month after she graduated, she headed off to Hollywood. People talked about it for years. We scanned the television credits looking for her name. It did pop up a few times, but never anything substantial. She played a dead woman on one of the forensics shows and she was once a customer on a fast-food burger commercial."

"Didn't Russell say anything? Tell people what shows she was trying out for?" Gary asked. If one of the Guzman clan acted in a show, his mom would have announced it in the local paper.

"No, he only rarely came to town back then. And, I don't think she actually got any speaking parts. More than a decade after she left, she came home with two kids—a boy and a girl. Lydia and her younger brother, Jace. Angela stayed a short while and then left again, just after her mother died. She convinced Russell the kids would be better off in Sarasota Falls with him, insisting she needed to move on." Aunt Bianca finished with, "As far as I know, the father wasn't in the picture. I think Angela struggled quite a bit, didn't handle being a single mother quite as well as your mom did."

"My mom had a lot of help." Gary remembered the days after his father left. His mother refusing to leave her bedroom. His older brother, Oscar, cooking hot dogs or canned spaghetti on the stove. His aunts and uncles coming to the house every day for two weeks.

Then, his mother went back to work, and took care of her brood as best she could.

Gary smiled at Aunt Bianca, remembering that same summer she'd taken him and Oscar in when things had still been too hard at home.

At the time, Gary hadn't wanted his uncles to fill the void his father had left. He'd wanted it to remain empty, grow black, fester even, as if his anger at his father punished his father.

Roberto Guzman never returned.

"You loved your brother didn't you?" Gary asked softly.

"Of course I did. He was ten years younger than me. When he was firstborn, I thought he was mine to play with. When he disappeared, I was so sure he'd be back. He'd always been one to head off on his own for a while. Your mother knew that. I knew that. We just didn't expect…"

She hadn't expected it to last forever. Neither had Gary's mother or his siblings.

Gary, though, never expected to see his father again. Maybe he'd be a better person, stronger, if he'd held out hope. Studying his aunt, he queried, "Which is why you neglected the cabin for so long?"

"It hurt to go out there. Just like with Russell, what we expect doesn't always happen.

But, we're not talking about me. You wanted to know Russell's story. Angela died about two years after she left Russell's again," Bianca continued.

Gary did some math. He knew Russell was in his early eighties, meaning he took on two kids when he was in his midfifties. "How did she die?"

"Car accident."

The things taken for granted, Gary thought. He'd spent the last week putting up with an old man, not realizing that he was looking at someone who'd not only been in battle—like Gary had—but who'd also suffered loss and come through it a better man because of it.

"Why are you asking all these questions?" Aunt Bianca finally asked. "Did Lydia come for a visit?"

"No, she tried calling Russell today and got no answer because Russell was at my house," Gary shared. "Eventually, she called the police station and Leann came out to do a wellness check. She seemed pretty concerned about Russell."

"Leann's terrific. She and her boys spend a lot of time with Russell. Her youngest would rather live in the middle of the forest than in town. Leann tries hard, but she's got a lot on her plate."

Gary recalled Leann's face this morning: the moment she stopped scolding Russell, the moment she'd exposed her true feelings of relief that he was okay.

He hoped her sons didn't take her for granted.

CHAPTER TEN

MORNINGS BECAME ROUTINE for Gary. He rolled out of bed at six and made himself breakfast. Then, he got to work. The kennels were finished and this morning, after searching online for home repair websites and videos, Gary had started on the cabin.

Russell had been correct; it would be a bigger job than Gary expected, meaning he might make Sarasota Falls home longer than he'd intended, meaning he'd have more time to mull over just how close he'd like to be with Officer Bailey.

He wasn't sure how long he'd been working away, but Goober's barking let Gary know something was amiss. Putting down the hammer, he wiped sweat from his brow, walked away from the supports he was reinforcing. This morning he'd uncovered all the furniture, pulled and pushed it into the yard and made two divisions: keep or discard.

Make that repair or discard.

All that before he'd decided to shore up two of the supports so part of the cabin roof didn't fall on his head.

"What is it, girl?" Wilma was running a wide circle around the camper, either chasing an imaginary rabbit or being chased by an imaginary monster. Goober let out another woof and ran to the road.

Gary checked his watch. Nine straight up, a good hour past the time Russell usually showed up. "Okay, I get it. We can go check." He snagged his truck keys from a table by his favorite camp chair and soon—with all three dogs—headed for Russell's.

His first inclination when he saw Leann's car was to pause, but the high-pitched cadence of bullets leaving a gun had him yanking the key from the ignition and leaping from the vehicle. He bounded around the house, heart pounding, wishing he had a weapon.

About the time that his brain reminded him that Russell did have a shooting range, he heard muted laughter and Russell saying, "You keep swaying to the left. Just a fraction. Your scope is not off. You are."

"Have I always done that?"

"Not like now, I don't believe. Maybe if you aim a bit—"

"Have you gained any weight since the last time…" The moment Gary started offering his advice, he wanted his words back.

Daggers, killer laser jets, and lightning shot from her eyes. Then, Russell whooped and jabbed, "You need to work on a better pickup line."

Gary blushed and said, "Oops."

"Not good enough, GI Joe," Leann said, but at least Russell's teasing had Leann relaxing enough to say, "No, I haven't gained weight. I know exactly what I need to weigh in order to fit the uniform as well as chase down a runner without getting embarrassingly winded."

"Sorry. I should have said don't change where you aim. Your primary goal is to develop good trigger-control skills. Have you spent any time lately working on your upper-body strength?"

She shook her head.

He didn't dare offer Leann any pointers. He knew darn well why she was here. She wanted to improve her shooting abilities in order to get the promotion to lieutenant. A part of him imagined Leann's expression if she got the job and his heart tightened in his chest.

Gary walked up to her. "I'll give you a

twenty-minute lesson as long as you promise not to tell anyone."

"I don't need a lesson from you. I can shoot."

"Ask him how many army marksmanship qualification badges he has," Russell suggested.

"I don't care," Leann groused.

Russell laughed. "Expert, sharpshooter, marksman and—"

"She said she didn't care." Gary should have felt relieved; instead, he felt a little insulted.

"He owes you," Russell reminded, "and his advice could make a difference." Turning to Gary, Russell added, "Her ability to shoot is just one hiring point. You're not interfering with Oscar's promotion. Heck, if he were here, he'd be helping her. As a matter of fact, he has been up here helping her."

"I have more badges," Gary muttered.

"Good," Leann said. "Give me some advice."

Gary pulled a penny from the pocket of his jeans and handed it to her.

"What? You're paying me to keep silent, not tell Oscar? Sorry, I won't do it for any less than a fiver."

Gary wanted to laugh. Why did this woman, the only one who'd piqued his interest in years, have to be up against his brother for a promotion? And why did he have to be in a position to help!

"Put the penny on top of the sight. Then, get the sight focused as best you can. It doesn't matter how often you have to shoot at the target. You need to do it until you hit it and that penny doesn't move."

A moment later, Gary was standing close enough that he could smell cinnamon, likely Leann's soft-looking hair. If he wasn't careful he'd be reaching out to touch it.

He realized she could all too easily make him want to feel again, love again, maybe even stay put.

Having given his advice, he quickly left. He didn't dare stay any longer because if this had been a shooting competition, she'd have just won the first round with a bullet where he was most vulnerable: the heart.

"PEACHES ATE YOUR alarm clock?" Leann looked from her oldest son, Timothy, to the giant dog that was supposed to be a golden retriever but everyone—including the veterinarian—referred to as one-third golden, one-third sheepdog and one-third bear. Neither kid nor dog displayed enough guilt in her opinion.

"I left my door open last night," Timothy admitted, "but really the dog hasn't chewed anything in here for months."

In here, meaning Timothy's bedroom, was the only room where Peaches still occasionally destroyed items, mostly because Timothy was her stubborn child who brought food into his room. He also had the smelliest feet, and he played tug-of-war with Peaches using items that shouldn't be tugged. All things Peaches loved. Looking past him, Leann studied the room that was half boy and half teenager. No, it was now one-fourth little boy and three-fourths teenager, meaning he could be more responsible.

"Did you walk Peaches last night?" Leann asked. "Or feed the hamster, the turtle…"

Now guilt became evident.

"No, because I was—"

"He got to the Royal Arena on Clash Royale on his video game," Aaron chimed in, excitedly. "It was awesome. We were both sitting on the couch, and it took almost an hour."

Leann closed her eyes. She'd moved back to Sarasota Falls hoping to find support, and yes, love for her boys. She was taking a chance, but luckily her friends and her ex-husband's parents—Tamara and Barry Bailey—were more than willing to lend a hand. The only downside to Tamara and Barry was that they were quite willing to spoil Tim and Aaron exactly the way they'd spoiled their only son, Ryan. Lately the real problem was their telling the boys that their father was coming home and looking forward to seeing them. A promise Ryan had never kept in the past.

"How much is in your savings?" Leann asked Timothy.

"No, Mom, you know I'm saving for a trampoline."

He'd been doing a good job of saving, too. She promised him that if he saved up his money and made it to just over a hundred dollars, she'd fork over the other half. He'd spent hours on the internet looking at different types and costs. Leann had spent hours convincing the Baileys that they couldn't just buy it and give it to him.

"If I remember correctly," Leann said, "that alarm clock cost me about seven dollars new, meaning it will take seven dollars to replace. You may pay me now."

Tim stomped off, no doubt recalculating what he had in savings and what he'd have left. He'd put aside all his Christmas money, leaving him twenty-five short of his goal. He'd not earned a single dime in the month and a half since then but had spent some—mostly on items he could live without. She'd offered him plenty of earning opportunities, too.

"Here." He returned and shoved a five, a one and four quarters in her hand. He turned, but before he made it to his bedroom door, she said, "Shower, no dawdling. Because you didn't take one last night. Am I right?"

It was already after six thirty. They needed to get ready for school, have breakfast, and she had to get to work. Leann was as frustrated with herself as she was with them.

"Mom, do I have to take a shower, too?" Aaron asked, all hopeful. "I have gym class today, first thing, so I'll just get dirty and smelly. Today's Friday, so tomorrow's the weekend and it's okay if I smell."

"Yes, you need a shower. No, it's not okay to smell. You can go use mine so we save time."

"I don't like yours. I always get the floor wet."

She gently nudged him in the direction of her bedroom. "Sometimes we have to make sacrifices. I'll sacrifice my floor, you can sac-rifice... What will you sacrifice?"

"My shower has cool *Star Wars* people on

the walls while your shower has boring sunflowers."

"Then, that's your sacrifice." She nudged a little harder and he took off.

Leann headed for the kitchen. At least once a month she managed to find the time to make ham, eggs and potatoes for the boys' breakfast. Usually, though, it was pancakes or cereal. Today was a cereal kind of morning.

Even though Timothy got in the shower first, Aaron was out of the shower and dressed before his big brother sat down at the table. Leann fed Peaches because the boys wouldn't have time. Poor ole mutt. He was just over seven and doing his best to pretend he wasn't slowing down. He'd still prance after the boys when they were in the backyard but he no longer was willing to spend an hour chasing a ball, more like ten minutes. And, he was gaining weight, which is why Leann had instigated the walk-every-night rule.

She should have been home last night; instead, she'd been at Sarasota Falls Meteor Park again refereeing her sister and brother-in-law. This time a friend had called Leann directly instead of contacting the police department. It had taken Leann almost an hour to convince them to go home and go to bed.

When she'd finally walked through her front door, all she'd wanted to do was go to sleep. She never got enough sleep, another reason why this morning was already bumpy.

She watched her boys disappear down the sidewalk walking to school, then jumped into her car and headed for work. Fifteen minutes later, she entered the station and got a cup of coffee while Oscar sat finishing up what looked to be a report.

"I thought you were leaving today," she said.

"Just as soon as I can finish this paperwork," Oscar said, a grin spreading across his face. He and Gary really did look alike, except Gary was a bit taller, a bit darker skin tone, and there was something else about the man that Leann couldn't quite put her finger on. "We took Little O to my mother's last night," Oscar continued, "and we're taking Peeve out to Gary. We need to be in Santa Fe by two to catch the plane. We'll be on the boat tomorrow. After that, we'll be cut off, limited phone access." He wiggled his eyebrows. "Shelley and I will be alone."

Leann took a long swallow of hot brew and waved away the brochure he wanted to show her. She'd seen it. Oscar had the photos saved on his phone and every Sarasota Falls officer had seen the cruise ship at least a dozen times. When he and Shelley got to Alaska, he had a jeep tour scheduled, a historic walk and a few other outings.

He handed over his open tickets from the graveyard shift and rubbed a hand over his chin. "About my brother," he began.

Leann didn't say anything, just raised an eyebrow.

"He doesn't talk much about his last tour of duty, but I know when he came back, he wasn't the same."

"What do you mean?" She took another swig, thinking that she didn't want Oscar to confide in her but also knowing that she'd listen because she had to.

Had to. Gary intrigued her.

"Most people act different when they return from duty," Leann pointed out.

"I know my brother, and he's more serious than I've ever seen him. Plus, he seems to latch onto a project and not let go."

So far, the Gary she'd witnessed didn't seem moody, or remote, or troubled.

"I'm impressed with what he's doing at the cabin. He's been there barely a week and look what he's accomplished."

Leann could only nod. She'd been more than

impressed by the kennels when she'd driven by yesterday.

"You know that Aunt Bianca's wanting us to find out what happened to our father. He might ask you for some help."

"I can help."

Oscar nodded. "Good, just don't let him get so involved that he forgets everything else."

Gary was often there in the back of her mind, fading in and out, trying to get her attention, making her think of him, and more. If she were in high school, she'd call him a crush. She's wasn't a teenager, though, she was a mom, a sensible mom, and so she kept pushing the attraction away.

Now, here was Oscar making Gary more human, someone hurting, like she had.

"This time," Oscar said, almost to himself instead of her, "Gary's a bit more vulnerable."

Leann nodded.

"I know my brother," Oscar defended. "When he came back from his last tour, he didn't hop on his motorcycle or quad and take off. Instead, he sold the motorcycle, bought an old truck and slept on the living room couch for a week before he could stay in his bedroom alone."

She had a picture of Gary stretched out on

a mattress, staring at the ceiling, his eyes seeing events he couldn't shut out.

"I want you to check up on him every once in a while I'm gone," Oscar said.

"I'm not sure I'm the one who—"

Oscar rolled his eyes. "He's adjusting to civilian life. Believe me, it's not easy. Shelley and I will only be gone a week. Please."

"He's getting along gangbusters with Russell."

"And Russell's a great help, but Russell's a million years old and has troubles of his own."

"I have troubles of my own. They're aged ten and twelve."

"Russell's grandson, Jace Blackgoat, spent the night in jail over in Springer. He allegedly started a fight in a bar, busted up a table. The owner's not going to press charges if Blackgoat pays for damages."

"I know Jace. He wouldn't—"

Oscar raised an eyebrow. "The Chief said the same thing, but the last two years, Jace has been in and out of trouble."

Leann frowned. She knew Russell had a soft spot for the boy.

"Since Jace is this close," Oscar continued, "he might show up at Russell's. We should maybe be on the lookout. I've already called my brother. Now I'm telling you."

"Bailey!" The chief stuck his head in the doorway. "What are you still doing here? Manager at Little's Grocery Store just called. They've got a shoplifter."

"Right, Chief." Leann rinsed out her coffee cup, set it on the counter and began her day.

AFTER FILING THE report concerning the grocery store, she was back on patrol and came across Oscar and Shelley's minivan on the side of the road. Her brother-in-law, Ray, was already there. "What's going on?"

"Just a tire change," Oscar said. "And we're already an hour behind." As if agreeing, Peeve, Oscar and Shelley's dog, barked loudly.

"I happened to be passing by," Ray explained.

"I'll leave you to it. Changing a tire's nothing for you."

Ray grinned.

"Wait," Oscar said, "there is something you can do to help."

He opened the car door, wrapped Peeve's leash around his hand, guided the dog to the cruiser and smiled hopefully at Leann. "My brother's agreed to watch him. Would you mind driving him out to Gary's place? You're going out there to talk to Russell about Jace, right?"

No, she didn't mind helping out with Peeve. The ten-year-old German shepherd was the best-behaved dog in Sarasota Falls, maybe the world. Peeve would never eat an alarm clock, ever. Unless it would somehow save the people he loved.

"I'll take him." Leann accepted the leash. "I definitely need to talk to Russell anyway. I just came from a grab-and-go. Little's Grocery Store has a surveillance camera that caught a shoplifter. One of the cashiers said he looked a lot like Jace Blackgoat. I did the math. It would have taken him an hour to drive here from Springer. The shoplifting occurred almost two hours ago."

"Russell doesn't need to deal with this at his age."

"No," Leann agreed, "he doesn't."

"What did Jace take?"

"A bag of cookies."

"Weird. You call me if you need anything. I'll have phone service for the next twenty-four hours." Oscar loaded a huge back of dog food, a dozen treats and some toys into Leann's backseat. Then he waved goodbye as he got into his vehicle.

Peeve looked at his leash and then at Oscar's disappearing vehicle quizzically, his expression saying, "Really? I'm going with her and not you?"

She radioed in her time and location, then took off to deliver Peeve and check on Russell.

She didn't even make it to the outskirts of town before she spotted a young girl on the sidewalk, looking a little distressed. The girl's thin T-shirt did nothing to ward off the weather and the jeans were faded and threadbare. Winter was the only time Leann halfway appreciated the thirty-five pounds of gear she carried.

Leann hesitated, watching, trying to decide if she could spot parents, any adult supervision. Nope. Leann knew almost everyone in Sarasota Falls as well as a lot of their relatives, and this girl didn't seem or look familiar. She hoped she was all right. Pulling to the side of the road, Leann stepped out of her squad car and approached slowly. "Hello, are you in trouble? Do you need some help?"

The girl had straggly red hair and dark circles under her eyes.

"Honey, are you lost?"

"I am not lost." No slur, no stutter, not a care in the world.

"Are you visiting someone in town?" Leann asked casually, not showing any emotion other than concern, although her mind quickly ran through the possibilities. "Can I call someone for you?"

"My father. I'm looking for my father." The girl fell to her knees, giggled a bit, then quickly stood up and gripped a streetlight pole for support. Leann couldn't tell what the matter was exactly. Didn't matter. This was a minor who needed help.

"You have ID?"

"Why? I'm not doing anything wrong."

"Do you have any ID?"

"Nope," the girl replied and again slid to her knees.

Leann helped her up and escorted her to the backseat of her car. The last time she'd had a teenager back there, it had been one of the Bouder brothers who'd spray painted I LOVE YOU KATIE on the outside wall of a women's restroom at the college. Leann wasn't sure Katie Nesbit approved of the location or the message.

Peeve scooted over.

Leann soon parked in front of the station,

escorted Peeve and the girl inside. The girl promptly sat at a table and put her head down.

"Are you hungry?" Leann asked.

No answer.

"Everything okay here?" Lucas asked.

"I'm not sure. She hasn't been able to tell me anything and possibly has no ID either."

"I'll call for a child advocate," Lucas said.

"Do that, but first we need to get this girl to the hospital and find out what's wrong."

"Right away." Lucas picked up the phone, but paused first to say, "Lydia Blackgoat, married name Whitefeather, has been in touch. She says to please call her. Her brother hasn't been in touch recently."

"Blackgoats aren't scared of anyone," the girl said.

"You know Jace?" Lucas asked.

The girl shook her head. "Nope, never heard of a Jace."

Leann couldn't stay; she was on patrol, but it was turning out to be an interesting day. "Call me when you find out who she is. And, if you can, find out how she's connected to Jace Blackgoat."

Leann finally left the outskirts of town and hit the open pavement. Soon, she and Peeve were on their way to Gary's. Funny, she was already thinking of it as Gary's place and of him as Russell's number one buddy.

Leann didn't respond to any calls, but Lucas phoned with an update on the girl. She was Trudy Gilmore and her last address was two years old.

Peeve kept his head poked out the lowered window and issued a soft bark to let her know they were close to Gary's.

Her tires crunched on rigid grass as she parked next to Gary's truck. Russell was asleep in a chair outside and Gary busied himself adding finishing touches on a well-constructed dog kennel. Wilma was already barking a welcome. Goober was at Gary's heels but left to come greet her. Gary didn't pause from his work, merely nodded at her, and continued on what looked like a door.

"Hey," she called, after radioing in.

"Hey back at you," he replied easily.

"Looking good." She nodded at the structure.

"That's what all the women say." Gary smiled warmly, as if really enjoying his own joke.

She let Peeve out of the back. Peeve and Goober did a doggy-type welcome, and together they walked toward Gary. She waited until he stopped hammering and asked, "Has anyone besides Russell been by today?"

"No. Why?"

"We think his grandson, Jace, might be in town. He could be in trouble."

"What kind of trouble?"

Quickly, Leann filled him in on the details of the grocery store incident and what had happened in Springer last night.

"I'll keep an eye out," Gary promised.

"Another thing, we found a young girl who recognized the name Blackgoat, although she's not from around here."

Before Gary could comment, Russell said from behind them, "Jace never comes to Sarasota Falls. And, he doesn't take what doesn't belong to him."

"We're pretty sure it's him." Leann studied the man who'd been more of a grandpa to her sons than her father had. She hated to worry him, but it had to be done. "One of the cashiers was pretty adamant about the identification."

"She's mistaken. Jace has been dealing with identity theft for the last couple of years. Every time he thinks he has it taken care of, it rears its ugly head again." Russell took a step toward Gary's truck, and then turned back to say, "Want to drive me home?"

Gary laid the hammer in a toolbox and asked, "Why do you want to go home?"

"It's time."

Leann could see Russell's hands trembling. "I'll take you," she offered.

Russell went toward the cruiser. Gary didn't hesitate. "I'm coming, too." He closed his toolbox, hurried to the camper, returned and then put the dogs in the kennel before locking up and slipping into his truck. To Leann's dismay, he didn't wait for her but started his truck, and was off before she had time to radio her time, location and intent.

Russell didn't say a word from the backseat. She didn't say anything either, instinctively knowing he'd not want her to debate.

The shoplifter hadn't offered any ID obviously, instead, all they had was the recollection of the cashier.

When they got to his cabin, his front door was wide open. Russell said a word he normally wouldn't say in front of Leann.

Leann wanted to say the same word because Gary was already out of his truck and to the side of the cabin, doing exactly what Leann should be doing.

She wanted to shout, "Get back here," but if anyone was inside, she didn't want to alert them to Gary's whereabouts.

Gary inched along, his back to the cabin

until he was right next to the open door. Then, he ducked down, positioned himself so he was looking into the cabin and thereby blocking any view Leann hoped to have. Leann simmered and exited the cruiser, and hurried to the cabin.

"All clear," he shouted from inside.

Yeah, he acted a whole lot like a cop, from how he moved to how comfortable he was giving her a status report.

She peeked around the front door left ajar. Gary was exiting the kitchen and heading up the stairs to the loft. How he acted reminded her of Oscar.

It meant a whole lot more now, knowing that in all probability, if her radar was working correctly—and it usually was, albeit a few weeks late—Gary had been military police.

In a war zone. Just one more Guzman trying to outpolice her.

CHAPTER ELEVEN

THE FROWN LEANN shot him didn't deter him. Didn't matter that she was police and he was now a civilian, his instincts to serve and protect had kicked in, just like hers.

It appeared she didn't agree. Leann came alongside him and said, "I checked the back. No sign of anyone. If there were tire tracks, I just drove over them."

The thought of her out there alone with no backup made him clench his teeth. Flashbacks of his days in the service flooded his mind... It would take just one shot from someone hidden in the woods.

He couldn't protect everyone.

Not even himself.

But, she was a good cop, he reminded himself as she gave him another dagger-like glare and marched out to her cruiser. A moment later, she escorted Russell into the cabin.

Gary's breathing didn't return to normal right away. That Russell had stayed put in the back of her cruiser while they came in told Gary just how vulnerable the old man felt. And, when Russell walked no more than three steps into the room before stopping, looking as if he didn't know whether to move right or left, forward or backward.

"Anything missing?"

Gary followed Russell's gaze as it went from the coffee table, strewn with magazines, to the floor, where shoes were atop a sheepskin rug and firewood leaned against the wall. The walls had framed pencil portraits and landscapes as well as the large window, its view of the forest breathtaking.

"Maybe." Russell slowly shuffled to the fireplace, nudged a lose brick and stared at the open area. Gary and Leann watched him, unmoving, until he sank into his recliner. "About a hundred dollars," he whispered.

Gary whistled.

Leann frowned and said, "Did Jace know you hid money there?"

"Yes."

"Anyone else?"

"My daughter, my granddaughter, Lydia, and now you two."

"Then, it's probably fair to assume that Jace has returned," Gary said.

Leann opened her mouth, probably to argue, but Russell wasn't finished. "It wasn't Jace. He wouldn't steal from me. Never has, never will. He sends *me* money, not that I need it. I put it in a savings account to go back to him someday."

Gary helped Russell up and then led him to the couch. Leann, all business, looked at Russell's shoes and then headed to the fireplace, studying something at the edge of the logs. Abruptly, she headed out to the cruiser and soon returned with a black bag. Silently Gary and Russell watched her take photos of the hole in the fireplace as well as of the one clear footprint in the ash. She then took a sheet of rubber from the bag and got busy lifting the print.

"It's definitely a man's shoe," Leann added. "I probably should have asked if anybody male has been by to visit you and gone near the fireplace."

"Just me and Gary," Russell said. "And, yes, he's been near the fireplace. No way he could have known about the brick, though. I didn't tell him."

"I'll give you my shoes if you want," Gary offered.

Leann looked from the print she was lifting

to the foot Gary was lifting. "You're about a thirteen?"

"Spot on."

"This is more a ten, on the small side, and a tennis shoe. You wear tennis shoes?"

"I own a pair. We can drive back to my place and I'll dig them out so you can eliminate me. I've only worn the boots since I started working on the cabin."

"You know what size shoe Jace wore?" Leann asked Russell.

"Same as me. Size eleven."

"If Jace is in town, we'll find him and sort this all out," she promised. She looked ready to say more but her phone sounded.

"Not if you're standing in my cabin taking pictures and playing in the dirt," Russell grumped. "Besides, if it were Jace who needed the money, he'd have asked, not stolen. So, go ahead and take the prints. They'll just prove my grandson innocent."

Gary checked his watch. Only ten o'clock. He admired her focus. As far as he could tell, she'd had a pretty full day already with Peeve, the girl, Jace and now this.

Russell's fingers twined and untwined. His face was a shade of red Gary hadn't seen before.

"You all right?"

"No," Russell said. "I'm mad. Somebody broke into my house, took my money, and it ain't right."

"You have money anywhere else? Because if you do, it might be time to take it to the bank."

Gary expected Russell to say, "I don't trust banks" or "I know what I'm doing." Instead Russell said, "Most of it is in the bank. I just keep a bit here."

Gary let out his breath.

Then, Russell added, "and there."

"Presumably Jace knows all the other theres?" Gary asked.

Russell shrugged. Leann finally got off the phone. "I picked up a young girl, possibly a runaway, earlier. We identified her as Trudy Gilmore. She's now in the hospital, pretty sick. There doesn't seem to be a connection between her and Jace Blackgoat."

"Why would there be?" Russell asked.

Going to her bag, Leann pulled out the tablet she'd used to take pictures and started asking Russell questions.

"Russell, do you have any idea where Jace is right now?"

"He's in Nebraska driving a mail truck."

"Can you call him, please? So we can eliminate him as a possible suspect."

Russell pulled out his phone, tapped a button and waited. He had to leave Jace a message.

"Does he call you back?" she asked.

"Yes, but sometimes it takes him a day or two. He sleeps days and drives nights."

Leann and Gary exchanged looks.

"Why do you think Jace left Sarasota Falls and never returned?" Leann probed.

"I've asked him a million times, and he won't answer. It's like he's scared of someone. Which makes no sense," Russell blustered. "Who is there to be scared of?"

"Why don't you come back to my place?" Gary suggested.

"No, I want to stick around here. If Jace is in the area and looking for me, I want to be home when he shows up."

"Russell," Leann said gently, "just to be safe. Please come to Gary's. You don't know—"

"Jace would never steal from me or hurt me."

"You don't know that," Gary said.

"I do know that." Russell escorted them to the door. "I half raised that boy."

Gary wished he could believe it. Wished that he hadn't seen evil so profound that he knew there were people with not one shred of good in them. For Russell's sake, he hoped the old man was right.

Leann didn't herd as well as Gary. She pivoted and moved next to the wall to stare at a group of pencil drawings. She pointed to a young man and woman standing in front of a tree. "I recognize Jace, but I don't remember his sister so much?"

"Jace was about seventeen in that one. Lydia's a year older. She'd just graduated and gone off to college."

Russell prodded them out the door. Gary watched Leann leave. She clearly wanted to stay longer if her dragging feet and constant looks were any indication.

He glanced back at Russell's cabin, but the old man had closed the door.

Ignoring his instincts, Gary got in his truck and drove home. In truth, he didn't think Russell was in any true danger. Jace, it seemed, had gotten in a bar fight. Heck, Gary'd had his share of those when he was younger. Stupider. Stealing cookies, while a crime, wasn't huge. Stealing money from his grandfather. Now that didn't make a whole lot of sense, especially since Russell would had both fed and given Jace money had he asked.

Gary couldn't get a handle on the whys and

what fors. He mulled the situation over for a while. He played catch with the dogs for a half hour and then went to work on the cabin, managing to tighten every hinge before he couldn't take it anymore. He was heading for his truck to check on Russell when his phone pinged.

Leann said, "Anything happening?"

"I left soon after you did," Gary responded. "I did note one other thing, though, while we were inside."

"What?"

"Those drawings on the wall. They're signed. Most are by Angela Blackgoat, but two are by Jace."

"Interesting, but not sure if they figure into anything."

"I thought I'd mention it. I'm heading up there now."

"Good. I've called twice, no answer."

"Any news on Jace?" Gary asked.

"No, but call me after you check on Russell."

She hung up before he could bark back a "Yes, ma'am." He'd gotten used to taking orders over the years. He rather liked taking them from her.

A few minutes later, Gary knocked on Russell's front door.

Russell didn't answer, and Gary didn't

blame him. No one could wound as deeply as someone you loved. And, it had been there in Russell's eyes. No matter if an unknown situation had sent Jace running years ago, Russell still cared.

Still worried.

Still hoped.

Scenarios that no longer lingered when it came to Gary and his father. The difference being that Russell and Jace were still in contact, even if they didn't see each other often.

"I'm still out here!" Gary called. "I'm not going anywhere."

Finally, he heard footsteps and the door opened a crack. Russell looked a decade older. "I'm fine. You don't have to check up on me."

"I got the feeling that if I didn't check up on you, Leann would drive out here again. I thought I'd save her the trip."

"Fool woman."

Gary could tell Russell didn't mean it. "She's worried about you."

"And I'm worried about Jace. I've been sitting here thinking about the boy. I've tried and tried to get him to tell me what happened right before his graduation." Russell's face grew even more creased, and tears filled his eyes.

"You don't have a single idea?" Gary asked.

"Only thing out of the ordinary was the visit from Leann's brother Clark. He'd never been here before that I know of. But, he was polite and left when I said Jace wasn't home."

"What did her brother want?"

"I don't know. He just asked me if Jace was here."

"You need to tell Leann."

"I never really thought much of it. Something funny, though," Russell said. "Wasn't but a few weeks later, Clark left, and he's not ever returned either."

CHAPTER TWELVE

LEANN WALKED THROUGH the station's door and headed for one of the computer terminals behind the front desk. Typing in Jason Blackgoat's full name, she waited for the information to load.

"The hospital says Trudy Gilmore," Lucas informed, coming to stand behind Leann, "has done little more than eat and snore. She is still insisting there is no one to call."

"No one?"

"We found a mother living in Abilene, Texas, but she's not answering her phone, and we can't find a record of employment. I talked to an officer there. He's sending a patrol car to talk to the mother or some of the neighbors."

"How old is Trudy?"

"Fifteen."

Only three years older than Timothy. Why wasn't a parent rushing to the hospital, thanking the police for finding their child, caring for her?

Maybe Trudy's parents were like Leann's, who found it easy to let go. Her sister had the most contact with their parents. Their older brother hadn't been in Sarasota Falls since he'd graduated high school almost two decades ago. Except for the occasional phone call, which she always instigated, he might as well have fallen off the face of the earth.

Leann had another hour before her shift was over and she wanted to check on a few things. Jace's file was still loading so she pulled out her phone and found a text from Gary with information from Russell about her brother and Jace. Immediately, she tried her brother's number, although she wasn't sure what she would say if he answered. Maybe she'd start by asking how well he knew Jace Blackgoat and end with—

Before she could finish the thought, a prerecorded voice stated her brother was unavailable and advised her to leave a message. That never worked. She started to leave one anyone, but instead was interrupted by a new call.

"Hey, Patsy," she answered.

"I'm just calling to remind you about tomorrow night. You're still set to help out."

"Looking forward to it." She was and wasn't. If she could go as just a mom, she'd love the school dance. But, should something go wrong, like a fight between two kids or underage drinking, she'd be the one to deal with it, which likely wouldn't earn her any points from her oldest, who would be embarrassed.

She ended that call and glanced back at the file loading on Jace. It was almost complete. She had other ways to find out information. She stepped up to the front desk and started to ask Lucas a question, but he was dealing with Mrs. Edna Templeton, Leann's third-grade teacher. Lucas unzipped a brown canvas backpack, saying, "Where did you find it again?"

"At the park next to the library. My dogs found it under a bush."

"I'm not seeing anything with a name," Lucas noted. "I think it must be a teenager's. Look, here's a book, a half bag of cookies, an art tablet—"

"Young man," Mrs. Templeton said, "simply put the bag in lost and found and be done with it. Someone will claim it or not." Then, she turned to Leann and said, "Don't pay attention to your mother. You're doing a fine job raising your boys."

Great, there had been witnesses to Leann and her mother's exchange outside the ladies' auxiliary meeting.

Mrs. Templeton marched out the front door.

"Was she your third-grade teacher too?" Leann asked Lucas.

"How'd you know?"

"Because she called you young man."

Lucas laughed. "You had a question for me?"

"Yes, did your daughter ever mention Jace Blackgoat or my brother? They'd have been near the same age, right?"

"My youngest was in high school with them, but I don't remember her mentioning anything."

"You ever attend one of the dances?"

"I did, once. I was always working, it seemed."

Sitting at her computer, she read Jace's details. Nothing about being arrested, although his stay in the Springer station had been noted.

There was also a flag on his record stating he'd been a victim of identity theft. Interesting. But, they still had an eyewitness's identification.

Picking up the phone, she called Lydia. A friendly voice turned worried after Leann identified herself. "No, no," Leann assured, "your grandfather's fine. We're just fairly sure Jace is in the area, and we're trying to decide how to proceed."

"What do you mean?"

"We'd like to question Jace about a shoplifting incident."

Lydia was quiet for a few seconds, then said, "I realize this is what you might expect me to say because I'm his sister, but truthfully Jace has a job and money. He has no needed to steal. Please call me if you do find him."

Leann debated with herself, but common sense told her it would be a good idea to share everything. "I just came from your grandfather's cabin. He's missing about a hundred dollars and he says Jace wouldn't have taken it."

Lydia muttered, "I told him not to hide things anymore. He's right. Jace would never have taken it."

"When was the last time you spoke with your brother?"

"A few weeks ago. He's working in Nebraska."

Which jibed with what Russell claimed. "Do you know the name of his employer? Jace says it's the post office."

"Actually, he works for a trucking firm they contract with. I don't recall the name."

"Could you try calling him today? And, give him my number if he answers. We would like to talk to him." Leann rattled off her seven digits. She wasn't through.

"Lydia, all those years ago, after Jace left Sarasota Falls, did he come to you?"

"No. I was living in a dorm at Arizona State University. Whatever was going on with Jace, he didn't want to mess things up for me. I'd have left school for him, though. I love him that much."

"Your grandfather has no clue why Jace left town. Do you?"

"No. And I've stopped asking. He's made it clear that he's not willing to tell me why. I figure it's just another small-town mystery."

Leann could only nod.

Her intuition told her the case she was working on hadn't started with a bar fight or stolen bag of cookies but had begun decades earlier.

SATURDAY NIGHT, GARY left Wilma at the cabin. Goober happily sat on the passenger side, tongue lolling, waiting for whatever the evening presented. Peeve was staying with Russell, as both company and guard dog.

Attending a school Valentine's dance as a volunteer was the last thing he wanted to do, but his brother's call this morning had given him little choice.

"How do you forget something as important as a Valentine's dance?" Gary had asked in amazement.

"When you get the chance to go away with your own valentine, you forget about everyone else's," was Oscar's long-distance response. "Besides, in my mind, I had it down as the weekend before Valentine's day. I forgot they had to bring it forward because of a conflict. Listen, I can't spend any more time talking about it. It's expensive to use your cell on these cruises."

Gary wanted to ask Oscar if Leann ever talked about Clark, but Oscar ended the call before he could.

The February wind carried a slight chill, and Gary was almost glad to be doing something besides practicing his German, working, or scanning the internet looking for information about Clark Crabtree, a single accountant who seemed to have no social media presence.

Jace Blackgoat's social media presence was much the same. Null and void.

The elementary school was aglow with sparkling lights and giant cardboard cutout hearts. Gary walked inside, Goober at his side, following the handprinted directions to the school's gym.

"Hello?" A woman with a name badge reading Patsy Newcastle hurried up to him, peering into his face, and said, "Oh, you must be Oscar's brother."

"Geraldo Guzman. Call me Gary and just tell me what you need me to do."

She stuck out her hand, gave a firm shake. "Your job will be the doors at the back of the gymnasium. With all the mothers here, I doubt you'll have anything to do, but this dance is for sixth through eighth grade, and we have a few boys who think it's cool to sneak off with their cell phones or a stolen pack of cigarettes and pretend they're grown up."

"I can handle that," Gary said.

"I believe it. Leann says you can handle just about anything."

"Leann said that?"

"She did. She's my best friend and said you could handle anything except for dogs. But, this one seems to be behaving for you." She bent down, rubbed Goober's head and said, "And this is...?"

"Goober. I'm watching her for a buddy."

Patsy made a face. "Goober?"

"Consider her my emotional-support dog."

"Okay," Patsy said slowly, adding, "By the way, thanks for pitching in."

"You're welcome."

He thought about asking her about Clark, Jace, too, for that matter, but decided to wait, build a bit of a relationship. Plus, he didn't want her mentioning to Leann that he was probing. Clark, being her brother, was something of a conflict of interest.

Someone called her name and she quickly pointed out the doors where he'd be stationed. There were no kids yet, except for ones attached to mothers who were in volunteer positions. Quite a few last-minute details were being completed. While her son loved on Goober, Gary helped one woman hang decorations. Afterward, he set up a table that had a particularly difficult leg. Then, Gary walked the auditorium, snagging a few desserts and wondering who paid for the roses that were for sale: boy or mom?

Oscar had always taken their mom to things like this. Gary never wanted to go. Too many people. Looking around, Gary took a deep breath. Would there be too many people tonight? Would he get that trapped feeling he used to get? Or, would the noise and the excitement rolling off kids and their parents overshadow the dread he seemed to feel, albeit less often lately.

That feeling that something was wrong

formed in the pit of his stomach. What, he
didn't know. Worse, there was no way to make
the unease go away. "One, two, three," he
counted, heading for the door he was supposed
to guard and continuing to count under his
breath, trying to control his breathing. Goober
walked stiffly, at alert, obviously aware that
something was going on with Gary.

"It's all right," Gary said, his voice sounding distant. He hoped no one else could sense
his unease.

Someone touched his arm, and Gary turned,
his fist as clenched as his teeth. "You all
right?" Leann peered up at him, her face full
of concern. Her reddish-colored hair hung past
her shoulders in a gentle curl. Her ivory blouse
was tucked into dark brown slacks. The jew-
elry was all flame green, matching her eyes.

"You all right?" she repeated.

"Yes." He wasn't, though. The room had gotten darker, maybe because the dance was about
to start but maybe because Gary was fighting
off the remnants of a panic attack.

Her hand went to his arm, her fingers wrap-
ping around, bringing warmth and grounding
him. Some of the tenseness left.

"Sometimes these things are a bit overdone.

I saw you talking to my best friend, Patsy. Was she giving you a hard time?"

"Not really. She did happen to mention that you didn't think I was too competent with dogs. She was also unimpressed with the name Goober."

Leann laughed loud and free. First time he'd heard it. It was sweet and musical. "I live with two boys," she said, "I get the name Goober. I don't appreciate it, but I get it."

"You volunteering, too?" Gary asked.

"Some, but mostly I'm here with my sons. They're over there." She pointed to a long table loaded with food. Two boys were busy running back and forth from the door to the table delivering desserts. The bigger boy looked like he'd rather be anywhere else. The smaller one looked around, erroneously determined that no one was watching and swiped not one but two cookies.

"Excuse me." Leann marched across the room.

Gary didn't blame the kid. Most of the sweets came from Shelley's bakery. They tasted great. Waiting until Leann had stepped away from the table busy telling her offspring "Just one!" he headed over and took two cookies for himself.

"You're supposed to wait." The smaller kid

appeared at his side and, completely ignoring his mother's "Just one" dictate, took another cookie.

"You going to tell your mom?"

"What? No!"

"I'm Gary Guzman." He held out his hand, looking the boy over and deciding that there was no doubt as to his lineage.

"Aaron Bailey. I don't like to dance, but I love cookies."

"Me, too."

"My mom says you have three dogs. I like this one."

"This is Goober. Unfortunately, none of them are mine. I'm watching them for other people."

Aaron looked at him suspiciously. "You're babysitting?"

"Dogsitting."

"Are you getting paid?"

It figured a teenager, or almost teenager, would ask the question that Gary apparently wasn't asking often enough. Because no, Gary wasn't getting paid. He'd just spent hundreds of dollars building a kennel and for what... temporary, nonpaying lodgers.

He didn't mind a bit when it came to Wilma or Peeve. Heck, Peeve would have carried the hammer for him, and Wilma? Well, Wilma was around for comic relief, and Max was his best friend. Goober, well, maybe he didn't mind her either.

Of the three dogs, she was at his side the most.

Gary looked around, found a group of ten boys gathered around Goober all vying for her attention. The dog chose that moment to step away from her adoring fans to check out Gary's whereabouts. Once she found him, the dog—content—returned to the children.

"There are a few things more important than money," Gary finally said.

Aaron appeared to consider that, then agreed, "Like dogs."

"Exactly."

Aaron shuffled his feet a bit and asked, "Did you ever give a girl a valentine?"

"More than one," Gary acknowledged.

"No, not like you gave every girl one and just signed your name. I mean did you ever give a real girl a valentine?"

Instinctively, Gary knew not to tease about the abundance of fake girls that had passed through his life. Instead, he asked, "You mean a girl you really like?"

"Yeah."

Gary thought a moment. Maybe he hadn't given any female a Valentine's card. "Hmm, I gave flowers once."

Aaron frowned. "Did you pick them?"

"No, bought them at the store."

"Too weird," Aaron decided.

"Hey, I gave my mother a special Valentine's card. Made it myself. More than once!"

Aaron sniffed. "Doesn't count. I gave my mom a Valentine's card. She said it was the only one she got this year. Then, she gave my brother 'the look'."

Gary knew exactly what look Aaron was talking about when it came to 'the look' and suddenly wished he'd thought to buy Officer Bailey a Valentine's card.

Patsy came up to stand next to him, sending Aaron scurrying away. "The doors officially open in ten minutes. Go ahead and take your station."

"Yes, sir. I mean, ma'am."

She gave him the once-over. "Leann said you were cheeky."

"Leann seems to talk about me a lot."

"No, I don't." Leann stepped up next to him. "It's just that my best friend likes to sensationalize any topic that revolves around single men."

Gary looked at Patsy's left hand: ring.

"Oh, not me," Patsy protested. "I'm happily married. I just keep hoping Le—"

"And I," Leann interrupted, "keep hoping that she'll find something more entertaining to do than bug her best friend about her love life."

"Lack of love life," Patsy corrected.

Gary couldn't help it. He laughed. The unsettled feeling dissipated, completely, as he walked to his corner and stood guard so that no one left or entered. A few times he was called over to lift something heavy, and once he had to fix an electrical issue. Both Patsy and another woman brought him plates of food. Patsy did it with a smile and a smirk in Leann's direction. The other woman—a tall brunette who looked like she'd be both loud and fun—had written her phone number on the paper plate right under the three chocolate chip cookies.

Ingenious.

A few months ago, he'd have chased her down. A few weeks ago, he'd have dialed the number. A few days ago, even, he'd have at least entered it in his cell phone for later reference. Tonight, Gary kept the cookies but not the plate.

Someone, Gary thought a math teacher, came over to offer a ten-minute break. Against his better judgment, Gary headed over to the side of the room where Leann stood talking to the woman selling roses.

"Gary, have you met Heather Riley?" Leann asked him.

"Ah, the chief's wife."

Heather smiled and reached out a hand for Gary to shake. She didn't look old enough to be Tom's wife. For that matter, she didn't look old enough to have a kid in elementary school. "Nice to meet you." She introduced the little girl next to her. "This is my niece. We're helping out."

"Mr. Oscar's told us a few things about you," the girl said.

"None of them true," Gary said. "You can't believe my brother."

"Mr. Oscar always tells the truth." The girl's expression said it all. Oscar was lollipops and Gary green peas.

"I want to hear some of these stories," Leann joined in. "I'm with Oscar almost every day. How come he hasn't told me the stories?"

"Guess he's afraid you won't recover from the shock," Gary teased.

"Aren't you supposed to be over there in the corner?" Leann pointed to his station; the math teacher waved.

"I'm on break. And, aren't you supposed to be dancing with your sons?"

"I'm on break."

Something about looking down at the top of that glossy dark red hair and the tilt of her face made Gary wish he'd kept the number from the plate. Because if he had done that it meant he was safe. His heart was safe.

But he'd thrown it away. Hadn't hesitated.

If Leann had put her number of the plate, he'd never be able to throw it away. And that scared him.

So, Gary told his feet to move.

They didn't.

He ordered his feet to move.

They didn't.

His hand, however, moved. It went in his back pocket and removed his wallet. A dollar later, he was the proud owner of a single red rose that he promptly handed to Leann.

It didn't escape his notice that while he hadn't hesitated to throw away a phone number, Leann hesitated to take the flower. Even now, she stared down at it as if thinking about handing it back.

Not the reaction he was going for.

A fairly slow song came over the speaker, the artist crooning something about girl trouble and woes. Great. Even the music knew what Gary was suffering from.

"Who chose the music?" he asked. "This doesn't seem like one of today's hot picks."

Leann finally smelled the rose and smiled up at him. Then, she giggled, something he'd not heard her do. Maybe he'd want to hear it more.

Acting on impulse, he reached out his hands out her, drawing her close to him, and he led Leann onto a dance floor, where people half his height moved out of the way.

"That's Timothy's mom," one of them said.

"Cool," came a response.

"Gross," one of the kids muttered.

Leann didn't drape her arms around his neck like he wanted her to, but she didn't bolt out the door and head for the hills either. Instead, she swayed, looking up at him and stating the obvious. "This isn't really the right kind of song."

"What would be the right kind of song?"

"Is there a song called 'Stop Messing with My Head'?"

He stopped, unsure if she was serious or joking. When she smiled, he relaxed.

"No," he replied, "but there's a song called 'My Mom Embarrassed Me on the Dance Floor Because She Didn't Really Dance.'"

Leann rolled her eyes and stepped closer, still swaying and seeming not to care that he was holding both her hands, careful not to crush the rose. Her fingers were soft, warm, and he had the feeling that if he let go, he would spend the rest of the night trying to reclaim them. He could tell she didn't want him to do anything but what they were doing. Standing on the dance floor, gazing at each other, touching, and with a half smile on her face.

He got it. She was as torn as he was.

But, she still didn't move away from him. Maybe because they were in a sea of adolescents, maybe because she was a cop, and maybe because she wasn't sure who he really was: friend, foe, stranger, admirer.

Sometimes he wasn't sure either.

And his feet refused to leave the dance floor.

Still she swayed, her hands in his, her eyes—ever the cop—scanning the dance floor and surroundings. Then, her eyes came back to his and stopped. She had what his mother called cat eyes: all knowing, flame green and beautiful.

Their swaying slowed, but still he stayed right where he was, so close to her, afraid of breaking whatever spell held them together.

She seemed to feel it, too, because a sudden look of doubt crossed her face. Their connection wavered and broke as she let go of him, stepped away and cleared her throat before saying, "I need to find my boys."

He could only nod as he returned to his corner and endured the slap on the back the math teacher gave him.

For the rest of the dance, Leann paid no attention to him. She was focused on her two boys—sometimes dancing with one and sometimes dancing with both. The rose was nowhere in sight.

Aaron seemed to like being near his mother. The other one, Timothy, kept drifting off and hanging with his friends. Most of them had cell phones out. All of them kept glancing around to see if any grown-ups were nearby.

About the time Gary decided to head over, the disc jockey called last song and one of the moms swooped down, culled a child from the group and merged onto the dance floor. Like magpies came more moms until only Timothy stood there, alone: no phone.

Leann waved to Timothy and he joined his mother and Aaron on the dance floor, so he could be considered part of the family.

Gary wondered if he ever would.

"Fun time?" Patsy queried. Gary wasn't sure cleanup had been part of Oscar's assignment, but somehow it had become part of his.

"Sure. The kids seemed to enjoy themselves," he managed, hefting a garbage bag over one shoulder and carrying a second outside. Leann followed him with two of her own.

"Where are your boys?" he asked Leann.

"Aaron was falling asleep, so I sent them to the car to wait for me."

"That's where my son is," Patsy joined in. She also had a garbage bag. "I told him he could either sit in the car or help, but he didn't get to be in the way."

The two women laughed easily. Then, someone called Patsy's name and she scurried off.

"I thought you might show up at my place today," Gary said, leaning against his truck and enjoying the way the wind sent her long hair blowing.

"Why?"

"Checking up on Russell."

Leann shook her head. "Instead I was busy checking up on his grandson. I've left him messages. Russell was right. There's a flag in his file about identity theft. You think we might be looking for someone besides Jace?"

"Didn't the grocery store clerk recognize him?" Gary asked.

"She did."

"I think you should stop by and talk to Russell," Gary urged. "Tell him the latest."

"I can do that."

"Good." He was tempted to ask her about her brother, but he'd loved dancing with her, and now he loved just being next to her. He didn't want to possibly change the mood by bringing up her family.

"Oh," Leann said suddenly, "I talked to Lydia, too. She has a hard time believing that Jace stole Russell's money. There's something going on… Something that I can't put my finger on."

"There are too many threads," Gary agreed.

"What we need to do is make contact with Jace—"

"I spent years doing reconnaissance. I'm great at finding people. Especially people who don't want to be found."

"Were you military police, too?"

"I think my brother talks too much. I started as military police. Fort Bragg. An opportunity came along that enabled me to attend ranger school. I took it."

She didn't look impressed, and he definitely wanted to impress her.

"Wow, I'm impressed," Patsy said, joining them. "No wonder we didn't have any trouble, not with you guarding the door. Everything went so smoothly."

"It was great." Leann smiled.

Patsy, looking from one to the other of them, finally said, "You both seem way too serious."

"We're talking about Jace Blackgoat," Leann said.

"Russell's grandson," Patsy supplied, "who's supposedly back in town and shoplifting?"

"Did you know Jace?" Gary asked.

"A little. He and my big brother were in ROTC together. I can remember Jace coming to the house a time or two because of some project he and Paul were doing. I thought Jace was cute."

"What?" Leann's voice was half indignant, half intrigued. Gary recognized it. She was torn between listening as a friend and listening as a cop. "You always told me when you had a crush on someone."

"By the time I realized it was a crush, he was gone. And, he only came over once or twice. Clark was there, too."

"Clark wasn't ROTC."

Patsy was saved from adding anything else when someone else said her name. She rolled her eyes, handed her bag to Gary, and said, "The cost of being in charge," before hurrying off.

"Clark wasn't ROTC," Leann repeated, but her words were no longer musing. Instead, Gary noted concern. Maybe now was the time to find out a bit more.

"Your brother was in school the same time as Jace? Then you can ask him about Jace, right?"

"That's not easy. Clark's in Los Angeles and hard to get ahold of. Believe me, I already tried."

Gary started to ask a second question, but Leann's stricken look stopped him. "What?"

"He left the day after graduation. Clark's never been back. Not even Christmas."

"Like Jace?"

"Not like Jace," she said. "At the end, he just couldn't stand our father. He just…"

"Just what?"

"Just hated everything about Sarasota Falls."

She left him standing there by the Dumpster. She'd gone from inquisitive to upset without taking a breath. And she'd uncovered something Jace and her brother shared more quickly than he'd expected.

But, she hadn't trusted him enough to explore the possibility of a connection.

CHAPTER THIRTEEN

HER BROTHER, CLARK, had never been one to answer phones calls, at least not when his family was trying to get in touch with him. It was Sunday morning; he should be home. Leann tried not to be irritated as she left another message and then went in to wake up her boys.

"Aaron, up. Timothy, up!"

"Moooom." The protest came from Timothy.

"Time for church."

That worked for Timothy. Leann had a vague idea that there was a girl in his Sunday school class whom he was starting to notice. *Starting* being an interesting word. Ever a cop, she observed he tended to "accidentally" fall in step next to the girl when they exited class. A few times, he'd sat beside her at a potluck or school event—always making it look random. At the dance last night, he'd stayed on the other side of the room. His avoidance of her so strategized that anyone but a twelve-year-old girl would have noticed.

The girl was clueless.

Timothy even more so.

It would be interesting next year when Timothy entered both junior high and the church youth group and suddenly had the older boys to look to for example.

Hmm, maybe Leann should lock him up in his room until he turned eighteen.

And, if Leann did any more thinking about Gary Guzman, maybe she should lock herself up, too. She'd not stood on a dance floor with a man in almost a decade. And if she was being honest with herself, she hadn't wanted the dance with Gary to end.

No, no, no. Not the time to think about that. It was time to get her boys up.

Aaron was a different story when it came to morning routine. He was her go-to-bed-at-nine, rise-at-seven boy. This morning, she understood his grumpiness a tiny bit. They'd had a late Saturday night at the dance and he'd not gotten to bed until almost eleven.

She'd not gotten to bed until midnight and then didn't go to sleep until almost two: she blamed Gary and the scent of some kind of woodsy aftershave that had stayed with her even after she showered and drenched herself in strawberry shampoo.

She also blamed the single rose, slightly bent from being in her purse, and now on display on the desk in her bedroom.

Her bedroom was much cleaner than her youngest son's. She stepped on two pieces of Lego and a dirty sock before reaching the bed to sit next to her youngest son. He didn't smell woodsy. He smelled of bubble gum, pizza and sweat. She snagged the covers from his sleeping form and tickled his side. He wriggled and giggled.

Ack, sometimes he looked just like his dad.

She'd not seen her ex-husband, Ryan Bailey, in years. Three years ago he'd caught a hop to Albuquerque and she'd seen him then, looking older and decidedly distant. The last two times the boys had seen him, Ryan's parents had driven them to California, once for a beach vacation and then for Disneyland. It bothered her because it bothered her boys. She had very little contact, thanks to his parents, who could keep him up to date on every milestone.

Tamara kept saying, "He needs to be here."

Well, he'd be here and soon. So, he must have finally listened to his mother. Leanne would believe it when she saw it. She'd put her trust in the man once. He'd broken her trust, smashed it, and she'd not trusted since. She needed to remember that.

Should she have tossed the rose?

"Get up," she whispered in Aaron's ear. "You've twenty minutes before I have breakfast on the table."

He didn't move.

"Peaches!" she called. The dog loped into the room, jumped on the bed and sat on Aaron. It was a routine they'd had in place since Aaron started preschool.

"Okay, Mom," Aaron groaned into his pillow.

Leann didn't attend the same church as her parents and sister. She and her kids attended another one a few blocks from the elementary school. She'd first walked through its front doors when she moved back to town and stayed with Patsy for a few months. Now, unless she had to work, Leann didn't miss. And, when she did miss, her kids went with Patsy.

Surprise, surprise, they were ten minutes early when they passed through the entrance. Timothy and Aaron headed off to Sunday school and Leann went to the auditorium, sitting in the back, off in the corner, and looking around. People gathered in small groups, catching up on the weekend, making plans for the afternoon.

Luckily, an emergency had never interrupted morning services; thus, Leann felt like church was her true relax time. Not that her job was ever far away.

Nor were the members perfect. Some folks wouldn't look her in the eye because she'd pulled them over for speeding or had cited them for some other minor infraction.

Yet, most of the people she knew didn't give up, strove to improve their situations, changed.

Even her younger sister was trying to change. There'd not been a call to the police station for over a week. Lucas had told her he'd seen Ray at the old train depot outside town. Leann knew there'd been an advertisement for workers. Could Ray have applied for one of the jobs? She needed to text her sister.

Speaking of siblings, she saw Paul Keller, Patsy's brother, enter the auditorium. She'd told herself to wait until tomorrow, visit him when he got off work, but she didn't want to wait. She exited her pew and followed him to the pew in the front that he and his family favored. "Hey, Paul."

"How's my favorite cop?" he asked, hugging her before sitting down.

"Pretty good. I have a question for you. Patsy said you used to hang around with Jace Blackgoat."

He laughed. "You don't waste any time. I heard Jace was in the area, and yes, I hung around with him some—not a lot—sixteen years ago. Haven't seen him since he left."

"He ever cause any trouble at your place? Maybe take something that wasn't his?"

"None of us could ever get up to much even if we wanted to. My mom kept a close eye on us. She's a worrier. Besides, Mom liked Jace."

Paul and Patsy's mother believed the family who played together, stayed together. Mrs. Keller wasn't above jumping rope or learning how to play video games just to figure out what her kids were interested in.

Leann tried to be just like her.

"Jace and I did ROTC stuff together," Paul continued. "He was a team player, always did his share. We probably would have hung together more, but he lived so far out of town that he didn't get to do much of anything else."

"Can you remember any of his friends, even those he just hung out with a bit?"

"He and his sister were tight. After she graduated, he palled around with us ROTC kids. There weren't that many. I think our unit was ten. We all thought Jace would be the first one to enlist."

"But he wasn't."

"No, only one of our gang went into the military. Sam Balliard."

Leann knew Sam. As a matter of fact, she'd seen his photo just two weeks ago in his dad's office. He'd become a lawyer just like his father, Fred.

She'd seen Gary in the hallway after that first meeting. Forcing herself to stop thinking about the man who invaded her thoughts way too often, she said, "I know how to get ahold of Sam. What about the other guys? Do you have their contact information?"

"I can get it."

"What about my brother? Did Clark hang with Jace?"

"Are you kidding? Your father dictated who your brother associated with. Jace wasn't on the approved list."

It was true. Leann's parents thought they knew whom their children should hang around with. They based their opinion on job description, money in the bank and social status. Which was why Leann knew how to get ahold of Sam; he'd been around their house some. Her father approved of him. After all, his dad was one of her dad's clients as well as a lawyer. You never knew when that might come in handy.

She also remembered that Sam didn't actually like Clark much. He'd come around only when his parents made him. Like the elaborate parties her parents used to throw, and the parents insisted their offspring attend.

To impress people.

Or, to keep from angering someone who could later prove to be a pain, like Leann's father.

Leann shook away the memory. "Patsy mentioned my brother was with you occasionally."

Paul frowned. "If he was, I don't recall. The only time I remember Clark coming to our door was to find you."

That was because Leann and Clark handled their parents in very different styles. Clark pretended to do their bidding. Leann stoically rebelled. Patsy was her best friend. Didn't matter that Patsy's dad was a lowly foreman for a lumber company and her mom a receptionist at City Hall, didn't matter that sometimes Patsy's family ran out of pizza on Saturday night and didn't have enough money to order more. All that mattered was they loved their kids and cared enough to ask Leann how she was doing and always listened to her answer.

"I'll talk to Sam. Maybe he'll remember something." She started to turn away, but Paul stopped her.

"You know, when Jace was leaving town, he came by our house. I gave him every dollar I had, about fifteen. Two months later, I received three fives in the mail, no message, but I knew the money had come from Jace. He paid me back."

Leann was getting a distinct picture of Jace Blackgoat. He'd left Sarasota Falls as abruptly as her brother. He'd been a quiet, "cute" boy who'd not gotten in much trouble. And, until recently, hadn't gotten into trouble with the law.

If the trouble was really "him". Leann needed to visit Trudy Gilmore and find out why the name Blackgoat had caused a reaction.

When church ended, she stopped at the Station Diner to feed the kids. They ordered their favorite—macaroni and cheese bowls. Her own salad lasted but a second, and later she didn't remember chewing.

"Where are we going?" Aaron asked when they were back in the car and she turned the opposite direction of their house.

"We're just heading out to check on Russell. He's getting older and needs visitors. He's probably going to be at...at my friend Gary's place."

"But, I don't need to do anything for my Cub Scout troop."

"Mom's taking us to see Russell because she wants to know about his grandson, Jace. Right, Mom?"

Timothy was getting way too wise.

"What makes you think that?"

"One of the kids in class said something about Jace Blackgoat stealing from the grocery store."

"Is Mr. Blackgoat hiding Jace?" Aaron wanted to know.

"I don't think so."

Her phone sounded, belting out the song she'd keyed in designating her father's number. Normally, she'd put it on speaker, but she knew from years of experience that she probably didn't want her kids to hear what Ted Crabtree—a man they didn't associate with the word *grandpa*—had to say. She stopped at the side of the road and answered the call.

"I hear Jason Blackgoat might be in town." Her father didn't start with "Hello" or "How are you?" or even "How are the boys?"

"There's a possibility he's in the area."

"Why?"

Careful to be vague, more for her sons than for her father, Leann replied, "A man matching his description shoplifted from Little's Grocery Store."

"So, he's still a thief?"

Still?

"Did he steal something from you?" she asked.

Her father didn't answer. Instead he demanded, "What are you going to do about him?"

"We're looking for him."

"And when you find him?"

"If there's enough credible evidence, we'll arrest him."

"Good." Her father wasn't done because he continued with, "I hear you've been seeing the Guzman boy."

"I've worked with Oscar for years." But she knew her father wasn't talking about Oscar.

"I'm not talking about Oscar. I'm talking about the other one."

"You mean Gary? No, I'm not seeing him." Leann certainly wasn't going to share that she was on her way to see him right now.

"I've heard from more than one person," her father snapped back.

"It's a small town. I might keep running into him because of his proximity to Russell."

"What?"

"Gary's restoring the old Guzman cabin."

Her father muttered something she couldn't quite make out. Then, he said, "He's not someone you should get involved with."

Had she been younger, her father's suggestion would have made her want to definitely get involved with Gary. She, however, was older and wiser. Plus, she had two boys to consider. But really, she didn't need to prove anything to her father.

Instead of answering like a daughter, she decided to question like a cop. "What's your issue with Gary Guzman?"

She must have surprised him because he responded, "I know the family. His father, disappeared. He must have been up to no good."

"I've worked with Oscar for almost two years now. Their father's been missing for more than fifteen and—"

"I expect you'll do the right thing." Call severed.

What had just happened? Why was her father throwing out accusations? And, what was his problem with Gary Guzman?

"Who was that?" Timothy asked.

"That was my father," she said.

"Oh." In the rearview mirror, Leann studied Tim's reflection. In moments like this, he seemed a lot more mature than twelve.

"I hope Russell has hot dogs," Aaron said, easily leaving the topic of her father behind.

"Well, we're really going to Gary's."

The words were barely out of her mouth when up ahead a thin line of smoke swirled toward the sky. He was probably grilling some lunch. She pictured him in jeans, a T-shirt, dark hair curling around his ears. She thought of the hands that had held her gently at the school dance.

"Cool, Mom, look at all the dogs!" Aaron rolled down the window and yelled "Fetch" just because he could.

"I count three, and one of them looks like Peeve," Timothy noted.

"It is Peeve. This is where Gary Guzman, Oscar's brother, is living. He's watching Peeve right now."

"Look at that furry black-and-white one," Aaron said. "What kind of dog is that? Didn't he bring that one to the school dance?"

"Yes. It's a border collie and..."

Gary stepped from behind the camper,

crossed his arms and looked at her. The only word that came to mind was *smoldering*.

"Look," Aaron said gleefully. "There's another one."

"That's Wilma," Leann informed her sons when a third dog joined the mix. "She's a bit high maintenance." Luckily, her boys didn't ask how she knew so much about Gary's dogs.

"Sounds like my kind of dog." Aaron had his seat belt off before Leann could come to a complete stop. The kids exited the vehicle and were soon chasing and being chased.

Russell stepped to Gary's side, his face serious. Likely he was anxious to know if she had any more news about Jace.

Gary sauntered over to open the car door for her. He lingered, his arm stretched out above her, resting against the top of the car. He gazed down at her. A slow smile reached his eyes, asking a question that he already seemed to know the answer to.

"Can't stay away?" he queried.

For the first time in years, Leann didn't have a comeback. Ever a cop, her eyes swept the landscape, taking in the solid kennels, the cabin already showing excellent signs of repair and the camper, which, just a few weeks ago, had the look of solitude and sadness.

Not any longer. Now, this plot of land had a homey, welcoming feel. One that took Leann's breath away. Maybe because she recognized the truth—she had looked forward to coming to see Gary.

CHAPTER FOURTEEN

GARY WATCHED AS Leann's oldest boy downed three hamburgers, almost without pausing. Impressive. Good thing Gary had a dozen thawed.

"How can you be hungry?" Leann chided. "You just ate in town not an hour ago."

"Leave a little room for ice cream," Gary urged.

Aaron beamed at Gary. Ice cream obviously meant instant friendship. Timothy still didn't look happy—maybe that was because the three hamburgers he'd devoured without chewing were lumped there in his stomach.

"Then we'll have some." Gary looked over at Leann, hoping for a permissive smile. Instead he was privy to watching a gorgeous woman and a well-behaved dog. Stupid dog never acted like that for Gary. Wilma fetched the ball and shook hands with her paw, as well as stayed. Wilma looked very much the way Peeve did going through the paces with Oscar. Except

Leann was much cuter than Oscar in her blue skirt and a cute blue-and-white-striped shirt.

He looked closer.

And heels.

This was yet another side to the woman who occupied too many of his thoughts. Gary forced himself to look away and head for the trailer to fetch ice cream; he needed something cold. A few minutes later, he focused on dishing ice cream into bowls.

And realized that for the first time in a long time, he was truly happy. He had people to care for, a cabin to rebuild and three dogs who needed him. Well, maybe not Peeve the wonder dog, who seemed to know that his job was to watch Russell.

He'd bet Goober had never been happier. She'd spent the last half hour keeping the boys from going into the woods, not that they really wanted to. If Timothy or Aaron stopped petting her, she nudged their hands until they started again. Didn't matter that one of them had hamburger grease on his fingers. That was a bonus.

Once the ice cream was devoured, a whole carton, the boys went walking toward a creek that ran the length of Guzman land.

Peeve sat his butt down on Russell's foot

and watched the other dogs. Wilma and Goober ran back and forth, circling in front of and behind them, hind feet skidding in the dirt and their barks complementing the boys' laughter.

"Now's as good a time as any," Russell said to Gary. "You both want to talk about Jace, so go ahead."

Leann pursed her lips. The relaxed stance she'd had just a moment ago morphed into cop professionalism. Didn't take even a second. She shot Gary a look; one that clearly indicated she didn't want to involve him in this conversation. Too bad, he was already involved—with both the case and her.

"Russell," she said, "everyone I've spoken to thought highly of Jace."

Except my father.

"He was an easy kid," Russell said.

"Then why did he leave all those years ago?"

Russell frowned and stared out into the forest, not answering.

"Tell me about his friends," she finally suggested.

"I know he set store by his ROTC teacher. Sometimes he worked for Ralph at the hardware store. He liked the kids in his shop class. Some of them came by. They helped build the shooting range in my backyard. I can't remember their names."

Leann didn't hesitate. "There was Sam Balliard and his crew. They were all in ROTC."

"Yeah, those boys. They came by fairly often. Then, there was your brother that once. Jace was already gone. Didn't look happy. I don't know what he wanted of Jace, but he sure expected to get it. Just like his old man, a Crabtree."

"You're not surprised," Gary said to Leann.

"Nothing my family does surprises me."

"Your father can be pretty heavy-handed," Russell said. "He offered to buy the Guzman cabin decades ago and was sent packing. I half expected him to try to buy me out next. Couldn't happen, of course. This is state land. The Guzmans and me are grandfathered in. Were we to sell, it would have to be to the government."

Gary looked from Russell to Leann. She was walking away, shoulders straight, letting him know she didn't need his help, didn't want it. If he were smart, he'd chase her down, ask her about her family.

Gary had never been good at waiting—especially once he realized that he loved a woman. Not that he loved Leann. He only liked her. A lot.

And that scared him.

LEANN WALKED PAST the cabin, past the shed and into the forest. Her emotions were churning. How were Jace and her brother connected? And, why had her father wanted to buy the Guzman property? The only thing he did outdoors was play golf.

It made no sense.

Her foot snagged in a gnarled root and she hit the ground. A rookie mistake. She knew better than to ignore her surroundings. She stood, brushed off her knees, pretended the scratches on her palms didn't exist and kept walking.

For a half hour, she walked, scolded herself for caring and mostly dredged up memories of a childhood she'd hated.

Clark had hated it, too.

Only her sister, Gail, had tried to embrace the lifestyle her parents dictated, but she couldn't live up to her parents' expectations and when she'd finally given up, she'd been the most lost.

Until recently. Leann had texted Gail last night and her sister had responded that she and

Ray were spending the weekend in Santa Fe, going to a rodeo, having fun.

Having fun.

Leann would like to have fun.

She finally turned, vowing never to keep her church clothes on when she next took a walk through the woods, and headed back to Gary's. Though she didn't want to ask any more questions of Russell. And she certainly didn't want to confide in Gary. Not at the moment. She wanted to talk to Clark first.

Luckily, while she was gone, Russell's face had relaxed into some semblance of the man her boys knew and loved. He continued to doze in his favorite lawn chair with Aaron sitting next to him, chattering merrily, playing a game on his phone and seemingly unaware that he had no audience for his "Look! I just leveled up" and "Oh! No, no, no, I lost the tower!"

Timothy and Gary played horseshoes. Leann decided not to join them because it was more entertaining watching her son interact with Gary. Right now, he stood at Gary's side, learning how to determine the weight of the horseshoe and the speed he needed to exert at release, as well as the best kind of arc. Timothy shed his goofy sixth-grade persona and was actually conversing in complete sentences.

Leann settled in one of the lawn chairs and pulled out her phone. She checked messages. She had an FYI from Zack, letting her know that someone had tried getting into Trudy Gilmore's room at the hospital. Whoever it was had managed to sit Trudy up and get her shoes on. Why? Trudy wasn't being detained and needed the care.

There was nothing from Clark. Leann responded to a funny video sent by Patsy and also clicked Confirm about an upcoming dentist appointment for Tim. Then, she snapped a few photos of her boys at play. Finally, she snagged a paperback from her purse and settled back to get some uninterrupted reading time. After ten minutes, she realized she'd turned the page only once and that her attention was on Gary and Tim.

Mostly Gary.

Oh, yeah. He was aware of her as a woman. She tried to pretend not to notice. And, she resisted feeling honored, attracted, interested.

She forced herself to return to her book and managed another page before her phone rang and Lucas ordered, "You need to get to Third and Main!"

"My day off," Leann reminded him.

"The chief was helping with a fender bender

when a white truck veered right into him and
then—"

"Is he hurt?" Her words were loud enough
to stop the horseshoe game.

"Yes, I just took the call. I need you out
there right away. Third and Main. And, keep
your eye out for a white Ford 250 truck with
no back bumper."

"How hurt is he?"

"I don't know! Zack's on his way there. But
he's never handled an accident. Go," he barked.
"Get out there."

"I'm on my way." She hung up.

"What happened?" Gary said, so loudly that
Russell startled awake.

"A vehicle struck Chief Riley as he was
helping with an accident. Hit-and-run. He's
hurt. I need to get there."

Her mind started racing. The kids' grandparents, Herb and Tamara, spent Sundays with
their niece in Santa Fe. They'd come if she
called them, but by the time they got here, she
might already be done.

Chief Riley had to be all right.

Quickly, she tried for a second option, but
her best friend, Patsy, and her husband were
at a dive match over in Taber. No sitter there.

For the first time she considered Gail and Ray, but they were gone, too. Stupid rodeo.

"Could you keep the boys for a while?" she asked Gary.

Russell spoke up, "I can help."

"Sure," Gary agreed.

"I'll call as soon as I know something." Leann waved to her boys and jumped in her car. She then stuck the siren on her hood, activated it and started the ignition.

As she hit the road, all thoughts of her brother and Jace Blackgoat disappeared. In all her years on the force, she didn't remember any incident that had made her heart thud like this one.

Traffic was nonexistent. Good.

She slowed down only when she reached the main crossroads just outside Sarasota Falls. When she got to the bank, she turned left and quickly assessed the scene. A blue Chevy with a smashed-in door was parked by the curb. A teary Maya Gillespie leaned against it. A motorcycle lay on its side in front of the car. Its owner, Jimmy Weston, sat on the curb, head in his hands, shoulders shaking. It took only a few questions to ascertain the kid was distressed over the hurt chief of police. His bike, luckily, didn't have a scratch.

Leann nodded at Maya, who worked for the dentist where Leann took both her boys, and joined Zack, who was in the middle of the road measuring skid marks.

"Did you see the chief? Talk to him?"

Zack looked up. His eyes were dim and red. He wouldn't appreciate her noticing that he'd been fighting tears. Her own eyes grew hot. "Well?"

"I saw him. He was on the stretcher already and he wasn't talking. He had a bandage over his skull." Zack gulped.

Leann nodded and went to Maya. "You all right?"

"No, I'm freaked out," Maya yelped. "I ran into the drugstore for just a minute. When I came out, of all things, Jimmy Weston ran right into the side of my car with his motor-cycle. Didn't hurt his bike but look at my door."

The door was crumpled; the bike looked fine.

"I called the station," Maya continued. "Sure surprised me when I got the chief."

Leann didn't mention how shorthanded they were without Oscar. She didn't want to think about how shorthanded they'd be without Chief Riley.

"Go on."

"The chief was bent over looking at my door. He straightened, took a step back. I swear there were no cars about. Then, this white truck came screaming around the corner. The side mirror got the chief and he went flying back. I still expected him to jump up and start chasing the guy."

Leann waited.

"He didn't get up. That's when Jimmy and I saw the blood. Lots of it. All over his face."

"Did you get a look at the plate?"

Jimmy walked up then and said, "No. It all happened so fast."

"Did the driver slow down at all?"

"Just a nano. That's when I saw his face. He had to have seen what happened to Chief Riley. Maybe even pedestrians should wear helmets."

Maya choked, stopped crying and just stared at Jimmy.

Jimmy shrugged. "Can't tell you much what he looked like though. It all happened so fast." Leann nodded and followed up with a question about the description of the truck, which Jimmy gave expertly, better than he had the driver, and then called Lucas to see if he had all the details.

"They found the truck already," Lucas said, "at least, if a damaged side-view mirror is a tell. It was abandoned out toward Springer. And, we already traced the owner."

Before Leann could do more than feel a moment's satisfaction, Lucas added, "Guy didn't even realize it had been stolen."

"Another coincidence that maybe isn't. Springer's where Jace Blackgoat was," Leann said.

"I'd forgotten that," Lucas admitted.

Leann hadn't. Lately, except for when she was thinking about Gary, most of her thoughts and deeds went back to Jace.

Didn't matter right now. Leann knew they'd be here for hours because not only did they have to ascertain the details concerning Tom's hit-and-run, but there was the accident between Maya and Jimmy.

Zack, the rookie, handed over the ST-3 Accident Form that the chief had started. Leann bit her lip as she noticed a drop of blood and the place on the form where Tom's handwriting had switched from actual words to just a jagged pen mark that fell off the page.

"I found it on the ground," Zack admitted.

"Good work." After that, Leann drew a detailed diagram gaining input from both Maya and Jimmy, who—no surprise—didn't agree on anything. After that, she approached each witness and took as many notes as she could.

It did indeed take Zack and Leann hours to accomplish all they needed to do at the crime scene. When they finished, Leann checked the time—almost ten on a school night—and headed back to the station.

With the station's emergency calls rerouting to Lucas at home, on call, Leann turned on the lights, checked for notes or instructions at the front desk and then headed for her cubicle. She had reports to complete and needed to connect with Lucas and get an update on Chief Riley.

First, she'd check on her boys.

She reached for her cell phone just as the front door opened. Had she locked it? Leann stood: instinct had her hand going to the handle of her gun. Lucas stuck his head through the doorway. "Highway patrol found Jace Blackgoat."

"How's he—"

"Not talking. Won't talk, not a word, and he wouldn't even give his name."

"Nothing about hitting the chief?"

"Nothing. He'll be wanting a lawyer. He'll stay at the Springer station tonight—it's closer—and they'll drop him off here first thing in the morning."

Leann nodded, glad they caught up to Jace, but wishing that Russell wasn't going to have to deal with the repercussions.

"I'll call the hospital again and let you know what they say."

Settling in her chair, with a bulk of paperwork in front of her, Leann tugged her cell phone from the belt clip and punched in Gary's number. Gary...the day had started out so differently from how it was ending.

"Hey," came his voice, sounding more awake than she did.

"I'm so sorry. This took longer than I expected."

"Don't be," he said, sounding reassuring. "How's the chief?"

"Lucas is calling the hospital for an update. We know he has a head injury, but nothing else."

"Any idea who did this?"

She hesitated only a moment. Gary had befriended Russell, and it would be better if he knew. "It might have been Jace. He's been located by the highway patrol."

Gary gave a whistle.

"We'll know more tomorrow," Leann said. "Thanks so much for watching my boys."

"We had a great time. We went up to Russell's for board games and sleeping bags. Then came back here. Right now, they're sacked out around the fire. Aaron was out at eight."

"He's my sleeper," Leann said.

"Tim held out until ten. He was so enthralled by some of Russell's stories about the Santa Clara Pueblo Indians that I didn't have the heart to tell him to go to bed. By the way, he wants to move out here. He finally nodded off when Russell got a call from his granddaughter," Gary explained.

"Did she have anything important to share?"

"I didn't catch much of the conversation, but I got enough to know they're worried about Jace."

They needed to be worried about Jace, Leann thought. "I have my paperwork to finish and then I'll come get Aaron and Tim. That okay?"

"The boys and Russell are asleep. How about I wake them and bring them to you. You gotta be dying for some sleep."

"Russell's there?"

"He's sleeping on the cold, hard ground in a bag that's been gathering dust for a decade."

Leann wondered if there was evidence out there they may have missed. Jace could have been at Russell's place while everyone was at

Gary's. She'd have to turn off her lights and drive slow, or Gary had want to go with her.

"No, I'll come get them. I want to check up on Russell. I'll see you in an hour or more," she said.

"Looking forward to it."

She disconnected. Her common sense told her to consider him a good friend and ignore his "looking forward" to seeing her comment. What she couldn't ignore was her looking forward to seeing him, too.

CHAPTER FIFTEEN

MIDNIGHT SENT A grayish haze across the deserted road that snaked its way along toward the Jemez Mountain that loomed in the distance. Tschicoma—the highest point—stood guard in the night.

A half mile from Gary's place, Leann shut off the headlights and used the moon to guide her. She could see well enough to stay on the road, although she managed to drive into or over every dip and bump.

Just past Gary's place, she ran into the biggest obstacle: Gary. He stood in the middle of the road with his flashlight aimed at the ground. Smart man. He didn't want to blind her. Never mind that she could have killed him.

She stopped her car and waited for him to walk to her window, which she rolled down.

"I heard headlights were invented for a reason," he mused.

"I kept them off because I didn't want to risk waking the boys."

"Seems you missed my place," he pointed out.

"I wanted to see if everything's all right up at Russell's cabin."

"Alone in the dark?"

Busted. He stared down at her, his eyes unfathomable in the night's hue. Finally, she opened the door, exited and stood beside him leaning against the side of her car. She wasn't sure if she was putting off going to Russell's cabin or acting on the invisible pull she felt whenever she was around Gary.

"Just me, my Glock and the years of experience on the force," she informed him.

One side of his mouth twitched. She wasn't sure if he was laughing at her or feeling chagrined. All he said was, "The place was fine at eight when we got the sleeping bags and games."

Usually, Leann expressed her thoughts quickly and cohesively, but there was something about the shadows of the night running their fingers through the surrounding trees. Either she blamed the shadows or she had to admit that Gary, standing so close to her, had her on sensory overload.

He deserved to know what was going on. Quickly, she told him what she knew about Jace's being located and the plan for tomorrow.

"I've sent Oscar a text to fill him in. I imagine he'll be getting back to me soon. I even called my mother, but she's not heard from him either. She says when a Guzman goes on a second honeymoon, he's bright enough to turn his phone off."

Leann smiled and pushed away from the car, away from Gary. "Jace might have been to Russell's while we were at your place. I want to do a check on Russell's…"

Gary was around the car and entering the passenger side before she could finish.

"You need to stay with the boys." Unfortunately, her voice cracked a bit, but at least it didn't squeak. Good. She swallowed and added, "Their safety is my first priority."

"Agreed. Russell's with them. He was in the 213th Field Artillery Battalion—"

"Eighth Army," she finished. "He's also three times your age."

She got back behind the wheel. Silently they drove up the curving road. Gravel crunched under the tires as Leann pulled as close to Russell's house as she could.

She opened her car door and stepped out before Gary could act all gallant. Taking the lead, she headed up the walkway. Thankfully this time, the cabin's door was locked. Gary produced a key. The house smelled of popcorn and Old Spice, somewhat comforting and definitely Russell.

Nothing seemed out of place. An old newspaper, dated last week, was on the coffee table. Candy wrappers were scattered next to it. Russell's bed was rumpled. He was as bad as her two boys. A few dishes were in the sink, and a giant convenience store plastic cup was on the table.

"Mine," Gary admitted, opening the back door.

Both their flashlights played across Russell's backyard.

"I was more than impressed the other day when we were shooting," Gary shared, almost sounding apologetic but not quite. "Russell told me about how hard you've always worked at building your qualifying numbers."

"I need to work harder, maybe come up here on my days off while the boys are in school." If he were anyone else, Leann would have swallowed her pride, asked for him to tutor her. But, he was Oscar's brother, and she knew why Gary so desperately wanted to get ahold of Oscar. It wasn't just that the chief had been hurt and they were shorthanded.

"Russell says you have potential," Gary finally said as they moved past the outskirts of Russell's yard.

"That's me, Leann who has potential."

"Russell also says practice will take you from potential to proficient."

"Russell talks too much."

"My brother says the only thing he has over you, when it comes to the promotion, is shooting ability."

Leann frowned. Now she knew why Gary sounded almost apologetic.

"It's not the only thing he has over me," Leann admitted. "He's got FBI training that allows him to see big-picture details that I miss because I tend to focus on what's in front of me."

"Focus is a good thing."

"If one knows when and how to use it," she agreed. "Oscar knows how to focus, too."

"You know, I could maybe help."

Leann was saved from answering when her knees encountered a small fenced-in enclosure. "What's this?"

They aimed flashlights and then stepped back, realizing they'd stumbled upon a small, private cemetery. Leann had heard that many Native Americans buried their dead on their property. But, she'd been visiting Russell for years. How had she missed this tiny graveyard nestled in a corner of his property?

"Don't go in," she warned.

"Why?"

"It's not right."

Instead, they aimed the flashlights on the small markers, noting the one that looked the most recent, which would be Angela's. Leann could only shake her head as she stared at the graveyard, imagining Russell caring for it with pride and love. They backed away. She listened to the sounds of the night as they walked to Russell's house.

"Nothing out of the ordinary," Gary said, reaching out a finger to trace her chin. It wasn't cold and the weather had nothing to do with Leann's shiver.

His hand cupped her cheek, and although she knew he wasn't doing anything magical, the movement seemed to draw her closer.

She reminded herself that, yes, they were opposites, and yes, it would be wiser to run, but her heart answered the pull.

His lips settled over hers: warm, questing. She felt the heat all the way to her knees. Right now, she felt so safe in his arms. She fit there perfectly.

One of his hands curled around the back of

her neck. The other gently rubbed across her shoulder blades. It had been so long since she'd felt this way. She reveled in his touch. Her lips responded to his.

Coyotes yipped, and Leann pushed against the desire that had her wanting to get lost in this man. She couldn't, not now. Out of breath, she whispered, "We shouldn't be doing this…"

"Why not?"

"I'm—I'm not ready."

She stepped back, managed to break their connection.

Gary nodded, let go of her hands and grinned. "You did kiss me back."

"Well, yes, I…" Her throat constricted. She had kissed him back, and more than anything she wanted to do it again.

But, the timing was all wrong, not to mention everything else on her plate. She had house payments, orthodontist bills, a promotion to earn and an ex-husband who was arriving back in town tomorrow.

"I gotta go," she stammered. Then, she turned and ran to her car, but she had to sit there, wait for him to open the passenger side door and join her. His presence filled the vehicle. Worse, his touch lingered on the back of her neck and his taste was on her lips.

IT WAS COLD. Gary sat in a chair and sipped coffee, thinking that if it weren't for Russell snoring away in his sleeping bag, that Gary would go inside the camper and curl under a dozen blankets for a real snooze.

Well after eight, Russell finally sat up, looked around and remarked, "I slept through Leann getting her kids. Why didn't you wake me?"

"No need."

"How's the chief of police?"

"As of last night, still the same. They're monitoring him closely in the hospital. It's a head injury. I can't find out anything else." Gary handed over a cup of hot coffee and gave Russell a moment before saying, "There's a chance Jace was driving the truck that hit the chief."

Russell shook his head. "Jace wouldn't leave the scene of a crime."

"He was found soon after. He's on his way to Sarasota Falls from the station in Springer."

"I don't believe it. First, Jace knows Tom Riley and would have stopped. Second, Jace has been one with the forest all his life. If he wanted to hide, he'd not be found."

"I hope you're right."

"I am." Russell set his coffee down on the

ground and crawled the rest of the way out of his sleeping bag. Gary hoped he was as nimble at that age. He'd taken longer to get moving this morning, and he felt like he'd not slept at all.

Russell had been making himself at home for weeks. This morning was no different. He headed for Gary's camper, disappeared for all of two minutes and then emerged to grab the coffee cup and order, "Take me up to my cabin, please."

Any other day, Gary wouldn't have blinked. Any other day, Russell would have wanted to talk. Yesterday, while Leann dealt with the situation with Chief Riley, Russell had been the center of attention, keeping the boys' minds off their missing mother. Gary had been transported back to childhood and catch football, stories and games.

"What are your plans?"

"I need to head to town, find out what's going on."

"I'll drive you," Gary offered, knowing that if he didn't, the old man would drive himself.

"I can get there. I'm not that decrepit."

"Didn't say you were." Gary emptied the last of his coffee, stood, stretched and motioned toward his truck. "I'll take you home first. If you're going to be looking for a lawyer, you'll need to shower and change your clothes."

"Nothing wrong with me or my clothes." Now Russell was getting annoyed.

"Didn't say there was," Gary responded easily. "You already have a lawyer in mind?"

"No."

"How about we stop by to see my aunt Bianca? If her lawyer's not the right fit, she'll have advice on who to recommend."

An hour later, they made it to the outskirts of town. "I used to know everyone here," Russell groused. "Now I don't know anybody."

"What did your family do?"

"We raised sheep," Russell said. "You take a look at all of those old trails back behind your place. Most of them are from the days we'd be taking the sheep back and forth from winter range to summer pastures.

"My mother got rid of most of the sheep when she was in her eighties. She said two years with no profit was enough for her. Plus, without us boys to help, her heart wasn't in it. I'm the only one who survived the war to come back to her."

"I'm sorry." Gary thought about his mother, how she'd prayed for him and Oscar when they were both in Afghanistan. She'd practically forbidden Hector to even consider the military.

"It was a long time ago," Russell said as the tires of Gary's truck skidded over the gravel that made up Bianca's small parking area. There were three newish cars parked. Since she had four rooms to rent, Gary hoped it meant she was full.

Gary parked his truck alongside the guest-house, turned off the engine and went around to help Russell out, help that Russell shook off.

Two families, complete with teenagers and one Chihuahua, were just leaving when Gary and Russell entered the dining room. "Hurry," one of the mothers urged, "or we'll miss the train."

They all waved at Bianca and left.

"When did the train start running again?" Russell asked.

"Today." Bianca headed for the kitchen, with Gary and Russell right behind. Without asking when they'd last eaten, she fired up the grill and took bacon and sausage from the fridge. "You want hash browns, too?"

"No, ma'am," Russell said, already scooping the leftover eggs she'd offered onto a plate.

"The city council's all excited about the historic train bringing more tourists to the area.

Gotta say," Aunt Bianca shared, "I have guests for each weekend the coming month. Course, most of them are friends of the family who are doing the renovation of the train."

"I rode that train many a day," Russell said.

"Me, too," Aunt Bianca shared. "I hear they're hoping to repair the line all the way to Santa Fe."

Russell nodded. "That would be something."

"But that's not why you're here."

Russell stopped eating, wiped his hands with a napkin and said, "I'm hoping you can recommend a lawyer. I don't think I really need one because it doesn't make sense what they're telling me Jace has done, but I want to be ready."

Bianca moved aside, motioning for Gary to take over. He took over turning both the sausages and strips of bacon. Aunt Bianca and Russell sat at the kitchen nook and Russell told her everything going on.

"Have you spoken to Lydia about how far this has gone?" Aunt Bianca asked when he finally finished.

"I'd rather not."

"Get out your cell phone. I know you have one."

"What?" Russell sputtered.

"You heard me. Get out your cell phone. Call Lydia. It's been a couple of years since her last visit and it's past time."

"She's working and has family—"

"You are part of her family."

"But—"

"This is for Jace. They were always close. If you don't call her, she's going to be hurt."

Russell took out his cell phone. His fingers shook a bit, but once his granddaughter answered, his forehead smoothed out and he relaxed a bit.

Sitting at the kitchen table, the faint sound of country music in the background, Aunt Bianca said, "You've made a good friend there."

"Yup."

"I hear you've a good friend in Leann."

"Don't match-make, Aunt Bianca."

"Oh," she laughed, "I don't need to. You've handled it all yourself."

Gary couldn't seem to find the words to disagree.

CHAPTER SIXTEEN

LEANN PULLED INTO the police department's parking lot, already feeling like she'd put in a full day. Mondays were never easy. Aaron bemoaned that the weekend wasn't three days long, and Tim, of course, remembered a homework assignment due this morning.

Fun.

Their father was due to arrive, and Leann wanted nothing more than to stay in bed, lights off, and worry. Instead, she was back to work. Her eyes felt gritty and her pants loose. Was she losing weight? It had been an unpredictable week and was about to become more so. Lucas had called a good twenty minutes ago, wanting her to report for duty, but not sharing much on the phone. She figured it had to do with Jace Blackgoat. Based on the noise in the background, Lucas was dealing with way too many people in the waiting room to explain.

After last night's adventure in Russell's backyard—Gary's kiss, his arms around her, the warmth—she'd crawled into bed at three and when she closed her eyes, it wasn't sheep she counted, but the minutes it might be before she'd see him again.

She was too old for this. Too busy.

Pushing open the door, she stepped inside, noted a line of people and promptly bumped into Jimmy Weston.

"How's the chief?" he asked.

"Same," she answered, wishing she knew more. "How's your motorcycle?"

"That's why I'm here. I heard Jace Blackgoat will be brought by. I'm wondering if I can sue him for the damages to my bike."

"Give us a day or two," Leann suggested. "We aren't even sure he was the driver."

Jimmy looked at the long line of people, at Lucas, who wasn't smiling, and then back at Leann. "Okay. I can wait."

He left and she wove her way through the small crowd, fielding questions like "When is the chief coming back?" or "Who's in charge now?"

"Don't know," she answered everyone because they were mostly friends and "No comment" seemed too impersonal.

Lucas waved her toward the back and turned the front desk over to Zack. She'd never seen

Lucas so red in the face. "Jace is due any minute. Sorry to have to call you in early."

She didn't miss that he was a little flustered, even though he was the oldest cop among them and had the most experience. "Things do seem a bit wild out there."

Suddenly, Zack called out, "Need a little help here."

Lucas grumbled, "I'm glad I won't be acting chief. I don't have the desire, the speed or the memory."

"I can do it," Leann offered. "I was planning to apply—"

"Leann," Lucas said softly; his words stopping her cold, "you're our most valued patrol officer with the strongest work ethic I've ever seen. I don't know what we'd do without you."

"What are you trying to say?" Leann knew Lucas, knew that he was soft-pedaling and trying to be both politically correct and honest. Two concepts that didn't necessary complement each other.

"This morning, I got a call from the mayor. I didn't want you to hear this from anyone else. For now, Oscar will be acting chief of police."

"Until Chief Riley returns?"

Lucas nodded.

"The mayor made the decision?"

Lucas nodded.

Leann took a deep breath. Thoughts tumbled in her brain, trying to come together in coherent reasoning. "If Oscar's the chief, that's not a job either of us applied for, so does that mean I still have a chance at lieutenant or..."

"I'm staying on as lieutenant until Tom returns and then I'll retire and my position will be open."

"But, if Oscar has been acting as chief, he'll have something new to add to his qualifications. It will hurt my chances..." Her voice got softer as she spoke. Oh, wow, she sounded like her kids arguing a point and insisting a situation was unfair.

And, this was unfair.

But, what was really unfair was Chief Riley's getting hit by a truck and winding up in the hospital.

"The mayor made the decision," Lucas reiterated. "It wasn't an easy one for him. You are a great cop."

It was what Lucas didn't say that Leann worried about. Lucas knew her, knew the challenges she faced as a single mother and how stressed she was because of Ryan's return.

As if reading her thoughts, Lucas continued, "It's a good thing Oscar just had a brief vacation because for the next month, he won't have any time off."

"I've been working every day," Leann inserted.

He nodded, face somber, before querying, "And, you're willing to work every day for the next few months?"

Was she? Ryan was due in town. If she worked every day, Tim and Aaron would be at their grandparents', with Ryan, every day.

No way was she admitting defeat. In truth, if the chief was going to be out for months, they'd have to hire someone, albeit temporarily. But, it took time—time away from her boys.

She'd been trained by Chief Tom Riley, the best, and she knew that right now, her reaction was make-or-break. Lucas had rated her a "great" cop. To keep his high opinion of her, she needed to acknowledge that Oscar had earned the position and that she applauded him.

"I understand."

He nodded and began. "It's been a wild couple of hours. I need you to stop by Bianca's Bed-and-Breakfast. I spoke with Bianca earlier, but maybe you can get across the urgency of contacting Oscar."

That was easy.

"Then, head out to Russell Blackgoat's place." Lucas took an envelope off his desk and withdrew a photo.

"I can't raise Russell on the phone. Could you please go and collect him? It's important he be here."

"Jace looks old," Leann observed after studying the photo. Much older than Patsy's brother. She'd even bet her brother, Clark, didn't look this old.

Odd.

Lucas waved her off and soon Leann was back in her cruiser and heading toward Bianca's. After that, she'd drive out to Russell's place.

She wouldn't stop at Gary's. No need. He was not part of the equation and right now she didn't need any distractions of the heart, even if her heart told her something different.

RUSSELL AND AUNT BIANCA were at the dining room table, with Aunt Bianca making a list of all the things she thought Russell should be doing to help Jace.

"Lydia will be here later this afternoon. She says to wait to visit Jace until she can come, too," Russell supplied. "I hate thinking he might be in trouble."

"Who hasn't been in some kind of trouble?"

Aunt Bianca pointed at Gary. "You think so much of my nephew. You think he's never been in trouble?"

Gary frowned. Russell now looked intrigued.

"Well, he's been in trouble, let me tell you. A lot more than his siblings, too." Aunt Bianca was really enjoying this. "He got caught skinny-dipping in a neighbor's pool. Thankfully not everyone had cell phones back then or his picture would be all over Facebook."

"Our next-door neighbors were supposed to be out of town," Gary protested halfheartedly. "They told me I could use their pool in exchange for feeding the cat."

"Not at midnight and not without clothes on."

"The only reason they called the police," Gary protested, "was because they didn't recognize me."

Aunt Bianca tsked. "Two weeks later, he pulled the fire alarm at his school junior year. Said he didn't want to take some test."

Gary wondered if he should set the record straight. He'd pulled the alarm because there was a drug deal going down just outside the PE doors, and he knew that one of his brother's friends was involved. Later, he'd collared his brother's friend and Gary had tried to set him straight.

"I thought his mother was going to ground him for life," Aunt Bianca said.

The hair on Gary's neck prickled and he turned to look behind him. Leann stood at the kitchen door. Exhaustion smudged the skin under her eyes and stray hairs escaped her ponytail. Something in him welled up, and had she so much as looked at him, he'd have taken her in his arms, held on tight and told her it would be okay.

He'd make it okay. That was his job. Keeping people safe.

She didn't look at him but said, "Setting off a fire alarm is a Class E felony."

"I wasn't charged."

Leann rolled her eyes.

"How's the chief?" Bianca quickly asked. "I've been listening to the news all morning, but they haven't said a thing."

"We got the call an hour ago. The chief's head injury is now officially a concussion. He'll be released in a week or so."

"Good to hear."

"He won't return to work for a while." Leann took a seat, scooting her chair in before he could assist, and shook her head at Aunt Bianca's offer of food. "Bianca, has Oscar checked in with you at all?"

"No, sweetie, and I've called him twice today already. He said before he left that phone service was spotty on the cruise."

"The police in Seward will meet him the moment he gets off the boat," Leann said wearily. "If it ever docks."

"You can always deputize me," Gary offered, only half kidding.

Leann looked like she wanted to say she wished she could say yes.

"Sarasota Falls isn't big enough for two Guzman boys to tote a badge," Aunt Bianca said.

"It would just be temporary." Even as Gary said the words, he remembered that Oscar's time in Sarasota Falls was supposed to be temporary. His falling in love with Shelley had turned it into something permanent.

Gary had already admitted to himself that he was half in love with Leann. Working with her would either make or break the bond. Maybe he really should step up and apply. *If*—and that was a huge word—he could handle anything rooted, especially being a cop.

Being committed to a cop.

"We, ah," stumbled Leann, "have our schedule for the next two days, but we're shorthanded, and we really need an acting chief. It's just that…"

"You're not acting chief?" Aunt Bianca gently prodded.

"No," Leann said slowly, in a tone Gary never heard her use before. "Lucas and I will be sharing responsibility until Oscar returns, and then he'll…"

An inkling of the truth dawned on him. "He'll what?"

Leann sat up straight and jutted her chin out. "Lucas will put off his retirement until Chief Riley returns as well as handle internal operations. In the meantime, Oscar is acting chief."

"That's strange," Gary protested. "If the position is temporary, just until Chief Riley returns to work, and you're here and Oscar's not, why not just give it to you? You've been here longer. Who made the decision?"

"The mayor. Lucas told me not even an hour ago."

Again, Gary's inclination was to take her in his arms, but he could see it took everything for her to hold herself together. If he took her in his arms, she'd fall apart. He knew it. And she wouldn't appreciate it.

"Why did the mayor—"

Aunt Bianca held up her hand, stopping him. Impatiently, he slid the bacon from the pan onto a plate, followed it with the sausages and set the food in front of Russell. Aunt Bianca passed the ketchup and asked, "The mayor's wife still good friends with your mother?"

Leann visibly flinched.

"Maybe it's time to talk to the mayor himself," Aunt Bianca suggested. "You have seniority and experience. Put the mayor on the spot. And don't go in there and say 'I'm sorry to bother you.' Go in there and lay out your experience and then ask him to give you the exact reasons Oscar was chosen over you. Write them down. Then, counter all his reasons with your expertise. Let him know you're not accepting his decision without a fight."

"Aunt Bianca," Gary said weakly, "um, Oscar's your nephew."

"Oscar's a grown man. He can take care of himself."

Gary's mouth opened and shut. While Aunt Bianca didn't seem inclined to put family first, Gary hesitated. This was a raise for his brother Oscar, who had a new baby on the way.

Russell shook his fork and said the words Gary should have said. "And, your ability on the shooting range has improved thanks to Gary and me."

Aunt Bianca gave Gary a smirk.

No one said anything for a few minutes.

Russell put his fork down, waited a beat and said, "You got any news about Jace? Did you bring him here already?"

"You were right, Russell." Leann almost looked relieved that the subject had changed. "Since Jace refused to talk and had no identification, the cops were able to take his fingerprints. They got the results back this morning."

"And?" Russell urged.

Leann took a black-and-white photo out of her pocket. She held it up so Russell could see the forty-something man. "It's not Jace."

"What?" Bianca chirped.

"I hate to say I told you so." Russell squinted, studying the photo. "Sure looks like Jace, but it ain't."

"The fingerprints belong to Brian Blackgoat. Does that name mean anything to you?"

"Never heard of him. Course, there's a few Blackgoats in Arizona. Distant cousins. Is that where he's from?"

"He's from California. There's something else, though. His name is Brian Russell Blackgoat." Leann leaned forward, put her hand on Russell's arm and asked, "Didn't your daughter live in California before returning here with Lydia and Jace?"

"Yes," Russell said slowly. "Maybe Angela

found a distant relative. She could have told him about me living here. Wonder why she didn't mention him."

Maybe because he was a criminal, Gary thought.

Russell's face was scrunched up as he took the photo and held it closer.

"Brian Russell Blackgoat should arrive any minute if he's not already here."

"Then let's go," Russell said with purpose and jumped to his feet.

It was true, Gary mused minutes later as he steered his truck down Main Street. You just never knew. He'd gotten up this morning expecting to help Russell deal with his grandson. Instead, he was following Leann, taxiing Russell to the police station to meet his grandson's lookalike. Russell sat in the passenger seat, coming up with a half-dozen scenarios. Brian Blackgoat might be a cousin, a nephew, a stranger with Jace's face or a grandson Russell didn't know about.

What was funny was Russell's attitude. He was excited about the chance his family might grow.

"He's likely a criminal," Gary cautioned.

"The first time I met you, I thought you were a criminal." Russell smiled. "And what about Leann? How did she feel about you? She's changed her mind, eh?"

Leann had changed her mind, but what concerned Gary the most was how he was changing because of her.

THERE WERE AT least a dozen cars in the police station's lot. "Rush hour," Leann murmured under her breath as she parked on the street so Gary and Russell could have the last spot. Hurrying, she met them at the entrance and led them inside. For his age, Russell was fast. Or, maybe it was the thought of meeting Brian Russell Blackgoat that had him moving at a snappier pace. Compared with this morning, the station was quiet. Zack was still at the front desk, answering a call. "Lucas is in his office." Zack muted the phone with his hand. "Head on back."

After handshakes, Chief Riley updates and a vague reference to the weather, Lucas said, "They've not arrived yet." Turning to Russell, Lucas added, "Never seen anything like it. I've looked at the mug shot of Brian Blackgoat, and I remember Jace from when he was in high school. If I didn't know better, I'd say they were twins."

Leann wished she'd have paid more attention to Jace when they were in high school.

Out of the blue, Zack appeared in the doorway. "Brian Blackgoat managed to open the door to the police van and jump out. They were near the Turner farm."

"How long ago?" Leann asked.

"Minutes! Just minutes!"

"Turner farm," Russell mused. "That's on the way to my place."

"And it's not a stretch to think that Brian's been there before."

Leann was already running to the door, with Gary and Russell at her heels. Behind her, she could hear Lucas on the phone telling their colleagues that they would take over. After all, they knew the territory.

Thanks to all her visits to Gary, she really did. What usually took almost two hours was just an hour. She left New Mexico State Highway 4 and slowed on the gravel road leading up to Russell's place.

Brian would be on foot, so she would arrive before him. She needed to get to Russell's and put the police cruiser where he wouldn't see it.

She blew out air, trying to calm herself.

Only twice before had she dealt with escaped prisoners. Both times, she'd been a nervous wreck. This time was no different. She drove past Russell's, parked in a heavily wooded side area and then quickly and quietly made her way to the cabin. She retrieved his spare key from under the front step and, gun drawn, entered the living room.

Silence greeted her. The air felt heavy, and Leann silently slipped from room to room, opening closets and looking under beds.

Given she was driving, and he was likely on foot, she'd figured she'd beaten him there.

She settled for the bedroom closest to the front of the house. Leaning against the wall, she had a side view of the driveway. She didn't know whether she wanted Brian to arrive first or Gary and Russell.

The best-case scenario was for her to get ahold of Brian, thereby stabilizing the situation before Gary and Russell got there.

The kitchen clock, a cat with a moving-tail pendulum, she recalled, loudly ticked off the seconds. The creaks and moans of the old cabin reminded her how alone she was.

She hated waiting.

A distant whir became louder. She affirmed her grip on her gun and waited. A quad pulled into the driveway. Gary stopped, helped Russell off, and then concealed the quad in a group of trees.

She let out the breath she was holding and went into the living room and opened the door. "Maybe you should wait—"

"My home," Russell said simply.

Gary jogged up and closed the door behind him. "Russell, all your firearms locked up?"

Good question. Leann wished she'd have asked it.

"They are."

Then, Gary surprised her. "Your call," he said. "Where would you like us?"

"Back in Sarasota Falls waiting."

He shook his head. "Not going to happen."

"I was in the front bedroom, looking out the window."

"I'll take the back bedroom."

"I'll turn the television on in the living room and act like it's a regular day," Russell volunteered.

"I don't want you in danger," Leann started.

"I won't be," Russell said calmly. "I have both of you."

Leann started to argue, but Russell cocked his head. "Birds are stirring up a fuss. Something's out there. You really want to argue?"

She shot Gary a stern look. "Please stay in

the back bedroom until I give you a call. I've got this."

He reached out a hand, moved a lose strand of hair away from her eyes and said, "I know you've got this. I'm just here as backup."

"I won't need backup."

The television was switched on, but Leann couldn't make out the show. Her whole body was on alert. Gary's fingers still caressed her forehead, his touch soft and kind. He cupped her chin. "You might not need backup, but I will always have your back."

Always?

What did that mean?

Before Leann had time to reflect, she heard someone run up the back steps and push hard on the door.

CHAPTER SEVENTEEN

GARY'S KNEE WAS firmly atop Brian Blackgoat's chest. The man wasn't moving. Easing up his weight, Gary flipped Brian onto his back so that Leann could take it from there. She did so, quickly, stating the Miranda and telling him to get to his feet.

Again, Gary was taken aback with Leann's efficiency and directness. She'd been calm in a tense situation. He'd seen less from some stronger types while serving. "You don't have to take him right to the station," Russell spoke up. "You can do your questioning here."

"Probably not a good idea." Leann's response was quick.

"Well," Russell said, matter-of-factly, "he didn't make so much as a sound when Gary here took him down."

"This needs to be done right." Leann reached down and, with little effort, got Brian to his feet.

"I can help," Gary offered.

"You're not a cop."

"I absolutely am a cop."

"Was."

"Once a cop, always a cop."

Leann merely gave him a look.

"I'm right here," Brian said. "You're talking like I can't hear you."

Leann shook her head, ignoring Brian's comment and addressing Gary instead. "I can handle this."

Finally, she looked at Brian, and Gary knew what she was thinking. If Brian had any sense of family, even a tiny thread, Russell would get through to him, but she wanted this to happen by the book at the station.

Leann looked from Brian to Russell, right versus reality showing on her face. She knew as well as Gary did that they were more likely to get answers here, rather than in a formal interrogation room.

"He's nearing eighty," Leann said, indicating Russell. "You upset him and you'll answer to me."

Brian didn't say anything.

She urged him toward the living room. He took two steps and stopped. Russell was in his way, but rather than moving aside, the older man enveloped Brian in his arms, not letting go.

Gary put out an arm, stopping Leann from separating them. He knew physical contact was against the rules, knew that Brian had already gotten away once and could see the benefit of him using Russell as a possible human shield in order to escape. But, there was something about the look in Brian's eyes that said it would be all right. Brian just stood there and let Russell hug him, not returning any affection. Finally, he said, "It's all right, old man."

"Please, let's go in the living room." Leann looked a little pale. She took Brian by the arm, led him to a chair. She settled on the end table right next to him. Russell slowly walked to the couch and sat. No one spoke for a moment. Then, to Gary's surprise, Brian cleared his throat and spoke to Russell. "I should have knocked on your door and introduced myself."

Russell nodded.

Gary would have loved to start asking questions, but Leann began with, "What is your relationship to Russell?"

Brian directed his answer to Russell, not Leann. "Unless I'm mistaken, you're my grandfather."

"How?" Russell's voice wobbled. His hands were clasped and turning red. Gary reached over and patted him on the shoulder.

"I only have part of the story. It's what got me here."

"What's your mother's name?" Leann asked.

"Angela. Angela Blackgoat."

Russell's hand went to his mouth.

"And your father?" Leann queried.

"I never met the man, but Angela told me his name was Roberto Guzman."

IF LEANN HADN'T been sitting, she'd probably have toppled to the floor. As it was, she didn't have time to topple anywhere. She stood just as Gary growled, "Liar!"

Brian shook his head and gave Gary a look that would have stilled a lesser man.

"Truth isn't always a friend, is it?" Brian said. "I know who you are. I've seen you working on the property. It's part mine, you know."

Leann pointed at Gary. "You either sit or I'll put handcuffs on you," she threatened.

"What charge?" he barked. His cheeks had gone a faint flush color, and Leann knew she had to remain in control.

"Interfering with a police investigation," she barked back.

"Calm down, Gary," Russell said softly.

It annoyed Leann a bit that Gary obeyed Russell's order without questioning it. She hadn't guessed that Brian wasn't just Russell's grandson, he was Gary's half brother.

Leann grappled with this twist in events. It was one thing to catch up to a person wanted for questioning in a serious crime. It was another for Gary to find out he had a new sibling. Once again sitting on the end table, she asked, "Would you know if he's still alive?"

"Who?" Brian asked.

Gary's mouth snapped open and then closed.

"Roberto Guzman." She couldn't stop her stomach from fluttering.

"I told you I've never met the guy." Anger laced Brian's words. "And why do you care?"

Russell, ever stoic, repeated Leann's question.

Brian sat back. He kicked his feet out in front of him. His well-worn boots showed mud and the beginning of a hole where the left big toe was.

Russell stared, his lips compressed, and his eyes grew stern. "I knew Berto, you know. He lived on the next property. I knew him from snotty-nosed kid to manhood. I believe Officer Bailey asked you a question. I'd appreciate you answering her."

"I've changed my mind about answering

questions. I think I want a lawyer. I have the right to one."

"At the moment, we're not talking about any crime. We are trying to ascertain if you're related to Russell Blackgoat. This is a courtesy." Leann had already compromised, and it had been a mistake. She stood and reached for Brian's arm. "My cruiser's right outside. We can end this now. Thank you for your cooperation this far. We will—"

"I didn't say I wouldn't answer," Brian retorted. "I just, er... What do I get in return?"

"Nothing," Leann said. "You are currently under investigation for theft and hit-and-run and—"

"I get it." Brian struggled a moment and then looked at Russell, and said, "Old man, where were you all those years ago when I needed you?"

Russell leaned forward. "If I'd known you existed, I would have moved hell and high water to come find you. Why didn't Angela bring you to Sarasota Falls when she returned home?"

"Dunno. She left me with the babysitter when she went to the hospital to have Lydia. Never came back."

"Then how do you know you have a sister named Lydia?" Leann was quick to ask.

Brian smiled, but it didn't reach his eyes. Something else simmered there; not emptiness or hate but despair. "That's something you're going to have to find out."

"She left you with a babysitter?" Russell queried. "Is that who raised you?"

"Yes."

"Doesn't make any sense," Gary joined the conversation. "What kind of babysitter keeps someone else's kid and doesn't try to find the parents or relatives or—"

"The kind that receives money every month, good money, at least until I turned eighteen. I just assumed it came from Berto Guzman, my father. Then, the money stopped."

Gary grimaced.

Russell cleared his throat. "So, my daughter raised you until you were...?"

"Five."

"Who told you Berto was your father?" Leann queried.

"My mother and then Willow, the woman who gave me a place to stay until I turned eighteen."

Leann noted that Brian didn't say "raised me" or "cared for me" or "gave me a home."

"I am saddened by my daughter's behavior," Russell said.

Leann nodded and struggled to keep professional. No mother, father, should ever desert a child. Even her husband had remained a presence in her boys' life, albeit long-distance.

It made her question her attitude toward Ryan. She should be more welcoming to him; he was going to be a bigger part of her boys' lives. She was scared. There were so many what-ifs and he could hurt her boys, get their hopes up and then let them down. She wanted to trust Ryan, trust any man for that matter. Trust Gary Guzman, who kept exceeding her expectations.

Looking across the room, she noted the vulnerability in his eyes. Oh, yes, he could identify with Brian. Feeling abandoned by a parent no matter the circumstances was a strong bond.

She tamped down her emotions and asked, "Why do you think your mother left you and didn't come back?"

"Her new boyfriend didn't want to raise someone else's kid. He was a B actor who had plenty of money and promised my mom help getting her acting parts and a big house. She made a choice."

"You remember a lot for only being five at the time," Leann observed.

"Sometimes Willow told me things. When I got older, I found more on the internet."

Leann figured one of the things Brian discovered was Jace's existence, most especially their likeness.

"Did you ever see a check with the name Roberto Guzman?" Gary asked.

Brian shook his head.

There was a lull in the conversation as all three men stared at each other. Gary was simmering, Brian angry, Russell contemplative. One thing was for sure: Leann would find Willow and track down whoever had sent the money for Brian. She seriously doubted it was Berto Guzman. Something just wasn't adding up.

Berto had fathered four children with Gary's mother and disappeared, what, more than a decade later? Leann couldn't wrap her mind around the logistics.

Why would he faithfully send money to one child but not continue to look after his other four? The ones he'd fathered with his wife? The ones he'd actually known?

Leann needed to step back, regroup and fit the puzzle pieces together. Switching to a different thread, she asked, "Did you burglarize Russell's cabin?"

Russell stopped staring at his hands and looked up.

Brian hesitated, but only for a moment. "Yes, I needed the money. We, er, I was hungry."

"How did you know where the money was hidden?"

"My mother only left a few things behind. A couple of books, some clothes and a photograph of you, old man."

Not much, Leann thought, trying to figure out the mind-set of a woman who could walk away from her child. Brian had been five. Five! Both Leann's boys had cemented a place in her heart mere seconds after their birth, making them hers for life.

"Still need to answer the question," Russell urged.

"One of the books was full of drawings."

"Angela was an artist," Russell acknowledged, pointing to a drawing above his head.

Brian nodded. "She had one like it in her book, smaller, of course. She drew everything about your place. I know exactly what her childhood bedroom looked like. I know what my father looks like. I know you have a sweet Ford truck older than dirt."

Russell nodded.

"She drew the fireplace. She even numbered

the brick where the money was hidden and drew a dollar sign next to it. It was a long shot, but I was willing to take the risk."

"Is that what brought you to Sarasota Falls? The money?" Leann asked.

"Yes, but I thought there'd be more than a hundred dollars."

"Why didn't you just knock on the door and tell me who you were and what you needed?" Russell asked incredulously.

"Right, you'd have been welcoming."

"I would have, yes."

Brian gave a tight laugh. "You know, I considered it. Angela did have good stories about her growing-up years. I thought I'd stay in the old cabin—"

"Mine," Gary said coldly.

"—take a few days to figure out what was going on but…"

"But?" Leann urged.

This time, Brian's words were cold. "He was there, along with Russell. Once I figured out he was a Guzman, I knew we wouldn't find any open arms."

"Yes, you would have." Russell's voice broke. "You're Angela's son. That makes you my grandson."

Leann thought of the small cemetery, of Angela's grave, how tenderly Russell took care of all of the graves.

Brian's expression changed. Leann quickly asked, "Why did you stay? Why not leave Sarasota Falls?"

"Because you picked up Trudy."

A puzzle piece snapped into place. Leann couldn't believe it. "Trudy Gilmore?"

Brian nodded again.

"You stuck around because of Trudy Gilmore? What is she to you? You do know she's in the hospital? The same hospital where you put the chief of police?"

She wanted to trigger a response from Brian. She hoped he'd say, "I didn't hit him that hard." Or, "It wasn't me." Brian, however, didn't say a word, just looked at her like it didn't matter.

Russell stood, came across the room and patted Brian on the shoulder. "I came to town this morning to get my boy a lawyer. I still intend to do that."

"This isn't Jace—" Leann protested.

"No, it isn't. It's Brian. And, if he's Angela's son, then he's just as much my boy as Jace."

"You're hiring me a lawyer?" Brian said, incredulous.

"I am." Russell checked his watch. "Lydia's flight arrives in just over an hour. Even if I—"

"We," Gary interjected.

"—leave now, I'll be late picking her up." He moved toward the door. "Officer Bailey, do you need help escorting Brian to your cruiser?"

"No," Leann and Brian said at exactly the same time.

"Then, it's best you go with her, Brian. I'll be by to see you either tonight or in the morning, depending on what I can get done."

Brian's whole demeanor changed. Before Leann could begin to guess why, Brian provided the reason. "Sir, instead of helping me, would you help Trudy first?"

"No," Leann protested. "We're trying to contact her mother—"

"Who will not come to get her." Brian shot Leann a hard look, which softened when he added, "This is the only place I knew to come. We arrived with no money, slept in the park once we realized he—" a cold look at Gary "—was staying at the cabin. Trudy needs a place to stay so she can get her health back and until we know what's going to happen to me."

"Because you were driving the truck that hit the chief of police?"

Brian affirmed, "Because I was driving the truck that hit the chief of police. It was an accident. At the hospital, I'd tried to get in to see

Trudy, you see. I couldn't even get close. I was mad, trying to decide what to do. I got scared someone would start asking me questions. I was hell bent on getting out of town. I looked down for a second and then wham. I'm more sorry than you know."

"Why didn't you just stop?" Leann asked. "All you're dealing with is a shoplifting charge. Russell isn't worried about the hundred dollars."

Brian's lips pursed and Leann thought he'd clam up again. But then, he said, "There's also the fact that I've stolen someone else's identity. It'll send me to jail and Trudy needs me."

"What do I need to do?" Russell asked. "How can I help?"

"Just take care of her until I get out of jail. She's—she's fragile."

Leann let go a long, pent-up breath. Never, in all her years of police work, had a case been so emotionally complicated.

Really, Roberto Guzman was Brian's father!

Now, instead of feeling like she'd had any control of the situation, Brian complicated the situation even more.

Redheaded, olive-skinned and short, Trudy Gilmore looked nothing like Brian or Russell. Not to mention the girl was barely out of her teens and Brian was in his early forties. They weren't exactly the likeliest of traveling partners.

"Who is she really?" Leann asked.

Brian directed his response to Russell.

"She would be your great-granddaughter, sir. My daughter."

CHAPTER EIGHTEEN

ONCE LEANN TOOK Brian and Russell to the station, Gary offered to drive her to meet Lydia's plane.

Gary checked his speed and turned onto the highway. Behind him, the Sarasota Falls' landscape disappeared completely, replaced by open spaces, distant mountains and occasional trees in varying shades of green. Next to him, still in uniform, Leann was busy on her phone as he sped toward Santa Fe to pick up Lydia Whitefeather.

A sign on the highway alerted Gary that he had thirty more miles until Santa Fe Municipal Airport. Any other day, he would have enjoyed the sight of Leann in the passenger seat beside him. He was dazzled by her kindness, impressed by her intelligence and captivated by her smile.

It amazed him that he could have these thoughts, today of all days, when he had other things on his mind. Leann had to tell only one person about Brian's lineage, and she was doing it as a cop. Her only personal connection was her friendship with Russell.

Friendship, in this case, was a whole lot different from family. Gary needed to tell his mom, his siblings and his aunt. He'd rather tell a whole platoon that they were going from four meals a day to two than tell his family that Berto Guzman might have cheated on their mother and that there might be a half sibling, one who was facing charges at a police station, waiting for a visit from the lawyer his grandfather hired.

After arranging for Brian's legal counsel, Russell told them he was headed to the hospital to sit with his great-granddaughter. Evidently, the paperwork had already begun in order to release her into Russell's care.

Leann finally put away her phone and looked at him. "You okay?"

"Sure. Why wouldn't I be?"

She frowned, a different frown than she usually gave him that showed he'd either annoyed or perplexed her. This time, it looked more like concern.

"I'm fine," he insisted.

"Are you convinced that Berto is Brian's biological father because if you are, it's—"

"I'm not convinced of anything," he interrupted. "I need to think this through. But, I also need to let my family know. I don't want them to be blindsided like I was."

She nodded.

"I'm fine," he repeated.

A sign for the turnoff to the airport appeared at his right. As he flipped on the turn signal, he again perused Leann's expression. The frown was gone, replaced by something else. Something he liked a lot more.

Concern had turned to compassion.

He focused back on the road and almost hit the curb, something he'd not done since he was fifteen.

Leann Bailey had her hand on his knee. If she'd just patted it a couple of times, that would be concern. But, no, her hand rested there and the half smile she gave him said I'm here for you.

This time he did hit the curb.

While Gary cruised, looking for a parking spot, Leann took her hand off his knee and got her phone out to study Lydia's likeness. She showed him her picture. "Now that I've seen photos of all of Russell's grandchildren, I'm spotting subtle differences between Brian and the other two."

Gary grunted. He didn't see anything of the Guzman side in Brian: not the nose, the chin, the height or the character—especially the character.

He finally parked.

"I've never seen Russell so driven," Leann remarked as she opened the door to the passenger side and got out.

"It's not every day that you find out you've a grandson and a great-granddaughter." Gary joined her, walking toward the main terminal, and tried to keep the bitterness out of his voice. He was genuinely happy for Russell; really, he was. Gary just wasn't happy for himself, what he might have to tell his family, about a possible half brother.

"I wonder what would have happened," Leann mused, "if you hadn't been at your family's cabin. Would Brian have simply set up camp there, cared for Trudy and eventually gone to Russell?"

"Well, we know that he likely stole from a grocery store and that he definitely stole from Russell. Not to mention what he did to the chief."

"He must have been feeling desperate," Leann said. "Fear and panic can cause anyone to make bad choices."

"He should have been feeling guilty that he spent the night in jail over in Springer and left Trudy alone," Gary countered. "He should have been thinking he needed a job, needed to make a home for her."

"Sounds like he doesn't know what having a home is."

"You grow up, make a home, especially when there's children involved. Brian has a lot to make up to that girl."

"Yes, and it seems Trudy's mother isn't in the picture. If that's the case and Brian is in jail, what will happen to her?"

"I feel for Trudy, I really do. It's just a lot to take in right now."

Leann nodded, took his hand and squeezed.

The quiet moment between them passed as Gary said, "Lydia has to be here already."

They entered the airport and located the baggage claim area.

"Lydia?" Gary queried, approaching a woman who resembled the photo Leann had shown him.

"Yes."

"I'm Gary Guzman. Did Russell tell you we'd be picking you up?"

"He did, but he said he'd be with you." She stood, looking past Gary, focusing on Leann, and then said sharply, "Where's my grand-father?"

"He couldn't come." Gary started to say more, but instead, he introduced Leann.

A busy airport terminal probably wasn't the place to find out about a new half brother, but Lydia took it stoically. At least, she had until finding out about Trudy. Then, she sat, hands folded in her lap, nodding. "Grandfather will save the Blackgoat clan, one errant relative at a time."

"I'm sure he's eager to see you," Leann said. "Let's go ahead and start the drive back. I've a few more questions. We can talk in Gary's truck."

Gary grabbed the luggage, following the two women and listening as Leann made small talk, asking about the flight and about Lydia's husband and children.

"I should have visited more often," Lydia bemoaned as they left the airport. She sat by the passenger window. Leann was in the middle. Her shoulder was pressed against Gary's arm and the intimate contact kept him so distracted, yet aware of curbs, that he didn't add to the conversation at all.

Right now, Gary didn't want to think about visiting family. Not his father's connection to

Angela Blackgoat or how he was going to tell his family, especially his mother, about the situation.

He'd come to Sarasota Falls to be alone. Instead, he'd managed to become part of Leann's family as well as Russell's.

Gary glanced at Lydia and thought back to Leann's earlier comment on the subtle differences between Brian and his half siblings. She was right.

Gary frowned.

"So," she said, "Brian might possibly be related to you, Mr. Guzman?"

"Call me Gary. It's what he claims."

"What does your mother have to say?"

"I haven't had a chance to call her. I'll talk to my aunt first. She's lived in Sarasota Falls all her life. She'll know more."

"She ever mention anything between your father and my mother?"

"She said Berto and Angela were friends."

Leann shifted in her seat, inching closer to Gary. He wished he could just put his arm around her. Why couldn't things just be simple?

"Brian told us the man she married didn't want him. At least, that's what the woman who raised him claimed," he said, trying to get back on track.

Lydia snorted. "He didn't want us either. As long as he could afford a nanny to raise us, it was fine. Best thing that happened to Jace and I was when we came to live with grandfather."

"And something drove Jace away," Leann remarked.

"Won't be for much longer. Grandfather needs him. Jace will be here tomorrow."

"You're kidding," Gary said.

Lydia looked at them, her eyes watering a bit. "I—I don't think Brian's existence surprised my brother. I think—I think it scared him."

The last few miles to Sarasota Falls were uncomfortable. Leann, Gary could tell, itched to ask questions. Lydia, however, stared out the window, her lips pressed together and her hands busily clasping and unclasping.

Leann finally said, "So, you have three children? I have two boys."

"How long have you been together?" Lydia asked softly.

"Well, my oldest is—"

"She means us," Gary interrupted Leann.

"We're not together," Leann protested.

But they were, Gary admitted to himself.

The last week they'd been together enough to work as one to get things done and...

He thought about the feel of her hand, the warmth of her next to him here in the truck, the kiss they'd shared in Russell's backyard. It had been a mistake, of course. One that haunted him because he wanted to make the same mistake over and over.

But he couldn't give her what she wanted. He was better alone, no chance of letting anyone down. Plus, he'd go crazy every time she went on duty.

He swallowed, amazed by the rush of emotion that thought evoked, and forced himself to banish the image of Leann and him together because in the midst of everything, her sons' father would be returning home today.

Yup, Gary admitted, once again his and Leann's relationship would change.

Not that they had a relationship.

Except for that kiss.

IT WAS AFTER six when Leann made it to her in-laws to pick up Tim and Aaron. She'd dreaded turning the corner to their house. Last time Ryan had returned to Sarasota Falls, he'd been in a Hummer, and the boys had talked for hours about the great drive he'd taken them on.

Her in-laws' street looked exactly as it did every day. Not a single strange vehicle was parked anywhere or in the Baileys' driveway.

Maybe her ex-husband, Ryan, didn't have a vehicle yet.

She parked and slowly meandered up the walkway to their door. It had been a long day, she was exhausted and she wanted nothing more than to get her boys home, cook them dinner, check homework and maybe play a mindless game of UNO. Before she could do that, she'd have to make small talk with Ryan and his parents, pretend everything was all right and avoid topics that were meant for the lawyers.

She knocked and then opened the door, calling, "Tim, Aaron!"

They barely greeted her, then gathered their belongings as they charged through the room—Peaches at their heels—and out the door to scramble into the car.

"They're sure in a hurry," Leann said to Tamara. "Did Ryan…?"

"Delayed," Tamara said tersely. "I told the boys he'd be here tomorrow. They're a little disappointed."

"Everything okay?" Leann asked.

Tamara gave a brief nod. "Fine. Will the boys be here tomorrow morning before school?"

"No, I'll be able to take them. Oscar's due back in a few hours, so things will ease up a little."

Funny, she'd resented his getting the promotion over her. But, now, looking at her boys sitting in the car, their expressions gloomy, she knew she had something more important to deal with.

"Any news on Chief Riley?" Tamara asked.

"Good news. He's healing slowly, but the doctors feel confident he should make a full recovery." She'd had two phone calls, one from Lucas and the other from Chief Riley's wife.

Tamara smiled. "We needed some good news today.

Leann agreed but thought that Tamara didn't know the half of it.

"He was supposed to be here," Aaron grumped when Leann slid behind the wheel.

"Did your grandmother say what kept him?"

"He's in California. She said he—"

In the rearview mirror, Leann watched as Tim roughly nudged Aaron. Something was up. She knew her oldest boy, and he was more than bothered right now.

"He's in California," Aaron repeated.

"Something came up, so he couldn't come here today."

"That's okay," Leann said as she started the car and pulled out onto the road. But it wasn't okay, not a bit. She looked in the rearview mirror again and studied not her youngest, who was doing the talking, but her oldest, who looked as tense as his grandmother had. Tim remembered his father more than Aaron did. Leann wasn't sure if he recalled all the arguments or the nights Ryan hadn't come home, but she knew he understood that Ryan hadn't really been a part of their lives: then or now. Still, her oldest had battled hopefulness with skepticism when told that his father was coming to Sarasota Falls for good. She hated that at just twelve, he already mistrusted the words of his father.

"He'll be here tomorrow," Aaron continued. "Grandma said she'd have Grandpa talk to him."

"I'm sure we'll find out something soon."

"Yeah, maybe after school." Aaron wasn't a skeptic, yet, and very much associated his father with good times. His disappointment at Ryan's delay was of the "you made me wait" and not the "you've let me down again" variety.

"Tomorrow will be here before you know it,"

Leann promised because she'd promise only things that "would" happen.

"Hey, there's Gary!" Aaron sat up, his father forgotten and a grin spreading across his face.

The small parking lot of Bianca's Bed-and-Breakfast was empty except for Gary's truck. Gary opened his truck door, stepped out and then moved aside for Goober, Wilma and Peeve to mass exit.

Peaches barked.

"Can we stop?" Aaron asked eagerly.

Any other day, any other time, Leann would have said no. But, Tim had looked Gary's way and Leann knew that the dogs would be just the type of distraction he'd need. Gary, however, might not welcome them. Tim's needs won out over Gary's.

She pulled in next to him and smiled weakly.

He returned the same but managed to act a bit more excited when Aaron tackled him around the knees. "Hey, bud."

"I hear you might need a couple of dog walkers?" Leann suggested.

"I don't—"

Please, she mouthed.

"I don't know when I've needed dog walkers more." It took Gary only a minute to hook leashes to collars. Tim somewhat unwillingly took Wilma, the problem child, while Aaron, although younger, took Peaches, Goober and Peeve.

"Mom," Tim whined. "I really don't want to walk the dog. Please."

Wilma, however, very much wanted to be walked, and started moving, pulling Tim until he was two houses away and forcing Aaron to hurry to catch up. Goober was thrilled to have people to herd. Peaches followed Peeve, clearly in love. Peeve took it in stride.

"What's going on?" Gary said.

"Their father didn't show. He's delayed in California. Aaron saw you and got all excited. I'm not too worried about him, but Tim's taken the news hard."

"Will Ryan be here tomorrow?"

Leann shrugged. "According to his mother, he will be. How's Russell?"

"He's okay. Brian apparently is cooperating. Jace will definitely be arriving soon, and Lydia has taken over. They should be bringing Trudy to Russell's place tomorrow. Lydia's already bought clothes and food and even some sort of tablet for Trudy. I ran Lydia to the store and then took her to the cabin. I also made sure Russell's old truck started. I grabbed the dogs and headed here."

"I take it you haven't told…"

Gary shook his head. "Figured I should do it in person. I'm telling Aunt Bianca first before I tell my mom or siblings. You, uh, haven't told Oscar yet, have you?"

"No. Lucas said he'd let you do it."

"Right. I'm hoping Bianca might know something she can add to the story."

"I'll go walk the dogs with the boys."

"No, come in with me. You can add any information I might miss. Or—" he paused "—you might be a bit more comforting than I am. I just want to yell at someone."

She put a hand on his arm, squeezing gently. He smiled, bent down and kissed her forehead. From anyone else, it would have seemed brotherly. It wasn't. The warmth and the gentleness of his lips made her almost miss a step as they started up the steps. It wasn't until he let go of her hand, to open the door, that she realized he'd entwined his fingers with hers.

"I saw you give the boys dog duty," Bianca said. "Come in, sit down. I'll pour us some coffee."

Leann shook her head, but Gary took a cup.

"News around town says Russell's had some excitement." Bianca placed what looked like a plate of her award-winning banana bread in the center of the table and sat down, looking at them expectantly. They promptly sat down, too.

Gary leaned forward. "Aunt Bianca, you said that Berto and Angela were friends when they were young."

Bianca nodded.

"Any chance they were something more?"

Bianca laughed before saying, "She was out of his league and way more mature."

"I've seen pictures of my dad when he was a teenager," Gary said. "He wasn't bad-looking."

"You look just like him, so I guess I'm going to have to agree. She came to him when she needed Russell's truck to start or if she wanted to make some other boy jealous."

Gary ran a hand through his hair, looking miserable. "Aunt Bianca, there must have been more to it than that. Brian Blackgoat says his father's name is Roberto Guzman."

Bianca didn't even pause before saying, "Not possible."

"Angela was pregnant when she left Sarasota Falls."

"That proves Brian doesn't belong to Berto. Your father would have fought to stay in the baby's life. To do the right thing."

"Not true," Gary said. "He let go of Oscar, me, Hector and Anna."

Bianca set her coffee cup down so suddenly that brown liquid splashed over the side, staining the white tablecloth. "I told you he wouldn't have deserted his family." She turned her attention to Leann. "I imagine a DNA swab has already been taken?"

"If not, I'm sure in the morning."

Bianca's eyes narrowed as she looked at Gary. "Don't you dare tell your mother anything until we find out for sure. Make sure Oscar doesn't either. You hear me?"

"Yes, ma'am. Loud and clear."

Bianca pushed back her chair and left the room.

"That went well," Gary said.

Leann rubbed his shoulder, wondering where this sudden need to touch him had come from. She quickly picked up the coffee cups and busied herself with the tablecloth, taking it to the counter, where she spread it and squirted dish soap on the stain before dabbing at it with a wet washcloth.

Outside came shouts, "Wilma's loose! Wilma's loose." Then came the sound of running feet.

"I'll take care of this," Gary said. "I've got my German down now."

Leann nodded as Gary left the kitchen. Aaron, all excited, busied himself with the three dogs he'd been in charge of, but soon joined her, diving for the banana bread.

Leann started rinsing the few dishes. Gary and Tim came into the backyard, leading Wilma, who now acted as if she were the most obedient dog in the world. In the silence of the evening, she could hear their words.

"A cat ran from a bush just as we passed it," Tim explained, his voice high and excited. "I couldn't hold on, and then she didn't come when I called her so I chased her."

"You did the right thing," Gary said.

"She ran in the street. I'm so glad there were no cars. I told Aaron not to chase her but go get you. I'm glad you came."

"I'll always come if you need me," Gary said easily.

What? Leann slowly set down the glass she'd been rinsing. Always?

"Will you come if Mom needs you?" Tim asked.

What?

"Yes," Gary promised. "I can do that."

"Tim's worried." Aaron had quietly, very quietly, come to stand beside her, gazing out the window at Tim and Gary.

"Why is he worried?" Leann whispered.

"I'm not supposed to tell. Tim said not to."

Leann merely raised an eyebrow. Aaron always told. He couldn't keep a secret, ever.

Aaron said in a small voice, "We overheard Grandma telling Grandpa that the reason Dad didn't come today is because yesterday, in California, he got married."

Leann looked out at Gary helping Tim remove Willa's leash. Life was about to get even more complicated, and it wasn't just her ex getting remarried. It was also Leann wondering if she was capable of believing that Gary would always come when they, she, needed him.

CHAPTER NINETEEN

BRIAN MADE BAIL. From the station's lobby, Leann watched as Brian and Lydia headed for the exit. Before they quite got there, Gary entered. Peeve was at his side, but only momentarily, as the dog moved past Leann and confidently through the foyer to Chief Riley's office.

Lydia didn't hesitate. She quickly gave Gary a hug and said, "Thank you again for picking me up at the airport yesterday and for getting Russell's truck to work this morning."

"My pleasure," Gary said while giving Brian a slow stare.

Brian returned the stare before following Lydia out the door.

"I—" Leann began at the same time Zack said, "They're waiting for you." The smile Gary shot her as he headed for Chief Riley's office was genuine, yet didn't reach his eyes.

She wondered how his greeting would have been if he'd not encountered Brian. And, she wondered how he'd take the news Oscar and Lucas would surely share with him now. An hour ago, she'd finally located and spoken to Willow Bartholomew. At first Willow had been defensive, but soon switched to complaining about the time she'd spent caring for Brian. No wonder he was messed up.

In the end, she'd verified that until Brian turned eighteen, he'd been under her roof—with his mother's permission, and yes she had documentation proving this—and she'd received a cash payment for his board in the mail every month. There'd been no correspondence, but Willow had been told, by Angela, that the money came from Roberto Guzman—Brian's biological father.

"Hey, Leann, come in here," Lucas called.

Oscar sat at the desk, his expression mirroring Bianca's from last night just before she'd walked out of the kitchen.

"I'm not convinced by Brian Blackgoat's claim," Oscar said drily. "Tell Gary about what you discovered."

Leann cleared her throat and repeated her morning conversation with Willow.

"We need to look into this more," Lucas said, deftly taking over the conversation. "Leann, we investigated Roberto Guzman's disappearance seventeen years ago. There should be re-cords and other evidence in the storage unit. I'd like you to head over there and—"

"I can do that," Oscar butted in.

"Conflict of interest and you have other duties," Lucas said firmly, never mind that Oscar was now acting chief.

"I'll go with her as a family representative," Gary volunteered.

"Good enough," Lucas agreed.

Oscar didn't look happy, but his phone pinged. He glanced at it and gave her and Gary a nod.

Instead of being on her usual patrol alone through town, she had a brooding Gary next to her as she drove to the station's storage fa-cility behind Little's Grocery Store.

He finally burst out with, "How did Willow sound? Was she nice? Genuine? Could you tell anything about her over the phone?"

"She didn't sound like anyone I'd let watch my kid," Leann said. "According to her, she hasn't seen Brian the Loser—her words, not mine—since he graduated high school. She did add that it would be nice if the ungrateful kid sent a little money her way showing his appre-ciation for her keeping him out of foster care."

"Tell me again how much she was paid for housing him."

"A thousand dollars a month."

Gary shook his head. "Couldn't have been my father. He didn't make that much. He gave his paycheck to my mom. She handled the money."

Two kids were playing catch in the street. When they saw Leann, they stopped and shouted, "We're sick, not playing hooky," before running across the street and up the steps into a house.

"The perks of being a cop." She parked alongside a golf cart bearing a for-sale sign and pulled a key from her pocket. "We're unit five, the biggest here."

"Is this safe? Couldn't someone break in?"

"There are no valuables stored here, just the remains of cold cases."

Something twitched in Gary's expression.

She inserted the key and turned the knob. Dust particles swirled about her face as she pushed her way in and switched the light on, Gary at her heels. She blinked against the stark, hanging bright bulbs. Steel shelves, three rows high, lined the room. Additional shelves were in the middle of the room.

"Chief Riley told me we'd be cleaning it

soon." Of course, he'd told her that a dozen times, starting with her first day on the job. Looking around now at everything from cardboard boxes to large grocery sacks to a few suitcases and even one garbage bag, she had to agree with the chief. It was past time. Probably most of this stuff could be disposed of.

"Some of this stuff is in alphabetical order," she said. "Other items are by date. I'm not sure how your father's things were stored."

It took them almost an hour to find the small cardboard box labeled Roberto Guzman.

Gary followed her to a table right by the door. He scooted aside two old newspapers and an empty water bottle. She set the box down and peeled old tape away from the edges. Dust flew when she lifted the lid. A sneeze sent it flying. Gary moved closer, watching her every move. She carefully opened the top and pulled out a few file folders that had the standard paperwork for a missing person's case. Below the documentation were a number of photos, a small calendar and a wallet.

"I remember this wallet," Gary said and picked it up. "It was usually crammed full of money, credit cards, old receipts. He had to take it out of his back pocket and set it on the console between the seats when driving.

Sometimes it fell on the floor, and I'd be on my knees looking for it."

She took the wallet from him, his fingers brushing hers. She opened it, and both of them stared at Roberto Guzman's driver's license photo.

"It's you," Leann said.

"Only I would never desert my family."

It made Leann lose her breath a little, hearing his words now and remembering his words last night. *I'll always come if you need me.*

Looking at the birth date, Leann calculated and determined that Roberto had been in his midthirties when he disappeared seventeen years ago.

She opened the money flap and found a video store membership and several photos encased in plastic. The top photo showed a bride and groom, young looking and happy.

"My parents," Gary acknowledged.

Then, there was a photo of four dark-haired children all looking impossibly young. Leann figured out Gary was the one grinning jauntily at the camera, already cocky and looking barely six years old.

Next came photos of Gary and his siblings.

"All of us kids."

She touched one photo. "Oscar?"

"Pretty sure. Look at that expression. He's the responsible brother."

She tapped the next photo. "You?"

Gary shrugged. "Absolutely. Look at that adorable face," he teased, going for a bit of false modesty. "I've always been the best-looking brother."

"Ahem, and the most humble, too."

Leann flipped to the next photo. "Then this must be Hector. What is he known for?"

"He's the smartest of the brothers."

The last photo protector bulged a bit more than the others. Leann knew it had to be Anna, the sister. Probably, as the only girl, Anna rated a few more pictures. Didn't matter. As a cop, Leann knew how to investigate. There was a saying about leaving no stone unturned. The same went for photos.

"Let's see what's behind it." Leann got out her fingernail file and started gently separating the photo from the plastic sleeve it was gummed to. It took even more time and care to extract the photo wedged next to it, but finally, she stared down at a photo of Angela Blackgoat, wearing an evening gown, holding a bouquet of flowers and sporting a tiara. Gary cleared his throat. His cheeks were a bit flushed red, his lips drawn together tight and his eyes unblinking.

She badly wanted to touch him, offer comfort, something, but his body language clearly said, "Stay back." She wanted to, though. Oh, how she wanted to. More than anything, she wished they could take their friendship forward, allow their relationship to reach the next level. If she was honest with herself, she was already half in love with him.

She hadn't seen him close himself off to her in weeks, certainly not since they'd started seeing each other every day.

Every day?

Yes, it was true. He'd become such a part of her life that she couldn't remember a day without him. She took tiny one step toward him.

He frowned.

Leann carefully put the wallet back in the evidence box and then took out the pocket calendar from the year Berto disappeared.

With Gary watching closely, she flipped through the pages. Roberto had been working the first few months, and he'd carefully written down where he was supposed to go, both address and start time.

"Was your father in construction? Is that why he worked so many different locations?"

Gary kept his voice even, no emotion. "He worked on cars, but he was especially great with transmissions, so often he'd helped out in other shops besides the one my uncles own."

The second week of May, Berto had actually written down the word *bus*, a number and a time.

She took out her phone and found the number for the bus company that serviced their area. It took a while of punching numbers before she got someone who could help her research what she wanted to know. Eventually, she hung up. The number belonged to a Greyhound bus that had left Hollywood, California, and arrived in Sarasota Falls at the time indicated.

She dialed Russell's number. He didn't answer. No surprise. She quickly called Lydia.

"Russell's right here," Lydia said.

"Yes?" Russell's voice came on the line. It sounded stronger and happier than it had in years.

"Jace here yet?" she asked.

"We're in the truck. Lydia's driving us to Santa Fe to get him. His flight arrives at noon."

"Think your truck will make it?" Leann said, half jesting, half concerned.

"Brian said it's in better condition than a

lot of others of the same age and make that he's seen."

So, Brian was good with cars, too. Just like Gary's father.

"Russell," Leann said, "do you remember when Angela showed up on your doorstep with Lydia and Jace? I mean the exact date."

"No, I don't. All I remember is I was sitting at my kitchen table eating chili, the next minute I'm staring at Angela, and she has in tow two grandchildren I didn't know I had. Wait a minute."

Leann listened while Russell shared the conversation.

Lydia took back the phone. "It was May. I missed the last two days of fifth grade, and boy was I annoyed because it meant I missed the class party. Plus, Mom only let us pack one bag."

"Why?"

"I guess, really, it was all we had left. People came and took the furniture, toys and stuff. I know we had a date to get out of the house. All Mom did was cry. We were totally out of money. We didn't eat anything on the bus from California to here."

"Where was your father?"

"They separated. I didn't know it at the time,

but we never had any contact with him after that."

"Your mom just had money for bus fare?"

"Not even that. She got it from a friend. He paid for the tickets, met us at the bus station here and brought us to Grandpa's."

Was the friend Berto Guzman?

Leann looked over at Gary. She knew he was listening intently while searching his father's cracked leather wallet.

"Do you remember what friend?"

"No, I only met him a few times, and it's been years. I know Mom grew up with him."

"What if I showed you a photo?"

"Why are you asking?"

"I'm following a lead," Leann said.

"Why don't you come to Russell's place for dinner tonight, sevenish," Lydia invited. "We'll be celebrating Jace's homecoming. I'll cook hamburgers and hot dogs for everyone."

Bring everyone? Her boys *might* be with their father and new stepmother. Leann was pretty sure Gary didn't want to be anywhere near Brian until the DNA swab result came in.

"I'll be there." She hated that she would be cutting in on Jace's reunion, but she'd also get to hear what Jace had to say, why he left.

"Be where?" Gary asked.

"I'm invited to Russell's tonight to talk."

On the phone, Lydia said, "Go ahead and bring Gary."

Leann wasn't quite sure how Lydia knew it was Gary. Could have been Oscar, Lucas, the mailman.

"Are you positive?"

"Of course. If Brian and Gary are related, they need to work this out."

In theory, that was true, but Leann wasn't confident that would happen. What Gary had learned about his family had affected him deeply.

Gary was watching her, waiting.

She swallowed, knowing if she brought him with her, she was admitting this could be a "relationship." If she didn't let him come along, then he was just a man who happened to be a part of an ongoing investigation, who happened to be the brother of her favorite co-worker, who happened to be handsome, single and likely to pop up at inopportune times.

"Okay," Leann finally said, "Gary will be there tonight, too."

After she ended the call, Gary asked, "Where will I be tonight?"

"Over at Russell's. We'll be celebrating Jace finally coming home."

Gary raised an eyebrow and shook his head. "I've got things to do."

"Like what?"

"Like work on the cabin, like look into Brian's claim, like—"

"You'd rather do that than spend the evening being supportive of Russell?"

"Russell wants to be surrounded by family.

"Russell considers you family," Leann said.

"No, not really."

"Yes, really. And if Brian turns out to be a relative that he shares with you, it will make the bond that much stronger."

"No. Russell was simply happy to have a neighbor around to talk to. Now, his family is here and he's not lonely."

"I don't think Russell was the only one lonely. And you've got family here also."

"You like to argue."

"I like being right."

"This thing with Brian isn't going to be quite that easy."

"No, but how hard it is will ultimately be up to you."

He didn't answer right away, so she continued. "I have no business giving advice on family. My relationship with my parents, my brother and sister, and even my ex means I'm not anywhere close to being an expert, but if it meant a change for the better for my sons, then I'd give it a chance."

"I'm only here temporarily. Oscar's probably better suited for dealing with this."

Leann flinched. She'd almost forgotten that he'd not put down roots. She closed her eyes, not wanting him to see her true feelings. "Well, I still like being right, so, you'll go with me tonight?"

"Yes."

It had to be enough.

For now.

LEANN RETURNED GARY to the station, saying very little. He didn't have much to offer either, images of his dad and how happy their family had been flooding his mind. Leann might be right about his attitude making the situation harder. He'd decided that were Brian truly a half brother, then so be it.

It was telling his mother that he dreaded.

She parked, and he followed her inside to the office that already seemed to belong to Oscar, listened to her report and watched Oscar's expression when Leann showed him Angela's photo.

He admired his older brother. Oscar had

to be reeling from the possible connection between Russell's family and theirs, but he remained professional and merely said, "Document everything, no matter how small the detail."

"Is our father's disappearance still considered a cold case?" Gary asked.

"Yes, but that might change. I feel like Brian has more that he could be telling us."

"You think Blackgoat might know something? Be involved somehow?"

"One way to find out," Oscar said. "Gain his trust. Tonight, be reasonable."

Gary's snort was cut short when Leann said softly, "Don't forget, every action you take will also affect Russell and Lydia."

Gary nodded.

Thirty minutes later, Gary was back at his cabin. He let Wilma and Goober out of their runs, gave them fresh water and hard food, before pausing to stand in front of the cabin. He was desperate to try to lighten his mood.

Goober ran over to him and arched her back until he reached down to pet her. Then she ran off to join Wilma again. The dogs were as restless as he was. He watched them playing for a long while, then whistled. Goober obeyed immediately. Wilma took a moment, proving her independence, and then came to him. He gave them both peanut-butter-filled bones, a treat usually reserved for special occasions. They settled down.

He didn't.

He changed into his work clothes and started on his cabin.

His cabin?

No, his aunt's cabin. Not really his. Even the dogs belonged to somebody else.

He was woefully behind; life kept getting in the way. What he needed to do now was take two of the cabin's interior walls down to their studs. He'd work off steam, maybe take the edge off the adrenaline.

Then, he'd shower and follow Leann up to Russell's house to learn more about Brian and figure out what he and Oscar would have to tell their family, their mother.

The sledgehammer was on his workbench. At least something in his life was where it should be. He hunted up the pry bar, donned gloves, then punched a hole in the middle of the first wall.

It was usually Oscar who took care of family matters, delivered both bad and good news. Gary had always been gone. This time, though, he had to be the one. This was his story. He felt it in his bones, just like he felt a solid change shifting in his own mind-set.

He'd been such a wanderer. When he'd arrived in Sarasota Falls, the word *temporary* had been his mantra. But now he was having trouble imagining leaving. He had things to do. Finish fixing up the cabin, his cabin; take care of the dogs until their owners returned—he was keeping Goober; and teach Leann...

Teaching was the furthest thing from his mind.

Kissing was more on his mind.

He stopped pounding the wall, enjoyed the feel of his muscles getting a workout and finally stepped back, thinking of the night in Russell's backyard: the walk, the tiny cemetery containing generations, the kiss.

He wanted more nights like that.

Letting out a long breath, he felt a hint of a smile. Until Brian showed up with his tall tale that wasn't looking so tall anymore, Gary had been smiling a lot more lately. Being in love had that effect.

Love?

He started working again, setting down his small sledgehammer and starting to pry apart aged—some rotting—wood.

No, surely not love—maybe intense like. He

really liked Leann, liked being with her, touching her, smelling her, seeing her smile.

His mom used to smile a lot before his father disappeared.

He paused, breathing in and out, sweat in the small of his back.

His mother had been smiling a lot more lately, mostly because of Oscar, who'd gotten married and started a family. Oscar had been smiling a lot, too, before all of this business began about their father.

Taking his phone from his back pocket, he punched Oscar's number. His brother answered not with a "Hello" or "Guzman here" or even a "Yeah," but with a "What have you learned?"

Looking around the cabin, his cabin, the one he needed to offer to buy, he said, "I've learned that family is what's important and if Brian is our half brother, then we deal with it."

"What?" Oscar sounded amazed.

"Take care of your people—they'll take care of the mission."

"Don't spout a code of value at me," Oscar sputtered. "This is Leann's fault."

Gary started to sputter back but didn't.

"Yup," Oscar continued, "all sappy. Figure out what's going on tonight. Do reconnaissance. We'll drive up and visit Mom in the morning."

"Sir, yes, sir!"

Oscar chuckled. "Little brother, you've got it bad."

Gary hit the off button. Tonight, he'd kiss Leann and tell her how bad.

CHAPTER TWENTY

With Brian Blackgoat out on bail, Oscar on duty and Chief Riley on the mend and giving orders via phone since he wasn't allowed back to work yet, the Sarasota Falls Police Station had almost returned to normal.

Leann relaxed. Maybe she'd catch up on—

"There's someone to see you," Oscar interrupted that thought.

Leann looked up from the report she was finishing. "Who?"

Oscar shifted uncomfortably.

"Hello, Leann." Her ex, Ryan Bailey, stepped into the room. His reddish-brown hair was still cropped short, his complexion still a bit ruddy and his smile identical to Tim's.

Leann rethought normal. "Ryan, what are you doing here?" This wasn't the place or time for a meeting. She'd envisioned it at the lawyer's office, or maybe at her house with him—all humble—apologizing for letting the kids down and seeing what a great life their boys had with a new trampoline in the backyard and Peaches standing guard at her side.

"I was hoping we can have a moment to talk without the lawyer, without the boys, or my parents—"

"Or your new wife."

Oscar raised an eyebrow, then interceded, "You finished with your reports?"

"All but one."

"Important?"

"Traffic infraction, failure to yield."

"You can finish it tomorrow. Go ahead and take off."

Chief Riley would have made her finish, but then, Riley knew Ryan and would have made him wait until she was off shift.

"Thanks, I need to get my stuff." Turning to Ryan, she said, "If you wait in the lobby, I'll only be a minute."

He nodded and left.

"You going to be okay?" Oscar asked. "Want me to call Gary?"

"I'll be just fine, and no, I don't want you to call Gary. Why would you even ask that?" The last thing she wanted was for Gary and Ryan to size each other up before she even knew what brought Ryan here, so hat in hand. Plus, Gary wasn't her boyfriend. In fact, she wasn't sure what Gary was to her....

She went to the locker room, got her purse and headed for the foyer.

Ryan fell into step with her. "Want to go to the Station Diner? Get some coffee?"

"No." Too many people would ogle them.

He tried again. "How about the tiny park beside the library?"

She nodded, half-afraid he'd suggest the park near her house if she didn't. Way too many memories there. They walked the short distance in silence.

School was still in session so the park was mainly empty. A mother and toddler were packing up to leave. Her third-grade teacher, now retired, sat on a bench. There was a book in her hand, but she was sound asleep.

"Thanks," Ryan said. "I'm sorry I didn't get here yesterday as promised."

"You got married."

"That's right. I didn't know you knew."

"The boys overheard your mom on the phone. Aaron spilled the secret."

Ryan shook his head. "Mom's pretty miffed that I didn't wait and invite them."

"Spur of the moment?" Leann asked, surprised that her voice sounded calm.

"Melanie and I had the license. We were going to do it in about two weeks, after I'd worked out…" He faltered a bit. "After you and I worked things out. I wanted the boys to meet her."

"But?"

"I don't know. We were at the beach. There was a couple exchanging vows. We watched, and it ended. The priest congratulated them and walked away. I don't know what came over me. I stopped him and asked him if he'd marry us. He was more than surprised that I had the marriage license in my car."

"So, you got married."

"We did. What's even funnier is the bride and groom from the original wedding signed as our witnesses. We're going to meet on the beach in one year and celebrate together."

"Melanie's idea?" Leann knew that Ryan wasn't much of a romantic.

"No, mine."

Okay, Ryan hadn't been much of a romantic with Leann. She got it.

"Look," Ryan said, "Leann, there was a time when we were friends, a time when we loved each other, enough to—"

"I get it."

Chagrined, he continued, "I met Melanie

over a year ago. So, we didn't hurry, though, of course, the wedding makes it seem like we did."

Leann could only nod.

"I want to be part of my boys' lives. I want to have a civil relationship with you, to make it easier on Tim and Aaron."

This Melanie must have quite an influence on Ryan. Leann closed her eyes and thought about Tim feeling that he needed to keep secrets. She thought about the help Ryan's parents were. She thought about her conversation with Gary and how she'd advised him to not make things harder than they needed to be. And, she recognized that change had to happen, even if it meant she had to accept her ex-husband back in her, their, boys' lives.

"All right."

"What? Really? Oh, I can't tell you how relieved I am."

Leann didn't tell him that she felt a little bit relieved, too.

"I haven't been home yet," Ryan continued. "I know my mother picked the boys up from school. Melanie and I would like to take them out for pizza tonight. Just show up and surprise them."

She hesitated, wanting to protest but realizing that she had the opportunity to make things easier on her boys.

"That would be fine. I—I have something to do tonight, so you could have them for the evening. They'll have homework," she warned.

He whooped, got out his phone and texted.

"Tim needs the most help with math. Don't let Aaron fool you into playing more than an hour on any of the games on his phone. They'll be spending the night at your parents' house since I'll be out late. I'm going to Russell Blackgoat's place."

Ryan nodded. "I remember Russell. He taught me how to tie a trucker's knot." Ryan motioned to a car that was parking nearby. A tall blonde woman exited the vehicle and hurried their way. With hands outstretched, she embraced Leann before Leann could move.

"I've seen your picture, Leann, and the boys are so handsome. I look forward to spending lots of time getting to know them."

Leann was a cop. More than anything she wanted to question, dig and, yes, believe the worst. No such luck.

Instead, she said, "Congratulations."

"I'm sorry we were a day late. We rented a condo by the beach for just one night. In February, there's lots of availability."

"Sometimes an opportunity lands in your lap and you need to embrace it." Funny, even as Leann said the words, she thought about Gary.

LEANN OPENED THE door to a too-silent house. Peaches whined, no doubt wondering where the boys were.

"They're with their father," Leann told the dog, her stomach clenching. She'd made the right decision. Too often she'd been called to various houses where the divorced parents couldn't work together. She wanted, prayed about, better things for her sons.

And she could hope that maybe Ryan had changed, grown up, settled down. Even more, she hoped she could swallow away the fear that came from knowing there'd now be another woman in her sons' lives. She'd been so worried about sharing them with Ryan, and now there was Melanie.

Melanie who wanted to spend time with the boys. Leann sat down on the couch. Peaches immediately put his head in her lap.

Time with her boys.

The worry about money had been so pressing that she'd pushed aside the need for time. Besides, she did a pretty good job. She always made it to school concerts, PTA meetings, and she took them to Russell's, of course.

Would she have time to do all that if she became detective.

Lucas's words came back to her. "I didn't get to chaperone much. I was working."

Time to rethink the budget.

Rethink priorities.

Leann took a quick shower, changed into jeans and a nice shirt and then headed out to her car. She was halfway to Gary's, picking him up for their visit with Russell, when she realized she was running early. And she bet, just bet, Oscar had called his brother, so there'd be questions.

She parked her vehicle behind Gary's and stepped out. The wide-open space, the swaying trees, the old cabin calmed her down. She loved it out here. Goober and Wilma ran up to her. She'd have to scold Gary again and remind him about the danger of letting dogs run loose out in the wilderness.

"Gary!"

She headed for the camper he called home. Country music played and she could hear some sort of echo. The door was open, so she stuck her head in and then backed out quickly. Gary was in the shower, singing to Garth Brooks, and not doing a bad job of it.

Goober walked with her to one of the chairs around the fire ring. She stroked the dog's head and watched as Wilma investigated a tree line. Finally, feeling more content, she took out her phone to check messages. She had sixteen. The first was from her sister, Gail. Ray indeed had a new job, working on the historic train that ran the old route from Sarasota Falls to Santa Fe. Things were great. The majority of messages, however, were from friends and neighbors letting her know that Ryan was back in town. A few mentioned the blonde woman with him, but none seemed aware that she was his wife. Two had seen her in the park with Ryan and wanted to know if she was all right.

The last text was from her mother suggesting a Saturday night dinner for Ryan and Leann.

Closing her eyes, Leann leaned back and hoped that she never, never, would be that clueless when it came to knowing what was really going on in her children's lives.

Since Leann didn't want another text about how she'd blown it, she decided to hold off on informing her mother about the new Mrs. Bailey.

"You look nice."

Leann opened her eyes to jeans, an unbuttoned blue cambric shirt and tan abs that made her want to reach out and touch. "So do you."

He pulled the closest chair up next to her, usurping Goober, who merely moved to the other side, and took one of her hands in his. "I hear you had a visitor."

"Oscar called you."

"And it took everything I had not to rush into town."

"My meeting with Ryan would have been over before you got there."

"How did it go?"

"Pretty good, actually . We agreed that he could watch the boys tonight. I met his wife, who seems too sweet to believe and especially too sweet to be with him—though he was definitely not acting like the man I married. No, that's not right," she said and stopped herself, "he wasn't acting like the man I divorced."

"He changed."

"We both did," Leann admitted. "We married so young and for all the wrong reasons."

"You loved him."

"In my own way, yes." She sat up straight, wishing she could undo the past and knowing she'd do the same thing again anyway because she couldn't imagine a life without Tim and Aaron.

"We were young, I was pregnant, and both sets of parents basically pointed to the altar and said, 'Go.'"

Gary smiled. "So you went."

"And if I admit it," Leann said, "I ran to the altar. I wanted away from my parents. I wanted to breath, laugh, love. I wanted to re-create my friend Patsy's family, but I didn't know how and neither did Ryan."

"Your home life was that bad?"

"It was *sterile*. That's the best word for it. My father was always working, and when he was home, we had to be quiet. Made no sense, because he was always in the study and unlikely to hear us if we dared laugh or knock over a lamp."

"And your mother?"

"Mostly gone. Why am I telling you all this?" Leann extracted her hand from his, checked her watch and started to get up.

His hand on her knee stopped her. He took both hands this time and said, "You're telling me because of everything happening now, and because I'm listening."

She shook her head. "It's a mess. I'm a mess."

"You're the most put-together woman I've ever met, and I've met plenty."

Leann was sure he had. As if reading her thoughts, he shook his head. "I mean in the military, and just wait until you meet my sister and mother. Picture Aunt Bianca times two. There, I made you smile."

"I'm going to text Ryan. See how they're doing."

Leann's fingers danced across her phone, texting Ryan, thinking that now she'd need to get Tim a phone so she could text him instead. Then, she settled back again.

"Tell me a good memory about your childhood," Gary suggested.

"No."

"Come on. You know about my father. He just walked out on us one day, never even sent a text that he was alive let alone sent financial support. And now we've this half brother who's appeared out of nowhere."

"You're awfully collected yourself for a man about to clear up some family mysteries," Leann observed.

"I've decided it is what it is. My family will deal with it, together."

"Together. I like that part." Leann couldn't help but compare her family who didn't do anything together. "Oscar's all the time talking about your mom and uncles. You were surrounded by family. Plus, you had Bianca."

"I'm realizing how lucky I was—am," Gary said.

He scooted his chair even closer, leaning forward, looking into her eyes. "I want to know anything and everything about you. Which shoe you put on first. What you have for breakfast. Why you still wear a wristwatch. And about your childhood."

It would take only the most minute movement to kiss him. But, she couldn't.

At least that's what she told herself. Her real fear was that if she kissed him, she'd want more. That she'd want forever.

Could she handle forever?

HE WATCHED HER WITHDRAW, happy that this time, instead of getting up and walking away from him, she only settled back in the chair.

"I put on my right shoe first, I usually have a Pop-Tart, I find glancing at my watch quicker than getting out my cell phone, and I grew up here in Sarasota Falls. End of story."

"No one's story is that brief." He smiled, hoping it would encourage her to continue.

"Mine is."

"Share one good memory about your family. Just one."

"Then you'll leave it be and we can go to Russell's for dinner?"

"For now, and don't worry, I won't tell your sons about the mistake you made when you were fourteen."

"What?"

He laughed. "Everyone sneaks out a window and tries to meet up with friends when they're fourteen."

"Except my kids won't because I'll nail their windows shut," she mused.

"A story about your family," he prodded.

She finally came up with one. "When I was about eight, my brother and I put my little sister's beloved Winnie-the-Pooh stuffed animal in a chair and dared Gail to save him."

"So, the preamble to your future profession was kidnapping?"

She grinned.

"And you remember that?"

"Both my boys now have the same bear."

"Go on with your story," he urged.

"You have to realize how much Gail loved her Winnie-the-Pooh, which, of course, meant Clark and I were forever taking it. This time, though, we went overboard."

Gary chuckled.

"My brother, Clark, guarded one side and I the other. Gail threw a fit and was trying to get Winnie. We, of course, maintained our ground."

"And this is one of your cherished memories?"

"I'm not done yet."

"Go on."

"Clarissa must have heard us because she came running into the room, slid like a professional baseball player aiming for home plate and hit the chair we had Winnie in. The chair fell, Winnie landed in Clarissa's arms and, when we chased Clarissa, she bested us at every turn."

Gary nodded, liking how animated Leann was getting as the story continued.

"Clark started laughing so hard that he forgot all about Gail, who walked right up to us and vowed to get Clark and me one day. Then, she ran and kissed Clarissa and pulled Winnie into her arms."

Although he'd heard the name before, Gary had to ask, "Who's Clarissa?"

"Our housekeeper."

"Where were your parents?"

Leann blinked, the last hint of joy seeping

from her face, but a half grin remained. "They were out of town."

"Oh."

"If they'd have been in town, for one, we'd never had been playing in the living room, and two, we wouldn't have involved Gail in the game. It took her longer to learn how to be invisible when it came to our parents."

No kid should ever have to be invisible. Leann, her sons, they'd never be invisible with Gary.

"Maybe someday we can play keep-away."

"Sure," she said easily. "I play it all the time with my boys, in the living room. We use the Winnie-the-Pooh from Aaron's childhood. And no one gets upset."

"That's nice that you got him a Winnie-the-Pooh."

"I didn't." Leann smiled. "Gail made good on her promise and gave it to him on his third birthday. He fell in love with it instantly. I'll never be allowed to forget taking her bear."

"Your boys are lucky to have you. I'm lucky to have you."

He moved closer, kissed her forehead, then the tip of her nose.

She whispered his name. Angling her lips

to his, surely she was wanting him to kiss her more.

Just then her phone pinged. Spell broken, she pulled out her cell, checked it and then held up a photo for him to see: the boys smiling over pizza.

She scooted her chair back and stood. "We'd better get going."

"I agree. You do know, it's okay to be fashionably late."

"But—"

"Let's walk."

"But—"

"Nothing is as soothing as the outdoors. It's not even a fifteen-minute hike."

She glanced back at his truck and then at him. He held out his hand, and she took it, fingers entwining with his.

She might be shorter but she kept up with him, easily stepping past rocks and dodging tree limbs. A few times Goober pressed against Leann, just sure she would stray off the path.

Walking behind her when the path narrowed, he marveled at how her hair glistened as the setting sun shimmered red orange. Her parents might be a piece of work, but they'd created someone beautiful.

"Turn left here," he advised.

She argued, "This isn't the path."

"No, it will take about five minutes longer, but it's neat."

"It's going to be dark soon."

"I have a flashlight."

"Are you always this prepared?"

"I wasn't prepared for you."

"What?" She turned, and this time he didn't kiss her on the forehead. He kissed her full on the mouth, until she nestled closer in his arms and kissed him back. This is what he wanted. Her. Forever.

The kiss didn't last nearly long enough. Up ahead Wilma found something worth barking at. Leann stepped out of the embrace, eyes hooded, smiled at him and took back his hand.

"Russell told me," Gary shared, "that these trails were made by his family as they walked sheep to pasture."

"There's a pasture?"

Gary frowned. "I should have asked him that. It must be farther along."

"How much of the land have you explored?"

"Not as much as I want to. I'm thinking about asking Aunt Bianca to sell me this place."

"Wow," Leann said, "This means you're staying."

"I've found everything I want here."

She didn't respond, which worried him a bit, but he knew she had trust issues, and he also knew—although he couldn't seem to stop himself—that the day her ex-husband returned wasn't the day to press for answers in this department. He changed subjects.

"William Benedict sent me twenty dollars, Goober's veterinarian history and a one-sentence note telling me that he's not returning for the dog."

Leann's feet stilled on the mud-colored New Mexico soil. "You've had Goober how long now? Over a month?"

Gary nodded.

"You do realize Benedict never intended on reclaiming Goober."

"I figured that out, but how did you know?"

"After I left your aunt's place, I tracked him down."

"What?"

Leann nodded. "I'm a cop. It's what I do. I went to the Station Diner. Benedict was there. He said your commanding officer was worried that you were having a bit of trouble adjusting to civilian life."

Gary stopped. "Why didn't you tell me this sooner?"

"In all honesty, that was only the second time I met you, and at that point I had no clue you'd be somebody I'd wind up being with every day. And, until this moment, I forgot. I've had other things on my mind." She started listing. "Trudy, Jace, Brian, my sister and brother-in-law, the break-in at Russell's, a promotion now lost, Chief Riley's accident, my ex-husband's return, Oscar being gone—"

"Okay, okay, I get it."

"Obviously," she continued, "I didn't believe it was important. Though, I do remember thinking back then that you were having trouble adjusting to civilian life."

"No way." One corner of Gary's mouth turned up. "Wait, did you just say, 'a promotion now lost'? You mean you've heard something? Oscar hasn't said a word."

"No, he wouldn't. And maybe lost isn't right. I just see the writing on the wall. And, truthfully, with Ryan back, I'm not sure I want to be working longer hours."

"But, this is what you wanted most."

"I had been wanting it. It's just that I'm wanting something else now."

"That's a quick turnaround."

"Sometimes when it comes to meeting the

needs of family, a quick turnaround is the only way."

"You really believe you weren't meeting the needs of your boys?"

"No, I was. But I want to keep meeting them. And be happy."

He nodded, tugged on her sleeve and drew her to him.

"We weren't fighting," she protested. "I'm not angry."

"I don't care. I still want to make up." His lips covered hers. She slipped into his arms, her skin tingling.

He didn't even notice that Goober gave a brief woof and then trotted toward the lights just ahead at Russell's cabin.

Some chaperone she was.

CHAPTER TWENTY-ONE

LEANN CLAIMED A second hamburger and settled back. Kissing had obviously made her hungry. Russell and Trudy sat at the picnic table. Trudy was draped with a blanket and still looking painfully thin, but the manic look in her eyes was gone and Leann watched as Lydia and Russell did their magic on the young girl. Every once in a while Russell would point at something and Trudy would nod. Lydia was handing Trudy food to try, wanting to know if it was good.

Great way to get a teenager who didn't want to eat, to eat.

If not for Gary sitting all tense by her side, she'd be enjoying tonight. She loved happy endings and it looked like Trudy, at least, would be getting one.

Russell was the busiest Blackgoat, intent on everyone getting along, but he had too many people to corral.

What amazed Leann the most was Jace's

reaction to her. She, truthfully, barely remembered him. He'd been her brother's age but not one of her brother's friends. Yet, Jace moved away every time she came near.

Brian looked much the same, expression-wise, walk-wise and tough-wise. Now, though, he'd showered, dressed in what had to be Russell's clothes and constantly reminded Trudy to stay under the blanket or eat more. With a whole lot of love and three good meals a day, Trudy could make a full recovery.

It was unsettling to see the two sides of Brian Blackgoat. He'd stolen and hurt someone. Yet, it all tied back to Trudy. He'd become an instant father without any guidelines or help. Leann couldn't remember her father telling her to stay under a blanket or eat more. It had always been Clarissa or one of the other staff.

Finally, food devoured and most of the dishes cleaned up, the chill of the night air sent them inside, and Lydia asked the question, "How is Chief Riley?"

Brian, who'd been bringing Trudy a glass of water, stopped but didn't look at Leann when she answered, "He's out of danger and should be released any day now."

"When will he return to work?" Russell queried.

"We're not sure. Gary's brother is acting chief right now."

Brian sat next to his daughter, no emotion on his face.

"We will make this right," Russell said. "Help with food and bills."

"Insurance will—" Brian began.

"Common decency and restitution are of the heart," Russell said. "You need to have courage, strength and know how to sacrifice before you can truly stand proud as a man."

"Where did you hear that?" Brian asked, smirking.

Lydia cleared her throat loudly. Surprisingly, Brian stopped.

"Courage, strength, sacrifice. It's a mantra from my boot camp days," Gary added to the conversation for the first time.

"You have a daughter to raise," Russell told Brian. "Children change everything. You'll need all the courage and strength you can muster."

Trudy looked uncomfortable and Leann wondered what all the girl had gone through before landing with her father.

"Speaking of children changing everything," Gary said, "Leann spoke to Willow Bartholomew today. She said she was under the assumption that Roberto Guzman was the man sending monthly payments for your upkeep."

"Told you," Brian grumped, sounding a whole lot like Gary. Leann checked to see if Gary noticed. He hadn't.

"Thing is," Gary said, "my father was an auto mechanic with four children. He wouldn't have a thousand dollars a month to spare. It makes no sense."

"Like I said, I never met Roberto," Brian told them, "and I barely remember my mother. I'm not sure she ever sang to me, read to me or anything else."

"She didn't do that for us either," Jace said.

"She was too busy trying to meet the right people," Lydia added, "and become a star."

Not unlike my parents, Leann thought, *except they had to control the right people and remain stars.*

Trudy spoke for the first time. "No one's ever read to me."

"I'll read to you," Russell said.

Lydia laughed and said, "He'll read you all the Walter Farley books."

"I read them to Angela," Russell remembered. "But, she never loved them like you two did. From the time she was little, she was always looking past the sunrise, not at it, except when she painted it."

"Think of all that she missed," Lydia mused.

"Like us," Jace said.

"I like reading about other worlds. Dystopian novels."

Leann wasn't sure if Russell knew many dystopian YA novels. Didn't matter because he said, "I'll read 'em."

Brian remained silent.

"You know," Leann said, looking at Brian, "it's interesting how you'd never met any of your family, but you knew what this place looked like because Angela drew it."

"Yes, she'd even drawn the little cemetery in the back with the graves."

"You also said you knew what your father looked like because she drew him. Gary, why don't you show him a photo of your father."

Gary took out his cellphone, found the photo his mother had messaged him, and handed it to Leann, who passed it to Brian."

"Speaking of photos," Leanne continued. "We found one of Angela, all dressed up, in Berto's wallet…"

"That won't mean anything," Russell spoke

up. "I know the photo you mean. She was so proud, she handed those out to everyone. He probably tucked it in his wallet to be kind and then forgot about it."

The room was quiet while Brian studied it. "This man was in the book, usually standing by some old vehicle or in your cabin."

"My father," Gary said.

"But," Brian said, "this man is not my father."

Gary dropped the iced tea he'd been holding. The glass didn't break but hit the floor and bounced. Liquid spread rapidly along with a cascade of ice cubes.

"Where is this book?" Gary paid no attention to the iced tea, or anything else but Brian.

"I'll clean it up," Lydia whispered.

"We lost the book. I told you. And how do I know? Well, when Angela drew your father, he was always doing something like working on a truck, or riding a quad, and once she drew him riding a horse. I liked that one. The man," Brian said tersely, "who fathered me was always drawn dressed nicely and Angela often put herself in the drawing."

"Angela never drew herself," Russell said.

"Well, I assume the woman with black hair, shadowed face and pregnant belly was my mother. The blurry face looked a little like I remembered her."

"She did smudge out faces sometimes." Russell stood, slowly walked out of the room and came back with a framed drawing that he showed to Brian. "Did it look like this?"

"Yes."

"You said 'we.' *We* lost the book. Who is we?" Leann asked.

Brian looked at Trudy.

"I lost our backpack when we were sleeping in the park," she admitted.

Leann almost jumped up from her chair. "The park next to the library?"

Trudy nodded.

"Was the backpack big, brown canvas, faded black in spots?"

This time both Trudy and Brian nodded.

"That was turned in to the station days ago. I remember when Lucas looked through it. He said there was a book of drawings, but no name."

Five minutes later, the entire party loaded into three different vehicles and all headed into town. The only one to hesitate was Jace, who'd said the least during the evening, and who now looked resigned.

Jace drove Russell's truck with Brian and

Trudy in front. Gary drove his own truck with Russell beside him. Leann drove her vehicle with Lydia next to her. Even as she contacted the station, alerting them that she'd found the owner of the backpack and they were on their way, she couldn't help but think they were a most unusual caravan.

"This is all so amazing," Lydia said. "I keep looking at Brian and Jace and thinking how sad I am for Brian."

"I could never leave one of my children behind. They're with their father tonight, for the first time in years, and it's all I can do to keep from calling every few minutes."

"I vowed that my children would know they were loved." Lydia took out her cell phone. Leann was pretty sure she was scrolling through family photos. "I've always said that my childhood began when we meet Russell. Not only did he see that we had everything thing we needed, but he gave of himself. I didn't marry until I was almost thirty. Took me that long to find a man who was like my grandfather, a man I trusted."

Leann almost said she was still looking for that kind of man, but that was no longer true. Gary was that kind of man. She needed to tell him. But now wasn't the time, so she changed the subject. "Jace seems a little distant. Has he shared why he left and never came back?"

"He's battling with himself," Lydia said. "Twice I've seen him next to grandfather, looking like he has something to say, and both times he walked away. I think having a half brother flummoxes him. He keeps asking Brian the same questions you have. Funny thing, though, when Brian mentioned your name, Jace clammed up."

So, Leann wasn't imagining Jace's hesitance when it came to her. "What do you mean? Think it bothered him knowing that a cop was coming over tonight?"

"I'm not sure. I can't for the life of me figure it out."

Leann and Gary arrived first. Jace pulled up a few seconds later. When they walked through the entrance, Zack waved them back. "Oscar's in his office."

She still wasn't used to hearing Chief Riley's office referred to as Oscar's. She went in first, with Gary just behind. The Blackgoat clan followed. The builders must not have taken into consideration numbers because nine people crowded around the police chief's desk and filled the room to capacity.

"Did you open it?" Brian asked.

"No," Oscar said. "I waited."

Brian picked up the backpack, unzipped it and then Trudy stopped him. Carefully, she placed the backpack on the desk and tilted it, removing a black sweater, a half-full bag of cookies, two young adult books, two full bottles of water, a box of tissues, a pocketknife, an apple and finally a dark brown leather book about an inch thick.

"That's Angela's," Russell said. "I used to buy the drawing books special at the Founders' Day craft fair. She'd do a dozen thumbnail drawings first and then if she liked a drawing enough, she'd redo it in her book. She filled a lot of them."

"Do you have any others?" Leann asked.

"No, she took them with her when she left."

Brian opened the book, thumbed about three-fourths of the way through and then handed it to Gary. Leann shifted so she stood close to him.

The drawing was near a beach and two people stood in the sand. Angela's face was smudged as Russell foretold, vague facial details, but her long hair was distinctive. She was barefoot and wore a flowered dress that didn't meet her knees but flowed out thanks to her pregnancy bump.

"Mom hated to wear shoes," Jace said, looking over Gary's other shoulder.

The man was shown in detail. He was older, probably in his thirties, of average height, with a full head of hair. He had a half smile Leann recognized.

"That's not my father," Gary stated, starting to hand the open book to Oscar, but Leann took it, staring at the button-down shirt, the two pens in the right pocket and the oversize watch on the man's right wrist.

The room was too crowded. Leann couldn't breathe. She moved away from Gary, turning, but she stopped because Jace's was looking at her, such an expression of pain and sympathy on his face that she had to ask the question. "You knew?"

He nodded.

"Knew what?" Gary asked, looking from her to Jace and back again.

"That the man in the drawing isn't your father," Leann whispered. "He's mine."

TRUST, THOUGHT GARY, was a powerful friend but its absence was an equally powerful enemy. He'd already figured out that Leann trusted very few people: she trusted his brother Oscar and she trusted Russell.

He'd hoped, based on the last few days, that he'd made the cut. But, she wasn't coming to him. Instead, she was sitting at Oscar's desk, Oscar at her side, busy asking questions with Oscar acting as her wingman.

Gary wanted the job. No, not job: honor, privilege.

Instead, he buried the urge to push Oscar aside and simply stood, watching events unfold, a spectator.

"How long have you known that my father was with your mother?" Leann asked.

Jace reached inside his jacket and pulled out a book that looked exactly like the one Leann held. "Well, I found this in one of Russell's hiding places when I was a senior in high school."

"Which hiding place?" Russell asked.

"The floorboard near the end of my bed."

Russell nodded. "I'd forgotten about that one. Why didn't you come to me?"

Jace shifted uncomfortably. "I wish I had, but I was young and stupid. All I could think about was Clark Crabtree, all loud and always boasting—" He interrupted himself, said sorry to Leann, and continued. "I thought it would bring him down a peg."

"You showed him the drawing?" Russell was incredulous.

Leann had pretty much the same expression on her face.

"Grandfather, I am so sorry. I've regretted the action every day of my life." Jace opened the book to an area where only a jagged tear remained. "There was a drawing of Ted Crabtree and my mother. The one Clark took was of her back, but I knew it was her. So did he. She had her arms around Mr. Crabtree and he had his chin on her shoulder."

"Why didn't you show the book to me?" Lydia asked.

"Because Clark annoyed me, bullied me, so I went right to him. I wanted to bring him down a peg. I've never seen him so mad. He grabbed the book. I didn't let go. He managed to tear out the drawing."

"Did Clark do anything with the drawing? Is that why you never came home again?" Leann asked. "Makes no sense. Clark never said a word."

"Oh, he had plenty of words," Jace said. "And so did your father."

"My father?" Leann exclaimed. "Clark went to our father?"

"I'd had an ROTC event after school that

day. Then, the truck didn't start. Grandfather's place was so far from town, so I started walking. I'd stick out my thumb once I got to the main road. Turns out, I didn't have to. Your dad showed up. Clark was with him."

"I can't even picture that. My father and brother didn't do anything together."

"I thought they were going to beat me up. Instead, your father did something worse."

Russell and Leann both tensed.

Jace went on, "Mr. Crabtree said he'd make sure Grandpa lost everything, all the Blackgoat land, if I so much as told one person."

"How did he know you hadn't told me?" Lydia asked.

"You were gone, in college. Even if I told you, you'd not have seen the drawing, so it would be hearsay. That's what Mr. Crabtree said. I believed him. Man, I wish everyone had cell phones back then. I'd have already told you, but—"

"He couldn't take my land," Russell sputtered.

"You didn't have the money to fight him!" Jace insisted.

"I have money, friends and right on my side—then and now. Believe me, that man would have a fight on his hands."

"I couldn't take a chance, Grandfather. You'd done so much for Lydia and me."

"You mean to tell me…" Russell shook his head. "…that Ted Crabtree is the reason you've not come home all these years?"

Jace nodded.

Leann's head was in her cupped hands. Gary knew she wasn't crying. No, she was too used to internalizing her sorrow and anger.

"Leann, your dad offered to buy the Guzman cabin forty-some years ago."

Forty years ago, Leann's dad probably wanted the cabin next door so that he and Angela could meet up easily.

"You know that Clark left, right?" Leann looked up and asked Jace.

"Grandfather told me. I just figured it was because of college and working someplace else."

"Clark never comes back either, and he rarely talks to any of us."

"Anything change at your house? Did your father ever—"

Leann interrupted Jace. "Nothing changed at my house except that Clark left, I left and my sister went a little wild." Leann rose. "I will take care of this."

"What will you do?" Gary asked. "Are you going to confront your father?"

Leann looked at him. He recognized the faint first sign of tears threatening to fall, but they were shored up by a will so strong that no one else would see her sorrow. Gary hated that she'd had to be so tough. He wanted to pull her in his arms and say, "Whatever you want to do, I'll go with you." He'd crossed enemy lines, pulled team members from burning buildings and taken in one enthusiastic dog for a man closer than a brother.

They'd not needed to ask for his help. Not really. He'd given it.

Leann didn't need to ask either.

But, she didn't trust him enough to let him help.

Too bad, because he intended to give it.

For the rest of his life.

CHAPTER TWENTY-TWO

Leann disliked returning to the neighborhood of her childhood, a house that wasn't a home and siblings who'd deserved more than they were given.

When this was over, whatever happened after she confronted her father, she was heading to California to visit her brother and find out the full truth of why he left. She hoped that Clark had realized that he didn't want to be like their father. Then, when she came back, she'd visit Gail and work on becoming a sister rather than a guardian.

She'd also visit her lawyer, sit next to Ryan and Melanie and work out terms that were best for their boys.

She opened her car door and stepped out, standing in the street in front of her childhood home and not utilizing the circular driveway.

She had no clue what to do.

Tim and Aaron had called to say good-night. They'd enjoyed the evening with their dad and stepmom, and now were fast asleep at their grandparents'. Oh, and they'd assured her they'd finished their homework.

Leann, alone, was out in the darkness, wishing the world was a better place but knowing she could contribute to the well-being of only her portion of the world. She'd made Sarasota Falls a safer place for her boys, her friends, her neighbors and, yes, her family. It should be enough.

But, it wasn't.

The front porch shimmered, spotlights reflected on fancy, pristine cushioned chairs that no one ever sat on. It was all for show. Not like the chairs on her front lawn that didn't match, or the ones inside her house that hosted her boys and their friends for pizza nights, video game playing and occasionally homework review.

Her mother's bedroom light was on. No doubt Allison Crabtree was going over her itinerary for tomorrow. Leann hadn't a clue about what her mother's day would be like. Should she have made an effort to try harder to find out?

"I can deal with this," Leann muttered to herself, yet she didn't move. Every time, every single time, she was called home to deal with family issues, it was a step into the past that she never wanted to remember, let alone police.

"I don't have a dog this time," came a voice.

Leann jumped. Cops were never supposed to be caught off guard, but she had been. Gary stood there, hands in his pockets, serious expression on his face.

"What are you doing here?"

He stayed a few feet away, hands at his sides, looking so serious that she almost went to him.

"Well," he said, "I watched you leave the station. I told myself that I needed to give you space, drive Lydia home, keep busy. Seems Lydia didn't need me. She and Jace jumped in the back of Russell's truck, so I didn't have any passengers, and quite frankly, there's only one passenger I want."

She'd not cried, not when she saw her father's likeness in the drawing, not when she'd told everyone at the police station, "A thousand a month would be nothing to him." And not when Brian Blackgoat had muttered, "I'd rather have been fathered by Guzman."

Gary, though, threatened to bring her emotions all crumbling down, and if the faucet turned on, she might not ever be able to turn it off. "It's not a good time," she managed.

"No, it's not a good time, but I'm not here for just good times. I'm here for bad times, too."

She shook her head even as he took a step in her direction.

"I have no clue how to help you. I've just discovered that I don't have a half brother, and you've discovered that you do. We've reversed situations. It took me days to come to terms with the scenario. I'd just decided this morning, thanks to you, that I would give Brian a chance and that my top priority would be helping my mother deal with it."

Leann tried to laugh but managed only a dry chortle. "My mother will choose not to deal with it. She'll tell my father to do whatever it takes to bury the problem."

"Only a few lights on." Gary looked at the house.

Leann could only nod.

"So," he asked, "what is your plan when you confront your father? You do have one, right? I can certainly understand why you hightailed it over here," he said. "However, in combat, the adrenaline rush, whether it's from fear or anger or some other emotion, is a powerful weapon made weak if not accompanied by a well-thought-out plan."

"Another mantra?"

"No, I came up with the saying just now."

She again tried to laugh but snorted, very unladylike, instead. "I don't have a plan. How do you plan for something like this?"

"What do you want from your father?"

"I want him to confess."

"What will that get you?"

Leann thought a moment, not liking her first inclination, which was putting her father in his place. He didn't have a place, not really.

"Do you want him to acknowledge the affair?" Gary asked. "Acknowledge Brian? Pay for Brian's court costs along with Russell?"

"All of it and none of it?" she confessed. "I just want…" Did she know what she wanted? Her father had never really been involved in her life. Why was she surprised that he'd had another child he'd not been involved with?

"What were you thinking about on your drive here? Besides confronting your father."

"I was thinking about talking to my siblings, drawing closer to them, cutting ties with my parents completely."

"Do you really have ties to your parents?"

"Only when they suggest to the mayor that their daughter might not be the best choice for chief of police."

"We can deal with that. My aunt's suggestions were spot-on."

We?

Gary wasn't done. "When was the last time you sat down to dinner with your parents?"

She didn't even have to calculate. "Over two years ago. We sat at the same table at a picnic to raise money for the new fire station."

"Did you act as a family?"

"No, my father had to ask which of my boys was the oldest."

Gary whistled. "Then I like your idea about drawing closer to your siblings. I like the concept of a big family."

She interrupted, "But—"

He took two steps and had her in his arms before she could finish. He tugged her upward, so she stood on her tiptoes, and that's when he kissed her.

"Just think how big our cookouts are going to be after we get married."

"Married! We haven't even really dated! And, this is a horrible time to propose! I'm standing in front of my parents' house. My father—"

"Trust me, your father will not be invited to the cookouts."

Later, Leann couldn't say whether it was

Gary's humor that had her considering giving a yes or the kisses that distracted her from where she was and what she needed to do. And, surely what had her so confused and even considering his being a part of her life, her kids' life, was he was such a rock in the middle of turmoil.

She should be on her knees crying. Instead, she was in his arms feeling a whirlwind of emotions and all of them making her feel strong and hopeful about the future.

"I'll eventually want a better proposal," she finally said between kisses.

"I can do that," Gary promised.

"Maybe," she said, "you can propose at a nice restaurant, or maybe at a cookout at Russell's."

"You do like your food." He kissed her, let her go and walking back to his vehicle. She watched as he opened the door and retrieved something. A moment later, he was holding out a pink envelope to her.

"What's this?"

"Open it," he urged.

She took it, slid a finger through the flap and pulled out what was inside.

"A Valentine's Day card! You bought me a Valentine's Day card."

"I did, but it's all wrong."

She shook her head.

Facing her, he traced her cheek with his finger. "When I bought the card, I wanted you to be my valentine. I was thinking no further than a little romance. Now I know that would never be enough. I realize it's only been a few weeks and I know your life has never been more chaotic, but, I've been with you every step of the way, and I'm offering to do the same forever."

She bit her lip and tried to breathe.

Gary checked his watch. "Eleven fifty-nine. You have just sixty seconds to say yes to a proposal given on Valentine's Day."

"Valentine's Day?"

"That's right. It's February fourteenth. Fifty-eight seconds. The perfect day to say I love you for the first time."

It was all going too fast, and just how was a person supposed to act when switching from hot anger to ecstatic anticipation in mere seconds?

Leann tried to rein in her happy thoughts. Love?

"Fifty-two seconds. But, trust me, I'll wait fifty-two days, weeks, years, if that's what it takes to get a yes."

"One knee," she ordered.

Gary Guzman got down on one knee. Leann let the tears fall, then, but not the hot blinding spill of emotion that had been threatening all day. No, these tears were cool, opening her eyes to a future with Gary Guzman. And, oh, would she have a story to tell about the timing of his proposal. She dropped down on one knee, too, and said, "Happy Valentine's Day, soldier."

"Is that a yes?"

She couldn't decide whether to kiss him, tell him she loved him, or say, "Yes!".

So, she did all three.

EPILOGUE

LEANN RUBBED HER STOMACH, stared across the arcade portion of the pizza restaurant and watched Aaron. He'd spent the whole evening running to her and asking, "Are you all right?"

The smell of tomato sauce made her ill.

He always followed his first question with, "Can I have another five dollars in quarters?"

Gary's mother turned out to be a regular piggy bank when it came to celebrating her grandson's birthday.

Leann checked her watch. Gary was due any minute. She'd not allowed Aaron to pass out the cake or open presents until his stepdad arrived. Ryan agreed. "It's gotta be hard for a cop to get his son's birthday off when half the station is related."

Leann smiled and nodded. In truth, Gary had gotten off work thirty minutes ago and was picking up the puppy that would belong solely to Aaron.

Max had returned stateside two weeks ago,

and Wilma was no longer part of their family. Leann wasn't sure the family needed a third dog, especially when she was about to have her third child, but she couldn't say no.

She rubbed her stomach again.

"More water?" Trudy offered her. In her neat red blouse tucked into tan pants and topped with an apron that read EAT MORE PIZZA, she barely resembled the troubled girl who'd arrived in town two years ago.

While Trudy was successfully navigating the ins and outs of her first job, her father was, of all things, starting to raise sheep. He had the best teacher in Russell. For the last six months, Gary, Aaron and Tim had spent a lot of time at Russell's place, helping with fencing and such. Jace even drove in once a month to help.

So far, a profit hadn't been made, but who knew what the future held.

"Russell's having more fun that Aaron." Gary's mother noted.

Both Aaron and Russell were seated before identical race car games. Their shoulders swayed back and forth as their cars careened across the screen.

"He's dismantling the shooting range," Leann said. "Trudy's afraid someone will accidentally hurt a sheep."

"She's got him wrapped around her finger," Gary's mom agreed. "Great granddaughters usually have that ability."

Just then, Gary entered the restaurant. He set a squirming laundry basket on the table and then bent to kiss her.

Melanie came and sat down next to Leann. *"Another dog?"*

"What's one more?" Leann noted Melanie's bulging tummy. They were due three weeks apart.

Just then, Shelley, Leann's sister-in-law joined them. Her husband Oscar was at the station. He'd swing by on his break. Shelley handed little Roberto over to her mother-in-law.

Leann gently brushed the soft hair from Berto's forehead. The last year had been nothing but one miracle after another.

She'd even become closer to her brother and younger sister.

She knew Gary was thankful for everything that had happened, too. He'd put down lasting roots. Joined the police force too. His goal for the next year was to build a larger house on their property so his mother could come live with them. She'd finally retired. And, best of all, there was closure for the whole Guzman clan. The remains of Roberto Guzman—husband, father, brother—had been discovered by hikers just four miles from the family cabin.

He hadn't walked out on his family. They might not know every detail, but the consensus from the forensic medical team was he'd fallen down an incline and died on impact.

Gary put his fingers to his lips and whistled. It brought everyone over except Russell and Gary's aunt Bianca, who'd taken Aaron's place at the race car game. Who said only the young knew how to have fun.

The puppy, however, no longer wanted to be in the laundry basket. It nudged the towel off the top, peeked out—to the delight of the partiers—and then scrambled right onto the birthday cake.

"Good thing we didn't light the candles," Leann said.

Gary started to get up, but between Brian, Trudy, and everyone else, everything was soon cleaned up.

"Have I told you today how much I love you?" Gary asked.

"Twice this morning and once on the phone," Leann affirmed.

"How did the visit to the doctor go? Wish I could have been there."

"I went with her," his mother said. "It was pretty spectacular."

Gary laughed. "Not how Leann usually describes the visits."

Leann agreed with his mother. "This one was pretty spectacular."

"Why?"

"Well," Leann said, "let's look around. We've got a Tim, an Aaron, and Little O, and your mother is holding Berto."

"So?" Gary said.

"All boys."

"Yesssssss." Gary sat up. "What? You're kidding."

Leann put her hands on either side of his face. "Not kidding. I hope you're ready for a girl."

Their kiss might have lasted longer except for Aaron dropping a frosting-covered puppy in Gary's lap.

Aaron nuzzled the dog's fur and wound up with frosting around his lips, which he licked clean. "Sorry, mom. I'll try to watch out for it better when we're at home."

"A girl," Gary breathed. "We'll get her a puppy, too."

* * * * *